LIVIA DAY
DROWNED
VANILLA

BOOK TWO OF THE CAFE LA FEMME SERIES

deadlines✳

First published in Australia in October 2014
by Deadlines

www.twelfthplanetpress.com

This novel © 2014 Livia Day
Design and layout by Amanda Rainey
Typeset in Sabon MT Pro

National Library of Australia Cataloguing-in-Publication entry

Author: Day, Livia, author.

Title: Drowned vanilla / Livia Day ; edited by Alisa Krasnostein ;

             managing editor Helen Merrick.

ISBN: 9781922101013 (paperback)

Series: Cafe La Femme series; 2.

Subjects: Detective and mystery stories.

Other Authors/Contributors:

             Krasnostein, Alisa, editor.

             Merrick, Helen, editor

Dewey Number: A823.4

For Cranky Aunty Lou
Because books are better with dessert

1

ICE CREAM FLAVOURS: A GRAND EXPERIMENT, BY TABITHA DARLING

Bluebelderberry (fruit + cordial)

Pepperberry Fizz (sherbet)

Caramel Surprise (how surprising do people want their caramel to be, seriously?)

Bacon

Vegetarian Bacon

Peanut Butter and Jelly Jam

Sweet Potato and Cinnamon

Pineapple Chilli

Crème Brulée

Black Forest ... something less obvious. Pink Forest?

Vegemite

~~Vanilla~~

Summer in Hobart starts long and dry at the beginning of December, and the sun just keeps getting brighter. Hats, sunscreen and ice cream are all essential.

Also? Any music with a salsa beat.

The music flooded out from the windows of my kitchen—probably annoying any of my neighbours who were home on a Wednesday morning. The day was already heating up as I danced around the table in a tank top and undies, scooping freshly made sorbet into tasting dishes. And then went to pounce on my housemate.

'Cee-ege,' I said in my best whiny voice.

He was at his computer as usual, in the same scruffy clothes he'd been wearing for three days. Since his horrible girlfriend (we do not speak her name in this house) dropped him, I'd been watching for signs of depression and non-showering. It was hard to tell, since staring blankly at his computer screen for eighteen hours a day making clicky click noises wasn't completely out of the ordinary for him.

'No,' Ceege said, not looking up. 'Whatever it is, no. You have to learn to entertain yourself.'

'I bring ice cream for tasting,' I said, at the most annoying wheedling girlie frequency I could. He tunes out all non-extreme sounds. 'You don't have to look away from the screen. Though you should, every fifteen minutes.'

'Yeah, yeah, ergonomics, very important, don't care,' he said, opening his mouth obediently.

I scooped up a small spoonful of a virulent purple sorbet and held it out for him to taste.

'Guh, what is it?' he said, pulling a face.

'Blackberry hazelnut.'

'Too complicated. Next!'

I offered him a bright pink one, and noted the look of vague horror that crossed his face. 'Raspberry vinaigrette. Bad?'

Ceege grabbed his ever-present bottle of Coke Zero, swilled and swallowed. 'Why would you even do that to ice cream? What's wrong with strawberry, chocolate, vanilla?'

'Vanilla is boring. I take it that means you don't want to try my spicy avocado gelato.'

'Not in this lifetime, Tabs.' He dragged his eyes away from the screen (a miracle!) and peered at my tray. 'What's that one?'

'Banana,' I said, all innocent. He opened his mouth. Three seconds later, when the true wonder of the experience had been tasted and swallowed, he gave me a reproachful look. 'Bananoffemato,' I admitted.

'Banana and toffee and tomato?' Ceege said with a wince.

'Banana and coffee and tomato.'

'My mouth hates you right now, just so you know.' He went back to his shiny computer screen. 'How much more of your day off is left?'

'Most of it.'

He picked up the phone and handed it to me. 'You fail. Make them take you back.'

I eyed the phone like a chocaholic staring at her first Kit Kat in a month. 'Maybe I'll just check in.'

'You do that.'

Ceege buried himself in a sea of clicky noises, and I returned to the kitchen, balancing my tray of icy goodness. I hit the instant redial button and Xanthippe picked up on the second ring. 'Nin has everything under control, one of the annoying arty waitresses is due here in ten minutes to swap shifts with the other annoying arty one, and I almost have the hang of the coffee machine. We don't need you, we don't love you, stay home.'

'You're mean,' I said, perching on the edge of my kitchen table. 'Let me come in. I've had like three days off already in cat years. And what do you mean almost? You're not allowed to make coffee until you can name all the components of the machine and you know how to spell macchiato.'

'Hate you too, no frigging way, and Nin said that was crazy talk. She let me loose on the latté.' Xanthippe's voice was unbearably smug.

Not fair. 'Can I come in after lunch?' I tried.

'Café says no to Tabitha Darling. Thank you and good morning.' Xanthippe hung up. I hate having a business partner. Correction: I hate having a business partner who doesn't shut up and stay out of my business.

I binned the sorbets and started flicking through my recipe books for the next trial batch.

'Vanilla!' Ceege yelled from the other room.

'Not in this lifetime!' I yelled back.

Ten minutes later, the phone rang and I leaped on it, not at all desperate for a distraction. 'Forget what I said,' Xanthippe said in a grumpy voice. 'We need you.'

'I'm sorry,' I said sweetly. 'I did not hearrrrr you.'

'People are crying, Tabitha. I can handle coffee, I cannot handle crying. Get in here now, or I take a blowtorch to the mural.'

'I'll think about it.' I hung up and bounced back into the living room. 'They need me! I am indispensable. I knew it.'

'Put some clothes on,' Ceege grunted. 'Don't want to frighten the customers.'

'And deprive them of the sight of my Batgirl undies?'

'Since when do you have...' Ceege peered closer and then squeezed his eyes closed. 'Holy batarangs, Tabitha, that's a terrible thing to do to a bloke who hasn't had sex in two months. If I start fancying you, I might as well throw myself off the bridge.'

'Fine, I'll put a skirt on,' I said, rolling my eyes. 'But only to avoid sunburn.'

'Whatever helps you sleep at night.'

When I was a little girl, my mum used to take me to this beautiful old fashioned bookshop in a sandstone building that sat squarely on a corner of two busy streets. I was sad when they moved the shop, but even sadder to see the array of uninspiring businesses that took over that building in the years that followed. Lawyer's offices, accountants, a surf shop. It seemed such a waste.

Three years ago, a smooth-talking mate of mine tried to convince me to go into business with him. My talent for goopy cakes, his talent for spending money. It was all far too good to be true, and when Darrow happened to mention that he had bought a certain sandstone building which was just crying out for an amazing café on the ground floor, I hung up on him and refused to take his calls for four days.

Getting your dream is scary.

Of course within a month of opening Café La Femme, I discovered that getting your dream actually entails a whole lot of hard work, and you don't have to worry about karma and hubris and 'life being too good' when you're getting up at 5AM to slave over a hot oven. More recently, I had to cope when Darrow handed over most of his share in the business to his ex, Xanthippe—a woman I would trust to protect the café against terrorists, but not to scramble eggs.

Seriously. How can you not know how to scramble eggs?

'What's the problem?' I asked as I burst through the door of my café, trying not to look too pleased that they had only managed half the morning without me. 'Who did Xanthippe make cry?'

'I resent the implication,' said my new business partner from under her perfectly stylish swoosh of dark hair. 'I almost never make people cry.'

'Just keep telling yourself that,' I said. 'Tears?'

'Kitchen,' said Xanthippe.

'Wuss.' I headed for the swinging doors, to see what the damage was.

My crew looked up at me, a haze of extreme innocence emanating from them. I looked from one to the other. No evidence of tears. 'Lara, why are you still here? Yui, why haven't you got your apron on yet? Nin, just keep rolling the pastry, you're good.' I folded my arms. 'Why are none of you crying?'

'We've gone well past crying,' Lara said helpfully. 'We've had vomiting.'

'Panic attacks,' Yui put in, sounding unreasonably gleeful.

Nin just nodded, working on her pastry.

My eyes narrowed. 'Yet ... I see calm and not chaos. The reason for this is?'

'It's not us,' Lara said. 'As if. It's Melinda.'

My crew all nodded enthusiastically, assuring me that yes, it was Melinda. Which was still unhelpful. 'Someone called Melinda has been crying, throwing up and panicking in my kitchen... What did you do, put her in the pasties?'

'We gave her to Stewart,' said Yui, wiping a blue hair extension back out of her eyes and smiling at me. 'You know how good he is with the crying woman thing.'

Stewart. I tried not to look as if I'd been kicked in the stomach. 'Courtyard?' I headed out before any of them saw anything completely wrong on my face. Crying and puking and panicking. All things to be avoided.

I stepped out of my kitchen door and stood on the steps, looking out at it. A quiet corner, my favourite little haven. I'd finally cracked and put a café table out here, but never let anyone use it but the crew.

Customers didn't belong here in this little patch of green surrounded by convict-era sandstone blocks, just a couple of metres from one of the busiest roads in the city. It was ours.

Stewart sat at the table, comforting a messy young woman. She had dark hair in bunches, and clothes that just screamed 'quirky fine arts student'. Who thinks it's remotely justifiable to bring back the poncho? More to the point, who wears a poncho in December, a month when the sharp sunlight cuts through Hobart like a newly honed knife?

I wasn't really paying attention to her. Stewart had let his hair grow longer, and it hung in his eyes. He was still a complete scruff, in jeans that should have been turfed to the Salvos years ago. Nothing had changed.

But I hadn't seen him in seven months, and he was really here, and oh, yes there was the panic welling up inside me, with a twist of guilt on the side.

I'd really screwed things up.

Stewart handed one of a small hoard of napkins to the messy art chick who blew her nose on it and wiped her streaming eyes. Then he looked up and saw me, grey eyes steadily on mine for a moment before his face broke into a grin. An entirely friendly, 'everything's fine' grin. 'Tabitha. Miss me?'

I ignored the question, because throwing myself into his lap right now would be bad. 'Here we are again,' I said, bouncing into one of the cast iron chairs. 'Should have known, McTavish. As soon as the crying women turn up, you roll into town to save the day.'

'I like tae be where my skills are needed,' he said solemnly.

I put my feet in his lap. 'Introduce me to your friend.' See, this was easy. I could do this. Friends, with occasional flirting and none of that stupid awkwardness that had wrecked it all for us, after the Kiss That Shouldn't Have Happened.

'Melinda,' said the girl, wiping her eyes and looking almost normal. 'Sorry for the fuss, I didn't mean to … explode at everyone. I'm pregnant, it's weird. I start sobbing at ordinary things, and when I get stressed all hell breaks loose. Really, I shouldn't be allowed out in public.'

'Hey, I have days like that,' I told her. At Stewart's startled look, I added, 'Not the being pregnant part. General emotional wear and tear. I'm Tabitha, by the way. This is my café. Mostly.'

Melinda nodded, dabbing at her eyes again. Someone had given her a cup of ginger tea, which smelled so good I had to resist the urge to ask if I could have a sip. No stealing from pregnant women, Tabitha. 'I know Lara and Yui from uni. They thought maybe you'd be able to help me.'

Help how? 'Does this involve cooking or shopping? Those are my two special subjects.'

'No,' Melinda said hesitantly. 'But ... we can't go to the police. Friend of ours has gone missing. We're really worried about her.'

I looked at Stewart, who nodded. Which was a lot of help. 'How long has she been missing?'

'Five hours,' said Melinda, and her lip started wobbling again. 'I didn't know what to do, but Yui was there and she said you had this stalker earlier in the year, and you were good at figuring out how to do things without the police, and...' She started crying again, messily. Stewart handed her another napkin. 'Sorry, I'm normally not this bananas, but I'm so very worried about her.'

Oh, hell. Is that what I had a reputation for now? Someone who solved crimes? That was nuts. Surely everyone knew I couldn't be trusted with that sort of thing. If not, I was going to have to release some kind of memo. Tabitha Darling is not a private detective, but she's quite good with coffee.

'Couldn't she...' I said, and trailed off.

Melinda gave me a sharp look. 'Yes she could have simply gone shopping, or run away for some mad romantic fling or any one of a dozen things. But she didn't. I know Annabeth. She's a predictable person. Quiet and nice and sweet and considerate and very, very predictable. Something's wrong, and I have no idea how to help her.'

I gave Stewart a pleading look. He gave a small smile. The kind of smile that makes you go warm from skin to bone, and inspires even the slackest of lazybones to attempt virtuous deeds.

Or maybe that's just the effect he has on me.

2

www.sandstonecity.org - posted by random_scotsman

I'm back in sunny Hobart, Sandstone minions! My Random Scotsman tour of deepest darkest Tasmania has taught me several valuable life lessons, which I will now sum up for you:

1) Apparently the platypus isn't just something that you people invented to lure in the tourists.

2) Asking for platypus is a good way to get thrown out of several leading 4 star restaurants across the state.

3) There really are towns on the north east coast with three pubs and no people.

4) You have a town called Penguin. I know this comes as no shock to you locals, but naming towns after nouns? What's next? Paper, Rock and Scissors? (still getting over Moriarty and Bagdad, you sick, sick puppies)

5) Why do mainlanders (see I'm a real local now, I call them mainlanders) always complain about the weather? This is one

of the sunniest places I've ever been. Admittedly all I have to
compare it to is Glasgow, London and Melbourne, but still...
Thanks for all the great feedback about my postcards from the wild,
but I'm back for good, settled into my squeaky chair and ready to dish
the dirt on the City of Sandstone. You know you missed me...

Comments: 28

Stewart would have come along to Melinda's place with us, but she patted him politely on the hand and told him no men were allowed. Which ... okay. Interesting. I made Xanthippe join us instead, because she might be useful in discussing matters like missing people and stalkers.

Yes, I had a stalker once. Yes, I was—kidnapped, I suppose, for about half a day back in March. I was scared as hell, and it meant a lot that people started looking for me as soon as they realised I was gone. If there was a chance I could help someone else in the same situation, I wanted to do that.

One problem: I'm not actually any good at this. If you need to construct a tower of profiteroles or coordinate a vintage outfit, I'm your girl. But I only escaped my once-in-a-lifetime-abduction situation thanks to luck, stupidity, more luck, a handy half brick and some incredibly loyal friends. I wasn't convinced I had the necessary resources to rescue someone else.

Also, I was not the police. Who are professionally equipped to deal with missing people. They don't even make you wait twenty-four hours here in Australia.

There were many, many reasons why it was important to convince Melinda and her friends that they needed to talk to the professionals. Including my love life, but we'll get to that later.

Melinda's house wasn't what I was expecting. Student share houses are rarely to be found in the elegantly restored properties of Battery Point. Sure, these houses were slums a hundred years ago, but since then they've been renovated, restored, skylighted, water-featured, and generally transformed into the natural habitat for high flying lawyers, doctors, retired politicians—you get the picture.

This tall brick house didn't look particularly fancy, but it wasn't a deathtrap kennel either. 'We'll have to get you to sign a waiver,' Melinda said apologetically as she unlocked the front door and kicked her shoes off. 'We can't let anyone in unless they agree to have their face broadcast online, and to preserve our privacy—no sharing our address, that sort of thing.'

'Okay,' I said slowly. 'Why is that?'

Xanthippe pointed past my face, up into a corner of the little hallway, and I caught her scent—coconut and lime today. I wish she'd give up the fruit perfumes. Whenever I spend any amount of time with her I get the subconscious desire to make jam.

'Webcam,' she said in a low voice. 'Yeah?' she added to Melinda. 'Either that or you have a really full on security system.'

'Both, actually,' said Melinda, passing me a clipboard. I signed the waiver, taking note of the wording. Xanthippe hesitated when I passed it to her, but she signed finally. Curiosity is her weakness. We have that in common.

'Shoes,' Melinda said, almost making it a question.

I slipped my sandals off easily enough, but Xanthippe took longer with her black lace up boots. To her credit, she managed not to look completely hacked off about this. We made our way through a living room to a large, sunlit kitchen and I saw Xanthippe's eyes flick around, locating the cameras as we went.

'So, this is The Gingerbread House?' Xanthippe asked. 'Unless there are more webcam houses in Hobart that I haven't heard of.'

'That's us.' Melinda pulled her poncho off before she started laying out cups and things for tea. You could definitely tell she was pregnant now—I'm not an expert in these things, but I'd say she was second trimesterish. There was a definite bump going on under her close-fitting top. 'Call me Cherry, by the way. While the cameras are on.'

'Cherry it is,' said Xanthippe.

'Okay,' she said, boiling the hot water jug. The day was too hot for anything but iced tea, but I didn't object. Rituals are important. 'French Vanilla was supposed to be here until noon. It's her shift. She's always really good about it.'

Melinda had already told us that her missing friend's name was Annabeth French—but French Vanilla? Cute, and a little obvious as a pseudonym.

'Her shift,' Xanthippe repeated.

Melinda nodded. 'One of us has to be here at all times, for the webcams. Vanilla's great with the rules, normally. She takes them really seriously.' She pointed to the fridge. 'We have a schedule. She's not the sort of person to leave without a note, even if it was an emergency. And there was the power cut. Which is suspicious considering the timing, and it just makes me think that maybe it's her stalker.'

'I think I'm going to need a few more bullet points here,' Xanthippe said slowly. 'What exactly is going on?'

Melinda set a cup down with a clink. 'Oh. Um. I'm not sure of the best way to explain it.'

'Try,' Xanthippe suggested.

'Cherry, is that you home?' called a voice from further into the house. A tall woman with a boyish haircut walked in, and took her top off. 'Who are your friends?' she asked, unfastening her bra and laying it on the couch, with her top.

'Ginge, this is Tabitha,' said Melinda, grabbing another cup. 'And ... Xanthippe? Yui thought they might be able to help us find French Vanilla.'

'Cherry,' said the bare breasted woman, sounding impatient. 'She's fine. You're worrying about nothing.'

'You're the one who said you didn't want to bring the police in here,' Melinda/Cherry said firmly. 'This is a compromise.'

'She's just gone off for a wander. She hasn't even been gone overnight!'

Meanwhile I was trying not to stare at the woman's nipples. Because that would be rude. But they were right there, what was I supposed to do, ignore them? Was ignoring them ruder?

Xanthippe accepted the cup of tea from Melinda with thanks. 'Is it hot in here, or is it just me?' she said archly.

The semi naked woman laughed, relaxing a bit. 'I'm Ginger. This is for the cameras,' she added, gesturing to her breasts. 'Pays the rent, you know.'

I hid my face behind my own cup, not sure whether I was in awe or appalled. It would have sent me screaming into the night. I mean, I consider myself a recreational exhibitionist. I wouldn't have as much fun with clothes if I stopped to think about the size of my thighs, and I certainly wouldn't enjoy food as much as I do if my mind was constantly on the way my tummy sticks out in front during a scone-heavy week. And yes, anyone who spends any amount of time on YouTube probably has seen at least six seconds of my boobs with smiley faces painted on them (don't ask!).

But being constantly under surveillance? Complete strangers watching me constantly, perving on me and my friends, critiquing every crease and curve? I think I'd have a nervous breakdown in a week.

'How long have you all been doing this?' I asked.

'Two years,' said Ginger, helping herself to coffee (never mind my other hang ups, I would definitely not handle hot water that close to unclothed tits!). 'Cherry and me, anyway. Vanilla joined us about…'

'Eight months ago,' said Melinda. 'We had another girl here before that, Pepperminty, but she got engaged to this super conservative bloke and he got funny about the webcam thing. We even had to erase her from the archives to keep him happy.'

'Can't imagine why,' I muttered.

Xanthippe kicked my chair. 'Don't be rude.'

'What?'

'We're in their house,' she said firmly. 'Not nice to judge.'

She had a point, but I couldn't help being squicked. 'I don't mean to be rude—I am sorry, Melinda—I'm really not used to being the straightest person in the room.'

Xanthippe looked at me, then shrugged and pulled her top off, revealing a black bra.

'I can't take you anywhere,' I protested.

'When in Rome,' she said, laughing at me.

'Yeah,' Ginger said approvingly, leaning over to clink her coffee cup against Xanthippe's.

Okay, I was officially out-cooled. Or something. 'Can we get on with this?' I said plaintively.

'I haven't told you about the stalker ex-boyfriend yet,' said Melinda.

Xanthippe looked troubled. 'There's a stalker ex-boyfriend and you didn't go to the police straight away?'

'A stalker and an ex-boyfriend,' Ginger corrected. 'I don't

know if the stalker even counts as a stalker; he's someone who has left creepy messages on our fan forums. And that doesn't exactly make him a special snowflake—we get a lot of creep attention. The ex-boyfriend sends postcards. I don't think they're the same person.'

'I do,' Melinda said firmly. 'It's possible for the same person to use the internet and snail mail. The postcards stopped a month ago, and now Vanilla has vanished? So not a coincidence.'

'She'll be fine,' Ginger insisted. 'Honestly. You're worrying about nothing. No reason to bring other people in on this.'

Stalker. Just the word unnerved me. If there was any chance that what had happened to me—or anything like it was happening to someone else… I hugged myself, feeling cold despite the hot day.

'Tell me about the power cut,' Xanthippe said in a businesslike voice.

Ginger went to sit at a desktop computer, calling up her webcam records. This was a good thing, because it meant her breasts weren't quite so obviously … staring at me.

'Cherry and I were out this morning. Vanilla was the only one here, and she knows that she shouldn't leave the house empty. At 9:02—an hour before I was due home for my shift—the power fritzed, by the look of it. Everything in the house went dead—we presume for four minutes. After which the cameras came back on … and Vanilla was gone.'

Melinda nodded seriously. 'She looked settled, in the footage, doing her readings for tomorrow. No sign that she was planning to go out. She's a history student. No one called the house this morning—she doesn't even look upset.'

On the screen, we saw an image of a blonde in a button-up shirt (in December?) with blonde curls pinned into a messy bun at the back of her head. She sat on the couch, reading, and the shot was from behind so we couldn't see her face. Her feet were bare. Was it deliberate that she wasn't posing for the camera? Had she forgotten it was there? I don't think I could forget, but maybe you got used to it.

The image went black.

'Four minutes later she was gone,' said Ginger. 'We checked all the cameras. And her stuff. She took a pair of shoes. She left behind her mobile, her handbag, everything else.'

I leaned back, looking at Xanthippe. 'What can we do? We're not exactly experts at this sort of thing. Like for example, the police.'

Well, I wasn't an expert. I wasn't entirely sure what Xanthippe was or wasn't qualified to do. The possibilities were endless.

'Could check out Mr Postcards,' Xanthippe said thoughtfully. 'Unless he lives in Belgium or Queensland or something.'

'A small town down south,' said Ginger. Careful that the cameras couldn't catch it, she wrote *Flynn* on a Post-it note, then the name *Jason Avery*. That's where Vanilla comes from. His family own a fancy vineyard. It's what, an hour's drive?'

She shrugged. 'I reckon that's where she'll be, to be honest. Where else would she go? But we promised…'

'We promised we'd never contact her family or friends at home,' said Melinda, chewing her lower lip. 'It was part of the deal. She's terrified they'll find out about all this.'

Was rural internet access *really* that bad? Even a town like Flynn with a thousand or fewer occupants had to have at least one web geek who'd figured out the connection. Still, let them keep their illusions.

I looked at Xanthippe who was intrigued. 'C'mon, Tish. There must be something food related down that way. Give us an excuse.' Oh, she'd cracked out the high school nickname (I used to dress like Morticia Addams). So she was keen.

'Some of the state's best honey farms,' I admitted. 'Fresh fruit, the beginning of berry season…'

'There you are! So many excuses for a road trip.'

'It's a lot of petrol for a bit of honey.' Though mmm, honey gelato. There was a thought.

'We can pay you,' said Melinda. 'We make pretty good money off the webcams, and…' she hesitated, looking at Ginger.

'What she's not saying is that our subscribers are going to start kicking up if Anna isn't back in the house soon,' said Ginger. 'We've already got a bunch of cranky emails clogging up the server. French Vanilla has her own following, you know?'

Xanthippe snorted. 'Why did she choose that particular handle?'

Melinda shrugged. 'Vanilla—safe—boring. She never strips for the cameras. Always buttoned up. Some watchers like that more than the blatant stuff.' She gave Ginger an arch look. 'Though I swear she gets more harassing messages and emails than the two of us put together. Sometimes it pays to take your top off.'

'So,' I said. 'The promise you made to her means you don't want to check out her family house yourself … but you're okay with us doing it?'

'Hell, if it will shut Cherry up, it's worth it,' said Ginger. 'If she's not there, and not home by the time you're done, then … well, it will be the police, I guess. We'll pay you two hundred dollars for the trip. Plus petrol.'

Not a fortune, but nothing to be sneezed at. There was a very nice pair of shoes I'd been saving up for.

'Roaaaad trip,' Xanthippe said in an undertone. 'It is your day off, Tabitha. What else were you going to do?'

She had a point, and Nin would probably do better at the café without Xanthippe underfoot. 'Can we take the Spider?' I asked hopefully.

Xanthippe grinned. 'Hell yes.'

3

BLUEBELDERBERRY GELATO

In case you're wondering, my definition of gelato is 'sorbet with a bit of cream in'. As long as I stay away from genuine Italian people, I'll probably get away with it.

Ingredients:

1 cup water

2/3 cup caster sugar

4 cups fresh or frozen blueberries, blended (most recipes would try to make you strain out the bits but are they HIGH? All that beautiful blueberry pulp going down the sink, no thank you. I tried once and couldn't bear it. This is SUPERFOOD gelato.)

3 tablespoons elderberry cordial (if you can't find it, 2 tbs of lemon juice will do but then you have to call it Bluebemon, obviously)

2/3 cup thickened cream.

Instructions:

Put blended blueberries, water, cordial and sugar into a small saucepan. Stir over a low heat until sugar has dissolved.

Chill in fridge until super cold, or overnight.

Whisk/blend glorious purple liquid with cream.

Turn into ice cream by a) putting in metal bowl in freezer and stirring every half hour until ice creamable, or b) following instructions of your friendly neighbourly ice cream maker. The latter takes about 20 minutes. The former takes at least 3 hours. And part of your soul.

There's one problem with convertibles, which is nicely illustrated by Xanthippe's new haircut. As we bombed along the Huon Highway in her bright red 1972 (almost completely restored, still waiting on a few parts) Alfa Romeo Spider, Xanthippe's short, shaggy dark hair looked casually rumpled and adorable. My longer, lighter and entirely unstyled hair flew behind me like an insane cape, and, judging by the irritated noises behind me, it was actually trying to strangle Stewart.

It was vital that we kept moving. I had no idea what was going to happen to my hair when we stopped, but it wasn't going to be pretty.

'Vanilla,' said Xanthippe.

'You're as bad as Ceege! You can't say vanilla,' I complained.

'Sure I can.'

'That can't actually be your favourite.'

'Why not?'

'Vanilla is boring.'

'Classic,' she corrected. 'You appreciate classic clothes—' I had thrown on my one vintage Chanel black and white dress for the road trip because it was the outfit I owned that was most worthy of the Spider. Style matters. '—and classic cars. Why not classic flavours?'

'Chanel is not vanilla,' I pouted. 'The Spider is not vanilla. The Spider is chilli cherry chocolate bombe Alaska with salted caramel topping.'

Stewart leaned forward from where his long legs were impossibly folded into the tiny backseat. 'I cannae hear a word the two of ye are saying.'

'Favourite ice cream flavour?' I yelled back, getting a mouthful of my own hair as I tried.

'Rum an' raisin.'

I resisted the urge to kiss him. Kissing him would be bad. Also it was currently physically impossible. 'That's a good answer. I mean, it tells me that you're a middle-aged dad who should be playing golf somewhere, but at least it's not vanilla.'

Flynn was just about twenty minutes past Huonville, which came as a surprise to me as I hadn't previously realised there was much of anything past Huonville. We were well into the deep green of rural Tasmania now, and passed three posh tourist farms on our way in—lavender, honey and berries. No apples in sight, though I requested a stop at least three times to buy fruit on the side of the road. Xanthippe put her foot down and told me I could buy pears and organic cherries in Hobart, which was deeply unfair.

We made it to Flynn, and sent Stewart into the corner shop/takeaway/milk bar/newsagent to ask for directions to the Sunset Springs vineyard, where Annabeth French's postcard-sending ex-boyfriend could apparently be found.

'Why did we bring Stewart again?' I asked, when he was safely inside.

Xanthippe leaned on the wheel, shaking her hair back into place. Damn her. Mine was somewhere between a dustbunny and a mushroom cloud. 'He hasn't been around for months, and it's nice to catch up with friends. Also I'm auditioning him for the role of my sidekick.'

'Hey!'

She gave me a look. 'Want to keep him all to yourself?'

'Of course not,' I said quickly. 'But … you're my sidekick. You're not allowed to have one of your own.'

'I am not your sidekick!' she said indignantly. 'Nemesis, I can accept.'

I glanced at the shop. Still no Stewart. 'You're not interested in him, are you?' Oh help, it was high school all over again. *Do you like him, you know in a like like way?*

'What if I was?'

I so wasn't answering that question. 'Are you?'

Xanthippe laughed. Lucky for me, she gets bored with playing chicken pretty fast. 'I don't go for emo indie boys. Too much hard work.'

My first reaction was relief. Uh-oh. This was not something I should be feeling relieved about. As a respectable almost-in-a-relationship-it's-complicated woman, I should be matchmaking Stewart, not being pleased my friends didn't fancy him. I should be setting him up with Xanthippe so they could run off together for wild sex and happy fun times.

Instead, I said, 'He's not emo indie. Is he?'

'He blogs for a living, he makes wall art, he lives on black coffee and what's with all those grey T-shirts? Believe me, he counts as emo indie even without me knowing what kind of music he listens to.'

'Also, he writes romance novels,' I said as Stewart sauntered back to the car with an armful of supplies.

'I have nothing to add to that,' said Xanthippe. 'Good man, that McTavish!' she added, loud enough for him to hear. 'Navigate me.'

Stewart threw a tourist pamphlet at her and squeezed into the 'not quite big enough for a human' backseat, then leaned forward to share his bag of chips. 'We haftae go up a mountain.'

'Excellent,' Xanthippe said happily, examining the pastel-coloured map on the brochure and then tossing it on to the backseat. 'The Spider likes mountain roads. We laugh in the face of inclines and flirt madly with sheer cliff edges.'

'I should have brought a jumper,' I said sadly. Hot summer sun was all very well, but as soon as we got into the trees, it was going to get chilly.

Stewart fell back into his seat, taking his chips with him, and we were off.

The Avery Grove vineyard was lush. We drove up a long driveway lined with dark green trees that looked like they belonged in a Jane Austen costume drama. No sign of the drought here, even after six weeks of fierce sunshine, though I hated to think what their water bill was like.

Australian grass should never be this green in December.

The driveway snaked up to a huge old house, and ... okay, were those peacocks on the lawn? Why would anyone have peacocks in the same place as their grapevines? Talk about style over practicality.

A couple of lads in their late teens were attacking a trellis that was choked up with all kinds of evil, spiky greenery. One of them strolled over to us, eyes sweeping speculatively over me before he settled on Xanthippe, grinning widely at her. Hot brunette in a sports car, yeah yeah.

'Can I help you, love?'

She pushed up her sunglasses, not overly impressed with him. Which was probably a good thing, because he was far too impressed with himself. 'We're looking for Jason Avery.'

'I'm more fun,' the cheeky bugger said, leaning on my window to get a better angle for checking out Xanthippe.

'Excellent to know, I'll be sure and remember that,' she said, and the sarcasm was such a thin, subtle veil he probably didn't hear it. Stewart was snickering in the backseat, which suggested he did. Smart man, that McTavish.

'Ey, Jase,' Xanthippe's new conquest said, calling to the other bloke. 'Some people for you.'

The other plant-wrangler strolled over, not looking bothered. Late teens, blond, clothes barely hanging on to his frame, and his hair falling into his face. 'Restaurant's closed this week,' he said. 'Accommodation too—we're renovating. Cellar's a little further down the hill if it's wine you're after—did you miss the turn off?'

'Actually, we're looking for Annabeth French,' I said. 'Do you know where we might find her?'

Jason hesitated. 'What do you reckon, Shay?'

'Thursday arvo,' said the charmer. 'Scallop.'

The words made sense. Individually. I smiled politely while we waited for further translation.

'Local pub,' said Jason. 'She's on the afternoon shift. Should be working until five.'

Huh. That was surprisingly easy.

We parked outside The Scallop Shell, a bog-standard pub at the edge of town. A shortish, curvy girl with bright blonde curls was clearing tables in the beer garden. 'That her?' Xanthippe asked me.

'Looks a lot like her.' To be honest I hadn't seen her face on Ginger's computer, and it occurred to me now that paying attention to what our missing girl looked like might have been helpful.

I would make such a bad private detective.

'One way tae find out,' said Stewart. He looked at me. Xanthippe looked at me too.

'What?' I protested.

'We all have our special skills, Tabitha,' Xanthippe said patiently. 'Mine is dragging important information out of impressionable young men who want to make out with my car. Stewart is here for coffee fetching and the Scottish accent. Your job is making friends with runaway internet porn stars and all that girly shit that comes so easily for you.'

Well, okay then. As long as we each had a niche.

'Be good,' I said as I got out of the car, using my fingers in a vain attempt to tidy my hair.

'Shame,' said Xanthippe. 'I was planning to molest Stewart in the backseat while you're gone.'

'I dinnae put out on the first date,' said Stewart.

Xanthippe grinned at him. 'I do.'

I chose to rise above their blatant flirting. None of my business at all. *Repeat after me: the cute Scottish boy is not yours, the cute Scottish boy is not yours…*

'Annabeth French?' I asked as I approached the blonde.

She looked warily at me, stacking the last of her plates. 'Yes?'

'I'm Tabitha. Ginger and Melinda—I mean Cherry—asked me to look for you.'

A look of alarm crossed her face. 'Really?'

'Well, yeah. They were worried. You vanished quite … unexpectedly this morning.'

'Oh.' She nodded, still nervous. 'Yes. I was, um. Sorry to run out on them. I couldn't take any more of it. I needed to come home.'

And that decision had taken four minutes during a power cut? Intriguing.

'I'm glad you're okay,' I said finally. Really, this wasn't any of my business. Sure, their webcam business might suffer, but the girl showed no sign of having been abducted. If she didn't want to be French Vanilla any more, that was up to her. 'They almost called the police.'

'Oh wow,' Annabeth said, sounding stunned. 'That's … wow. Overkill. I'm fine. I was just over the whole … thing.' She glanced around nervously. 'No one around here knows about that. The Gingerbread House, I mean. I'd rather they never did.'

She thought she could keep a secret like that in a small town? Again, none of my business.

'You might want to give the girls a call—work out what to do with your stuff. They've got your phone.' Wallet, most of her clothes ... she must have got out of there fast. Ten to one there was a bloke at the heart of it.

'I will, I totally will,' said Annabeth. 'I'll borrow a phone and text them tonight. It was nice of them to send someone looking for me. I sort of thought they wouldn't miss me that much.'

'They were really worried,' I told her. Huh. So much for the 'she's so responsible, never misses a shift' Vanilla that Ginger and Melinda had been so certain would never walk out of her own volition. This girl seemed like a completely different person.

'I feel so bad, omigod,' she assured me. 'I'll call.'

Fair enough.

I made my farewell and headed back to the car. 'She's here, she's fine, no drama, wasted trip.' Don't get me wrong, I was glad she wasn't dead in a ditch or tied up in a cellar somewhere. But it still felt like it had been a pointless trip.

'Not wasted,' said Xanthippe. 'We made some cash, and look.' She pointed across the street where a huge orange sign proclaimed: Best Ice Cream Parlour In Tasmania. 'See? Completely worth it. If you're going to make ice cream, you have to research the competition.'

In other words, she wanted an ice cream.

'Fine,' I said. 'But you're not allowed to pick vanilla.'

'Fascist!'

4

From: Nincakes

Tabitha, what is that pink muck in the freezer?

From: Darlingtabitha

That is my attempt at bacon sorbet. LET US NEVER SPEAK OF IT AGAIN.

From: Nincakes

get it out of the freezer before I dob you into the health inspectors.

From: Darlingtabitha

If only I could think of some ethical and environmentally friendly way to dispose of it…

From: Nincakes

WHY ARE THERE SO MANY CATS IN THE COURTYARD?

It was getting on for evening when I got home, all windswept and interesting. That was one way to spend a day off. I had no idea why Xanthippe was so hell bent on playing detective, but if it kept her out of my café it couldn't be a bad thing.

Anyway. We were done. False alarm, red herring, whatever.

I wandered through my kitchen, thinking idly about what to cook for dinner. Something easy. French toast.

Dinner. Holy crap. I ran for my staircase, scrambling up to my attic bedroom. As usual, the floor and bed were covered in random clothes. As was ... becoming less unusual, there was also a police sergeant on my bed, wearing a suit and looking impatient.

'I am SO sorry,' I said, pouncing on him. 'There was this whole...' Hmm, non police people investigating missing girl was just the kind of thing that my ... Person Who Is Not My Boyfriend tends to get cranky about. 'Ice cream emergency,' I said finally.

Leo Bishop looked amused, which meant I wasn't too late. Good to know. 'You have more emergencies than anyone I know, Tish, and they're always delicious.'

I kissed him thoroughly, arms winding around his neck, and his hands sliding up my back. 'Favourite ice cream flavour?' I asked breathlessly when we finally came up for air. 'You're not allowed to say vanilla.'

Bishop kissed down my neck, mouth all warm and teasing against my skin. 'What's wrong with vanilla?'

'Oh you are kidding me.'

He laughed. 'It's a classic.'

'It's a conspiracy is what it is,' I muttered.

He drew back, eyeing my 'road trip in hot sports car' Chanel dress. I loved it to bits, from its black and white scalloped bodice to its mad, flouncy flared skirt. The threads were starting to go a bit, and it had a piece of duct tape holding the hem together, but it was still gorgeous.

'Is that what you're wearing?' Bishop asked. I could practically hear him trying to be tactfully enthusiastic. The fancy dinner we were supposed to be going to was not the place for creative fashion choices.

'No, no, I have a real dress,' I assured him, jumping up. 'It's on a coat hanger and everything.' I'd searched ages for something a bit more conservative than my usual style, but still looked cute on me. Little black dress ahoy. 'I even have boring shoes,' I said proudly as I unzipped the Chanel and let it fall in a flouncy puddle on the floor, leaving me only in a long black slip as I hunted around for the boring shoes.

'Oh, oops.' One of said boring shoes had ended up in an abandoned half-full cup of coffee. Ew. 'Might have to go with interesting shoes.'

Bishop walked over to me, one hand sliding over my hip, wrinkling the light satin fabric of the slip. 'I can live with interesting shoes.' He dipped his mouth down to mine again.

We were late to the fancy dinner.

Really, really late.

✹

Back in March, I kissed two men on the same day. A kiss is just a kiss, right? It doesn't have to mean anything. Except that one of them did, and I'm almost certain I made the right choice.

No, I know I made the right choice. I've been crazy about Bishop for years. My skin heats up when he steps into a room. He was head of the queue. Hell, he was the entire queue.

Stewart is a good friend, who makes me laugh and has a hot Scottish accent. But I'm sure now we weren't ever meant to be more than friends. It's not like he even made much of a protest when I told him that Bishop and I were together. He shrugged. I mean, who does that? If you really fancy someone, you don't just shrug when they tell you they are hooking up with another bloke.

It took Bishop and me a while to figure out some of our issues. We tried being boyfriend and girlfriend and not having sex, but that was a disaster. We got back on the rails when we decided to leave the boyfriend and girlfriend words out altogether, and just get on with the hot sex and occasional dating. It's good, so far. It works just fine.

Stewart disappearing on his unplanned blogging trip around Tasmania made everything less complicated, because then I didn't have to think about the fact that I was spending a lot more energy flirting with the friend I wasn't sleeping with than the one that I was.

Oh, and when Stewart's around, somehow we always end up investigating mysteries together. And I really don't need that in my life. Give me a hot police officer who disapproves of me getting tangled in such things any day of the week.

I slept late, which was bad. I've been doing that a lot lately—it's an unfortunate side effect of having a warm snuggly man in bed with me. Getting up for the early food prep is a struggle, even with daylight blistering into my bedroom before six AM.

I'm supposed to get up at *five* AM.

The alarm went off and I hit the snooze button before snuggling back under the doona. Mm, warm arm. Warm chest. And was that the second or third time I had hit snooze? Damn. I was going to have to check.

The phone rang, somewhere in the house. Bishop grunted a little and pushed back the doona. I promptly flipped it back over us. 'Ceege will get it. He's probably still up.' My housemate had gone seriously nocturnal in the last few weeks. 'Or Xanthippe. She has to be at the café as early as I do.'

'Mmm, good.' Bishop turned into me, his jaw grazing against mine. 'Very good.' He looked seriously at me for a long moment, those dark eyes holding mine, and then he started kissing me.

Say anything you like about the man, once he kisses you, you stay kissed.

Things were starting to get interesting—hands sliding over heated skin, lips and teeth and tongue getting in on the action, when my mobile rang. I reached out and switched it off without breaking the snog, rolling on top of him as I did so.

A minute later, Bishop's phone started to ring. Damn it. The trouble with shagging a police officer is that when his phone rings, he can't ignore it. I slid off him so he could lean down and pull his phone out of his discarded jacket. He answered briefly, then passed it over to me with an odd look on his face.

'McTavish, for you.'

I blinked, and looked at his phone. Slowly, I reached out and took it like it was going to bite me, or at the very least, judge me quite hard. 'Stewart?'

'All right, Tabitha.'

Well, this was awkward. I pulled the doona up to cover my breasts, not looking at Bishop. 'What's up?' I said into the phone.

'Ye haftae read the paper,' said Stewart, and there was something in his voice that made me realise there was more going on there than a massively embarrassing moment between the men in my life.

'What's happened?' My stomach pinged with anxiety as he paused far too long before answering.

'Just read it, and get back tae me.'

✼

Xanthippe was in our kitchen, putting on the coffee. Ceege was at the table, drinking his 'just this one and then I crash into bed' early morning beer. They both looked at me.

'What?' I glanced at the paper, which was folded on the table. 'Everyone is weird today.'

I didn't want to unfold it. Not with the 'we don't want to be the ones to tell you' vibe. I should have just read it on my phone from bed. But peer pressure is like a bravery pill. Or something.

I flipped open the paper, and read about a nineteen-year-old girl who had been found drowned in Lake Serenity in the town of Flynn yesterday evening. She had been identified as Annabeth French, and her boyfriend Jason Avery had been arrested for her murder.

'Oh,' I said faintly.

'Yep,' said Xanthippe.

'Is that all you have to say?'

She gave me a long, measuring look. 'Yep.'

I looked at the paper again. 'Oh boy. Do you think having a conversation with a murder victim a few hours before her death is … something that I should tell someone about?'

'Depends,' said Xanthippe. 'How much do you want to lie to your boyfriend?'

'Really a lot right now,' I said, eyes on the shiny picture of Annabeth on the front page. 'Might be hard to explain.'

'Always is,' said Xanthippe, who had a long history of explaining the inexplicable to Bishop. What with being his half-sister.

'And he's not my boyfriend,' I added automatically.

'Tell it to the judge.'

Bishop strolled into the kitchen, hair damp from the shower, still buttoning up his shirt.

'My eyes!' Xanthippe complained. 'Keep your pectorals to yourself, Leo. Some of us are related to you and choose not to know about your sex life.'

Bishop laughed, and leaned down to kiss me. I kissed back, trying not to look too distracted. 'Got to get in to the station,' he said to me.

'Mm, I'm running late. Nin will kill me.'

'No, she'll blame me,' he corrected. 'Last time I made you late she came after me with a rolling pin.'

'You know you love the attention.'

I waited until he was gone, then turned my guilty expression in Xanthippe's general direction. 'I'll tell him later.'

'Uh huh.'

'If the subject comes up. Specifically.'

I went to work. Just another day of serving up coffee and macarons, and trying to find a viable alternative to hollandaise sauce now that Hobart is finally over the Great Hollandaise Sauce Frenzy of the early 21st Century.

The good thing about working a café is that if you need to not think, there's always something to keep you busy. Lara and

Yui were both freaked out about Annabeth, but it turned out that neither of them knew her that well, it was just the fact of her death that had knocked them off their socks.

Nineteen years old. Yeah. That was quite a fact.

Every time someone mentioned her, I announced a kitchen emergency and walked away from them. Eventually they got the message. Tabitha Darling was not at home to conversations about dead girls. Not even on her tea break.

It shouldn't have got to me as much as it did. Right? I barely knew Annabeth. We'd had one conversation, and we hadn't exactly clicked.

Stewart dropped in a few times—he was back working in the office a floor above the café, and this had been our normal routine back before he pulled his disappearing act. I would have relished the normality of it, if not for the fact that he wanted to sound out how I felt about the Annabeth French story, and I wasn't up for it. I poured him a double espresso every time, and kept moving.

He got the message too, and stopped asking. It's good to have people in your life who know when not push.

The push came after work. I lay on the couch with a book, to the comforting background noise of Ceege clicky clicking. Ceege at least had no interest in probing how I felt about the latest mysterious death in our lives.

'Did you know that more than fifty percent of the desserts sold worldwide contain vanilla?' I said to him, flicking pages.

'Told you,' he said without looking up. 'Everyone loves vanilla.'

'Yeah, yeah.' The universe was telling me I had to learn to make the perfect vanilla ice cream. Ceege was being unreasonably smug about this. 'Did you know that ninety-seven percent of vanilla used in food or perfume is actually not real vanilla at all?'

'That must be what gives it that delicious plastic flavour.'

'Philistine.'

'Hey, you're a chef who doesn't appreciate vanilla, I don't think I'm the philistine here. Isn't that the sort of thing that gets you put in the stocks with people throwing bocconcini at you? Bad enough that time you banned capers and caused the Great Smoked Salmon Riot of 2011.'

'If you ever bothered to look up from your keyboard, you would know I am sticking my tongue out at you.'

'If you were reading my Twitter feed right now you would know how much that hurts my feelings.'

'Did you know vanilla is an orchid?'

'There are no words for how much I do not care. Busy here, Tabs.'

'Busy playing games with your imaginary people! I'm a real person, Ceege, talk to me.'

'My internet peeps are not imaginary.'

'Apart from that guy in Auckland.'

'We promised to never mention that again.'

'You have to put up with my boring you senseless with vanilla trivia,' I said. 'You started me on this.'

'I also like chocolate.'

'Shut up.'

The phone rang and I didn't even bother suggesting that Ceege could answer it—that would mean moving two metres from his chair that was developing some very intense bum-cheek grooves. 'Hello?'

'Tabitha.'

'Stewart.' Apparently we didn't even say hello to each other any more.

'I've bin looking at the archives o' The Gingerbread House website.'

All the fun drained out of the evening, just like that. 'I'm kind of busy...'

'Aye, can ye suspend yer avoidance tactics fer a few minutes?' he said abruptly. 'Ye'll be interested in this.'

I sighed, returning to the couch and putting my feet up. 'Okay, fine. Hit me. You have been looking at pictures of a dead nineteen-year-old because...'

'She's nae dead.'

Okay, that I wasn't expecting. 'Come again?'

'The dead girl in the lake wasnae French Vanilla,' Stewart said simply.

Well, fuck.

5

'You realise you sound ridiculous,' I said to Stewart, which was something of a relief. Usually I'm the one who sounds ridiculous.

'Check out the site, Tabitha,' said Stewart. 'I'm lookin' at it right now, and there is nae way that French Vanilla is the same girl they pulled from the lake.'

I blinked. 'So which one did I talk to?'

'Ye tell me.'

I was already moving to Ceege, tugging on his T-shirt sleeve. 'Budge up, I need to use my ten minutes a day computer time!'

'I can't log off now,' he protested. 'I have literally tens of people waiting for the new chapter of my Captain America fanfic.'

'And they'll appreciate it all the more if they have to wait a little longer for it.'

He glared, and did some rapid typing. 'What do you need it for, anyway?'

'I need to look at webcam footage of topless girls.'

Ceege moved out of the chair so fast I think I was hit by a sonic wave. Either that, or nacho crumbs. 'I am completely okay with that.'

'Why, thank you.'

I put Stewart on speaker phone and sat down, typing in the address he read aloud to me. The Gingerbread House. Cute. In a disturbing kind of way. The home page that blinked up displayed a cartoon gingerbread house with the various options displayed in windows—Chat, Archives, Hot Hits, Profiles, Forums and of course the veiled promise of Subscriber Only.

'Check out Profiles,' Stewart said through the phone speaker, and I clicked over to images of Gingernutz (away from the cameras we had been told her real name was Libby), Cherry_ ripe (Melinda) and a sweet looking blonde girl calling herself French Vanilla.

'Bloody hell.'

'Nae the same girl, is it?'

'Ceege, get me the paper from the kitchen.'

'What did your last slave sue you for?'

'Ceege!'

My lazy-arse housemate muttered under his breath but went hunting for the paper. He really didn't need to. 'No,' I said into the phone. 'Really not the same girl.'

'Should I come o'er?'

If I hesitated—and let's be clear on this, I did hesitate—it was because solving mysteries has not been a healthy life choice for me in the past, and had nothing to do with how there was this giant 'we kissed, and I got together with someone else, and you vanished for half a year' hole in our friendship right now.

'Of course,' I said, cheerfully enough that we could both pretend there hadn't been a really awkward pause.

Deniability is a wonderful thing.

Xanthippe came home late. I don't know where she goes—I imagine her posing gorgeously in nightclubs too cool for anyone else to have ever heard about, drinking cocktails that haven't been invented yet, that sort of thing. Either that, or she works nights as a security guard somewhere.

She walked in on me as I was in the middle of throwing raw vegetable sticks at two of the men in my life. 'I made dipping sauces!' I yelled at them.

'Vegetables, Tabs,' Ceege complained. 'We're men, we need meat. Or at least bacon. But if bacon, also cheese and grease.'

'Xanthippe,' Stewart yelped as I pelted him with slivers of carrot. 'Vote fer pizza! We want pizza.'

She leaned over the kitchen table and picked a piece of celery off his shoulder, biting into it. 'Tish, let the boys order pizza. You know they'll eat the vegetables while they're waiting anyway. It's a win win situation.'

I sulked, but took the phone out of my bra and relinquished it to Ceege.

'Classy,' Xanthippe noted. 'So what did I miss?'

'A mystery,' I said as Ceege started ordering far more pizza than four ordinary sized people should ever hope to eat. 'Again. Apparently it's what we do now.'

'Sounds promising.'

'The girl who went missing from The Gingerbread House wasnae Annabeth French,' Stewart said. 'Annabeth French wasnae French Vanilla.'

'Right,' said Xanthippe, sitting on the kitchen counter,

because she can't just use a chair like a normal person. 'That's unexpected.'

'It means our missing girl is still missing,' I agreed. 'For some reason, French Vanilla was pretending to be Annabeth French from Flynn.' I thought about it some more. 'Annabeth must have been in on it. She pretended to know what I was talking about, when I asked her about Ginger and Melinda. So she has to have known about it.'

This was bad. Really bad. I had thought I was so clever, going to bed safe in the knowledge that I hadn't done anything wrong—sure, I'd gone haring across country to search for a missing person on very little provocation, but it had been a red herring, no one was missing, and the world was a right and proper place.

But the world wasn't a right and proper place any more. French Vanilla was still missing, whoever she was, and the person whose name she had borrowed was drowned in a lake only a few hours after I talked to her.

I was starting to get the feeling I was living inside a Hitchcock movie. Did that mean I needed to bleach my hair a few shades blonder?

Ceege looked from one to the other of us. It was rare that anything happening in this house was interesting enough to drag him out of his cozy gaming-and-fanfic post-breakup world. 'So what are you going to do?'

'Stewart's going to blog about it, and Tabitha's going to

agonise about what she does and doesn't tell her boyfriend, right up to the point where her boyfriend reads Stewart's blog and has a blazing row with her about it,' said Xanthippe. Fair call, really. Apart from Bishop not being my boyfriend, but I'd given up with her on that point. She stood up, striking a heroic stance, all righteous and dramatic. 'Meanwhile, I'm going to find French Vanilla.'

'How are you going to do that?' I asked her. 'We don't even know who she is.'

'No,' said Xanthippe. 'But I think Libby and Melinda—or Ginger and Cherry or whatever they want to call themselves—know more than they are saying.'

'So what can we do?' I asked, hoping she could come up with something that sounded vaguely comforting. 'If Vanilla's still missing, and there's a connection to the murder inquiry, we need to tell the police. Before they hear about it on Stewart's blog.'

Not telling Bishop was starting to loom large and problematic in my head. Last time something like this had happened, I kept information from him longer than I should have done—okay, he hadn't made it that easy for me to confide in him, and he completely didn't believe me when I did confess all, but still. It was my bad.

This time around, it was worse, because we were kind of sort of (well okay, completely) an item, and I didn't want to screw things up irretrievably.

'No,' said Stewart in his low burr. 'Ginger and Melinda need to tell the police. We cannae be involved in that part. It isnae our business.'

'So what we need to do is persuade them,' said Xanthippe. She looked at me. Pointedly.

I sighed. 'Does my niche really cover that too?'

'Talking people into stuff has always been your superpower.'

For this visit, both women kept their tops on, which helped with the seriousness of the situation. Melinda had to keep getting up to run to the loo to wee or throw up in that pregnant lady way of hers, which broke the conversation up whenever it felt like we were getting somewhere.

'It's nerves,' she said when she returned for the eighth time. 'Sorry. I just can't stop thinking about Anna—or whoever she was.'

'Why would someone lie about being someone else?' Ginger said, not for the first time. 'I don't get it.'

'It does seem odd,' Xanthippe agreed. 'There are a lot of reasons why someone might want to pretend to be someone else … but if she wanted to hide, putting her own face on the internet on a daily basis wasn't the smoothest plan.'

'Maybe Anna was the one hiding,' I said. 'I mean, the real Anna.' The one who had been alive yesterday, and now wasn't.

'How can we report someone missing if we don't know who she was?' Ginger said in frustration.

Xanthippe and I looked at each other. 'We could find out who she was,' Xanthippe said with a gleam in her eye.

Melinda and Ginger did not know her well enough to know what that gleam meant, but I did. 'We're going to need to look in her room,' I said.

Why yes, I am a nosy person.

You can tell a lot about a person from their bedroom. French Vanilla (I couldn't call her Annabeth, just about the only fact we knew about this girl was that she wasn't Annabeth French) kept a tidy personal space, with a real patchwork quilt thrown over the top of her bed, piles of uni books on a shelf, and a laptop on the desk. A stack of postcards were neatly piled up beside her desk, a rubber band holding them in place.

'Hey,' I said thoughtfully, sitting on the bed and picking up a psychology textbook. 'Melinda said she was a student. How does that work? Did she steal Annabeth's identity to attend university in her name? What would be the benefit of that?'

Xanthippe nodded, already opening the laptop. 'Maybe she was paid to do it. Annabeth's dumb at exams, pays someone else to do uni for her, literally buys herself a degree.'

'So hard to pull off,' I argued. 'I mean—so much paperwork. Was she getting Centrelink payments too? That's major fraud.'

'Let's just see, shall we?' Xanthippe made a cursory inspection of the desktop. 'This is tidy too. Neat sort of person.'

'You're neat, that doesn't mean you're hiding a big secret.' Or did it? I wouldn't put it past Xanthippe.

'Tabitha, if you don't want to be here…'

'I do,' I said indignantly. 'I can snoop with the best of them. No conscience here, I am all about the random invasions of privacy.' I eyed the wardrobe, but that felt a bit too randomly invasive.

'Bags postcards,' I decided, snatching the bundle. Postcards were good. Anyone could read a postcard, it was hardly an ethical issue at all. Postcards practically begged to be read by complete strangers.

'They're from Jason,' I reported a little while later, after flipping through several. 'Well, we knew that. Melinda told us…'

'I don't know that I believe a word those two say,' said Xanthippe. 'They're too nice. I don't trust nice people.'

'I'm nice,' I pouted.

'No, Tabitha, you just smile a lot because you sell more coffee that way. Deep down, you're as cynical and broken as the rest of us.'

Hmm, interesting point. I wasn't sure if I agreed with her, but we weren't here to debate my personality. I kept reading the postcards. 'He definitely thought Annabeth was living here. Asks her to give up uni—she knows she's going to hate it, why doesn't she just come home … ooh.'

Wow. I almost never blushed, but this was… 'Okay, who writes stuff that personal on a postcard?'

'Is it smutty?'

'It's past suggestive and heading towards smutty. Teenagers these days! Can't they just sext like normal people?'

'Good for Jason,' she said, and then I saw her expression change as she recalled that Jason had been arrested for Annabeth's murder, back in Flynn. 'Oh, crap.'

I looked down at the postcards. 'I shouldn't have touched these, should I? I mean, they're evidence. The police can—fingerprints, and…' Fuck. Bishop was not going to be pleased. 'We really need to get out of here.'

'Hang on,' said Xanthippe, producing a memory stick. 'Just let me copy these files.'

'Oh, you're so not.'

'I want to find French Vanilla, don't you?' A few minutes later she shut the computer down, pocketing the memory stick again. 'I have no problem with turning all this over to the police, but that doesn't mean I can't have my own investigation.'

'You hate working in a café, don't you?' I accused.

Xanthippe nodded solemnly. 'I have developed a phobia of sugar packets. It's time for a new challenge.'

'Private detective?'

'If the awesomely retro fedora hat fits…'

6

random_scotsman posts in Sandstone City:

WHO IS FRENCH VANILLA?

One week ago, Annabeth French (19) from Flynn, Tasmania was found dead in a lake near her family home. Annabeth's family say she was a bright, happy girl who had been enjoying her holidays from university. Annabeth's boyfriend, Jason Avery was arrested in connection to her death, but was later released without charge. The police are not ruling out death by misadventure.

But questions remain about the life and death of Annabeth French. While her family believed her to be spending the year in Hobart, studying Arts/Law, the University of Tasmania has no evidence of her enrolment. More crucially, Annabeth gave her address to her family and boyfriend as a residence now known to be the infamous live webcam site The Gingerbread House. The quiet blonde Gingerbread Girl known as french_vanilla was not Annabeth French, though this was the name her housemates knew her by.

French_vanilla herself went missing from The Gingerbread House on December 5th, twelve hours before Annabeth French was killed. The police are publicly advertising for anyone knowing the whereabouts or identity of french_vanilla. Neither the Missing Persons Unit nor the team responsible for investigating the death of Annabeth French has confirmed whether they believe the anonymous french_vanilla is Annabeth's fellow victim, or her killer.

Comments (166)

My ice cream-making experiments, on the whole, were a lot more successful than my mystery solving. I made one batch every night, served it up via the Specials Board the next day, and sold it until we ran out.

Ginger honeydew, lime green tea, triple salted caramel and cherry cheesecake were all super popular. I never quite got evil enough to serve up the raspberry vinaigrette, though I did manage to pull off wasabi avocado. Well, opinions were divided as to whether I pulled it off, but I feel pretty secure about it.

I still hadn't perfected the vanilla. Which was annoying, because everyone kept requesting it. I had put up a Tabitha's Ice Cream suggestion box: vanilla, french vanilla and vanilla bean were the ones that turned up most often. They weren't even in Xanthippe's handwriting, which cannot be said for many of the other suggestions, including 'screwdriver' and 'crunchy frog.'

Vanilla was hard.

'Why's it French Vanilla anyway?' Stewart asked one quiet evening at my place. I came home from a long day at the café to find him playing *MarioKart* with Ceege. Then, after Ceege fell asleep on the couch because he'd pulled three all nighters in a row, Stewart came into the kitchen and sorted the suggestion slips for me while I made a batch of lemon meringue gelato.

I was pretending I hadn't noticed that Stewart had slipped in three extras that all read 'triple espresso, hold the ice cream'. 'Is there something particularly French about vanilla?' he went on. 'Or is it a thing that fancy ice cream makers say tae make it sound less boring?'

'That's what I always thought,' I said. 'Before I started researching it. It's America's fault.'

'Doesnae surprise me in the least.'

'All these fancypants people in Philadelphia became obsessed with ice cream, and hired French chefs to make it for them. Thomas Jefferson imported the vanilla from Paris during the French Revolution rather than getting it directly from Mexico or the Caribbean like a sane person. They called it French for snobby reasons. Also to distinguish between French ice cream which had egg in it, and Philadelphia ice cream, which didn't.'

Stewart grinned at her. 'Yer like an encyclopedia of dessert.'

'I've been called worse.'

I'll admit the trouble with me creating the perfect vanilla ice cream was that, despite all my deep and committed research, I still couldn't buy the concept that vanilla was interesting.

The *story* of vanilla was fascinating. Pirates and smugglers and slaves and orchids—brilliant stuff. Worthy of a good old bodice-ripping adventure story.

But the flavour itself bored the pants off me. Every time I started on vanilla I'd get the itch to add a touch of cinnamon or chilli chocolate and before I knew what I was doing, it wasn't vanilla any more. Or at all.

Lemon meringue on the other hand ... now that was a flavour I could get behind. Tangy sour scoops of dark lemon sorbet, surrounded by a creamy concoction of broken meringue pieces and something vaguely vanilla-ish as garnish. But only vaguely.

A cop out, maybe. But it was a delicious cop out.

'Much response to the French Vanilla story on the blog?' I asked him.

'Aye,' said Stewart, binning several requests for banana-related ice creams (he had a moral objection to them—I'd always suspected he had depth) and pushing the pile of Stewart-approved slips in my general direction. 'Turns out The Ginger-bread House has a massive local following. Girls, mostly.'

'Girls?' I said in surprise. 'I thought it would be more...'

'Dirty old men? And fourteen-year-old boys? Aye, I thought so too. Turns out that—Ginger taking her top off nae withstanding—most of the appeal isnae the sex. People watch them for entertainment. Listen to their conversations. The whole storyline where Melinda got knocked up by her ex and decided to have the baby on her own practically melted their server. It's like a cut price *Big Brother*. And…' he hesitated.

'Spit it out, Stewart,' I told him. Before the Bishop thing reared its head, we were excellent at being honest around each other.

'They earn their money wi' subscriptions. Highlights of the week are available on the site tae all viewers, but only subscribers get access via the live feed. D'ye remember they said they might lose subscribers without French Vanilla? Because she had her own fan following? Well, since the investigation intae her disappearance began, their subscriber numbers are up 20 percent.'

'Wow,' I said. I took a mouthful of sour lemon and puckered my mouth. Possibly too sour. 'Wow,' I said again. 'So they benefited financially from their housemate going missing?'

'Aye, tha's my thinking. 'Course, I have a nasty suspicious mind.'

'Yes you do,' I told him, and made him taste the lemon. 'But that doesn't mean you're wrong.'

'Wrong about what?' Xanthippe asked, strolling into the kitchen just as Stewart made a horrible face about my lemon sorbet. 'I love how you're too original to make ice cream flavours that people actually like, Tish.'

'Hush, vanilla-lover,' I said to her. She looked nice. Suspiciously unlike a hired assassin, which is to say she was actually wearing a plum-coloured top instead of something black or so-navy-blue-that-it-might-as-well-be-black. 'Going somewhere special?'

'Just dropping over to Ginger's,' she said casually.

Stewart and I looked at each other.

'By Ginger's you mean the house that is wired for image and sound, where every move you make is documented and broadcast to nearly four hundred paying customers, with edited highlights available to the entire web and averaging about 10,000 unique visitors per day?' I asked, to clarify.

Xanthippe gave me a look. 'That's the one.'

'Ye wouldnae be planning tae discuss the missing person case tha's provided them with a substantial increase in their hits and paid subscription o'er the last week?' Stewart asked, stealing some of my cracked meringue cream to take the taste of lemon away.

'The subject might come up. While we're hanging out socially. But I don't work to a script.' Xanthippe folded her arms. 'If you have something to say, just say it.'

I didn't say it. I thought really loudly about how it seemed convenient that she and 'Ginger' were getting along so well, and how regular visits from Xanthippe to The Gingerbread House couldn't help but keep the online viewers thinking about the missing person case. But Xanthippe was too smart to be used like that, wasn't she? Maybe she was playing them. Maybe there was a plan.

And it was really obvious that she wanted me to ask her what that plan was. I am not exceptionally good at doing what other people want, if it's not a specific customer-is-always-right scenario.

So I said nothing. I exchanged innocent glances with Stewart, and then stole back my meringue spoon, rapping him over the knuckles with it. 'Have a nice night, Zee.'

We sat in silence for a few minutes after she left. Stewart and I never used to do awkward silences, but recently we're becoming expert at them. 'So,' he said finally. 'Have ye subscribed tae the live feed yet?'

'Of course not,' I said sternly. 'That would suggest a morbid fascination with something which is none of my business.'

'Aye, right.'

'Ceege, however…'

Caught off guard, Stewart laughed. 'Does Ceege know he's a subscriber?'

'He'll find out about it when he gets his credit card statement.'

Served him right for falling asleep in front of the Playstation. Honestly, that boy had to get out more. Though at least gaming with Stewart felt like a slight improvement on him staring at a computer all night, every night. Was he coming out from his black cloud, perhaps?

'Yer a bad person.' Stewart beat me to Ceege's chair, settling into the scary butt grooves with a smug look on his face, and leaving me to lean over his skinny shoulder if I wanted to see what was on the computer.

Which I did, of course. Not leaning over his shoulder would have meant something I totally didn't mean it to mean. Or anything. My hair brushed his shoulder as he found the website.

'You don't really think…' I said.

'That French Vanilla was an elaborate plot device used tae spice up their reality web series? It's worth considering.'

Yes, yes it was.

'Ye figured that out yerself, though,' Stewart went on.

'Obviously.' If we were considering sinister possibilities, I could also start wondering whether Melinda and Ginger had locked dear little Vanilla Girl up in a cupboard somewhere to boost their income.

Stewart flicked around the site, figuring out how the live feed worked, checking in on the different rooms in the house. 'They dinnae have one in the bathroom,' he reported.

'Ew. Thank goodness for that.'

Ginger was in the kitchen, making something that looked like pasta. Melinda sat on the couch, reading baby magazines on her iPad.

'Want sound?' Stewart asked.

I moved away from the screen (and him), settling on the couch so I still had a view of the computer, but not quite so intimate. 'This feels wrong.'

'It's nae like they dinnae know people are watching. People are supposed tae watch.'

Libby and Melinda were so relaxed. How did they do that? It made me feel all scratchy, like bugs were crawling on my skin. Even if they were inviting it, it was so voyeuristic.

I could of course justify it by saying I was looking out for

Xanthippe. Yep, that was the reason. Nothing to do with being a nosy person at all.

My phone rang and I felt guilty the second I saw Bishop's name come up. Really, I had to stop doing that. I was perfectly entitled to spend the evening with a friend, watching women through webcams and speculating about an unsolved crime.

It wasn't like Bishop was my boyfriend or anything.

'Hey,' I said in my best innocent voice. 'What's up?'

Stewart, darting a look at me (ha, he knew my innocent voice meant trouble), stood up and went to get some more coffee, or something equally discreet.

'Wanted to let you know I have to stay late after all,' Bishop told me. (How much did I suck for forgetting we had vague plans tonight?)

'I'm sure I can think of something to do. I have a new ice cream flavour to play with.'

'Aren't you sick of ice cream yet?'

'That's the silliest question you've ever asked me.'

My attention was diverted by the computer screen. Xanthippe had arrived at The Gingerbread House already—hardly surprising, as the place was a five minute drive away.

'So I can trust you not to get into any trouble left to your own devices?' Bishop asked, only half serious.

'Mmmhmm,' I said. The second he hung up, I was going to turn up the volume on the computer. I really wanted to know what they were saying. 'I'll probably just read up on the history of artificial vanilla chemicals. Throw things at Ceege. The usual.'

Spy on Xanthippe, spend the evening with Stewart, eat lots of ice cream. None of those things counted as getting into trouble. I wasn't lying to him at all.

I could probably get off on a technicality.

7

GINGERBREAD FORUMS: Q&A

KrazeeKween: Cherry, I love your hair so much OMG! Where do you get it done?

Cherry_ripe: Hey KK. I always go to Tresses in Nth Hobart, but I haven't had any colour put in since I got pregnant, so that's all natural!

Ishtaa1988: question for all of you, are you really super close friends like you seem, or do you secretly hate each other?

Gingernutz: well I hate everyone. Of course I can only do it between 2am and 4am when Cherry and Vanilla are sleeping

Cherry_ripe: *smacks Ginge*

Gingernutz: heeee *sticks out tongue*

French_vanilla: I think it would be horrible if we weren't friends. Not just living together … living with someone you don't like SUX.

Gingernutz: yeah, and why else would we put up with Cherry blubbing through daytime soaps + throwing up all the time? If she wasn't super sweet, we'd have kicked her to the kerb months ago omg!!

French_vanilla: totally. Also, Ginger snores.

Gingernutz: I do not. U pick your teeth.

French_vanilla: only when you're there.

Gingernutz: *hits with pillow*

French_vanilla: *hides behind pregnant lady*

Cherry_ripe: Children, behave! People are watching us!!!

Gingernutz: they ARE?

This was dull. Seriously. Xanthippe was having dinner with two women. They were chatting. Eating pasta. All very pleasant and innocuous. They hadn't even mentioned French Vanilla yet, or poor old Annabeth.

Stewart and I were playing tiddlywinks. And no, that's not a euphemism.

'How can she hae covered everything?' Stewart asked, lying on his stomach on the floor to get the best angle to flip the big red tiddlywink into the bowl. 'Her real identity. She must hae left some trace of it. She lived with them for wha', nine months?'

'It was deliberate,' I said. 'Must have been. Xanthippe has the entire contents of French Vanilla's computer on her laptop—there was nothing worth looking at. A half finished novel, a few months of browser history, mainly related to The Gingerbread House site. Nothing personal. She used webmail only, and we don't have her passwords.'

'Tha's suspicious,' he said. 'The neatness. Almost as if she was expecting tae leave her computer behind.'

'We're back to her being a fake, then?'

'She was always a fake. But who else was in on it wi' her?'

I held up my hand to quiet him. Xanthippe had finally steered the conversation around to topics relevant to our interests. 'So have you heard anything about French Vanilla? Your French Vanilla, not that poor kid who died.'

'That's my girl,' I said cheerfully, relieved. Xanthippe was not falling under the sway of the seductive new webcam friends. Xanthippe was on the case.

'She could be asking as a concerned pal,' Stewart pointed out.

I hit him with a pillow.

'The Missing Persons Unit have been great,' Melinda replied to Xanthippe. 'Really great. They arranged for counsellors, they've been giving us support…'

'Ha, despite the fact that you threw up on that sergeant who tried to talk to us about Vanilla … Anna … wow, that's hard to get used to,' said Ginger. 'We don't know what to call her.'

'I mostly missed his uniform,' said Melinda.

'Do they have any idea yet, who she was?' Xanthippe asked.

'There was nothing on her computer,' said Ginger. 'They told us that, a few days after they took it.'

'Really?' said Xanthippe, swallowing some pasta and sounding convincingly surprised. 'How can you have no identity information on a computer?'

'She bought it second-hand, not long after she first moved in,' said Melinda. 'It was registered to the bloke she bought it from.'

'She had a bank account,' said Ginger. 'But it was in Annabeth French's name—the other girl must have set it up for her.'

Stewart passed me a mug of coffee and I drank it automatically. He'd put milk and sugar in which was oddly touching. Usually he refuses to support other people's unholy desire to adulterate the most important substance on earth (direct quote, can you tell?).

Was Xanthippe trying to draw more out of the Gingerbread women, figuring out what they knew or didn't know? Or was she playing dumb to help get their little mystery narrative across to the viewing public? It bugged the hell out of me that I wasn't sure which side she was playing.

'Does it bother you?' she asked now, her fingers circling the stem of a wine glass. 'That she lied to you, all this time?'

'Yes,' said Ginger, at the same time that Melinda said, 'No.' They looked at each other.

'Interesting,' said Xanthippe.

'I don't understand it at all,' Ginger said. 'She must have been on her guard the whole time, only pretending to be our friend. There's no excuse for that.'

'There could be a reason, though,' Melinda said gently. 'There are always reasons why people do what they do. I can't help wondering what she was running away from, what was so important that it was easier to take on someone else's name?'

'She has to have been messing us about,' Ginger snapped. 'She lied. Every day. She pretended to be doing uni work, for the whole year, and it turns out she wasn't even registered as a student. She wasn't our friend. We ... we did a lot for her, we stuck our necks out to help her,' she added fiercely. 'Misplaced trust if ever there was any. And our viewers—she lied to them too.'

Melinda shrugged. 'She was the one who tried ten different teas to help me through my morning sickness, and sat up with me when I had a really hard decision to make. She always listened when I wanted to talk, and she didn't hassle me when I was stressed. She was my friend no matter what else she was lying about. I miss her.'

Ginger swallowed down half a glass of wine. 'I miss her too,' she said in a low voice. 'But she wasn't real. How do you know she wasn't laughing at us the whole time?'

'I don't,' said Melinda. 'Isn't it nicer to think that she wasn't?'

'I know which one I'd want on my jury,' Stewart told me as the dinner conversation moved on to another topic.

Xanthippe came home late, and I was waiting for her, feet propped on the couch, and a cup of hot chocolate on the table beside me. It had gone cold an hour ago. 'Hey,' I said softly.

She gave me one of those inscrutable looks she's so good at, and glanced across the room to where Ceege was back at his computer screen, tapping away at his RPG, seemingly oblivious to us both. 'Your room,' she said, heading for the staircase.

The first thing she saw as she stepped into my bedroom was the little black cocktail dress I had worn to the fancy police dinner the other night. 'What the hell is that? That's not you.'

'It could be,' I said defensively. 'How do you know that isn't exactly what I fancied wearing that day?'

She eyed the label. 'You bought it new in Myer. New. In Myer. You.'

'Shut up.'

'I thought you were physically incapable of buying clothing that wasn't from adorable little vintage boutiques, and hipster market stalls. Aren't you worried that impressing my brother with your new mainstream style will lose you retro credibility points?'

'Can we stop talking about this right now?'

Xanthippe sat on the edge of my bed and flopped backwards, her dark layered haircut fanning out over my, yes, okay, vintage Japanese bedspread that had indeed been purchased from a market stall that almost certainly qualified as 'hipster'.

We hadn't done this in forever. Yes, she had a part share in my café now, and she'd been living in our third bedroom for most of the last year, but we rarely hung out, just the two of us. We were best friends in high school, but we had been distant for a long time. You don't get back something like that—or at least, we hadn't tried all that hard.

'Aren't you going to ask me what I found out at The Ginger-bread House?' she asked finally. 'Or did you watch it live?'

'I don't know what you're talking about,' I said, joining her on the bed and grabbing my hairbrush and hair ties. I can't sleep without braids these days, even if it makes me look like a deranged Heidi in the mornings.

'Good, you watched it live, then. Saves time.' Xanthippe looked wretched. 'I can't help myself. Can't turn off wanting to figure out what happened. I think I upset them both, though, talking about it like that.'

I clamped my mouth shut so as not to point out that discussing the missing 'Anna' was good for their income stream. 'Maybe it helps for them to talk about it,' I said instead. Ah, tact.

Xanthippe glared at the ceiling. 'They're confused, like they don't know how they're supposed to feel. They don't even know who she was. Who to miss.' There had been a pause just after the 'm' sound which made me think for a minute she was going to say 'mourn'. Possibly I was imagining it.

'It's only been a week,' I said finally.

'Eight days. It's been eight days.'

'In a way,' I tried, 'It's better that no one knows anything about her. It means they can tell themselves she had a plan, somewhere safe to go. Isn't that more comforting?'

Xanthippe glared at me. 'Comforting that they can come up with some pretty fantasy where a girl they lived with for most of a year just appeared and then disappeared like Mary fucking Poppins?'

'If I were them, I'd take what I could get,' I snapped back.

'Yeah,' she said after a minute. 'Me too.'

What we weren't talking about was Carly. Carolyn Denver was one of our high school's goodiest good girls. She always got As, even in subjects she wasn't great at (she worked so hard you could see the steam coming out of her ears), she was talented at music and art. She even participated in team sports, which I couldn't understand at all.

For a couple of months in grade ten, she started dropping by the shady spot behind the gym where Zee and I used to hang out, reading magazines and talking shit. We didn't know what to make of her at first, but it turned out she was kind of funny when she wasn't completely stressed out. We got used to her sitting with us, even though when it came time for class, she would ignore us as she went back into the orbit of her super normal friends.

Three days before the end of year exams, Carly didn't turn up to school. By the next day, the police had been called, and we were all called into the guidance counsellor's office one by one for informal interviews.

It was in the papers for a long time, until it wasn't any more. Every now and then, Carly's parents would set up some kind of information appeal, but eventually they stopped too.

Every year or so, around December, I Google her name and run it through Facebook just to see if she is miraculously—I don't know. Living in Peru and married to a plastic surgeon, or something. But, no. There's still a website set up by a family friend that chronicles the search for Carly, but they haven't updated it for a while.

It's ten years since she disappeared. Chances are she's not coming back. But I'd been thinking about her a lot since this Annabeth thing started, and I figured Xanthippe had as well. Now would be a good time for us to admit how deeply Carly's disappearance had affected us both.

But we don't do the serious conversation thing, her and me.

Eventually Xanthippe said, 'Okay, I'm going to bed.'

And I said, 'Sleep well.'

She looked at the dress again and snickered on her way out, so I threw a magazine at her. I guess we were doing okay. For a given value of 'okay'.

8

GINGERBREAD FORUMS: Q&A

Seelyluvs: so how'd you come up with The Gingerbread House idea?
(can I steal it?) How did you all get together?

Gingernutz: steal away, though be careful what you're getting into.
Living your life live on the web isn't for everyone.

Cherry_ripe: About two years ago, me and Pepperminty (the other
founder of The Gingerbread House) answered an ad Ginge put up for
a 3 bedroom uni share house. It was still going to be a push for us
to pay the rent, and we talked about how hard it would be to get jobs
and manage our classes at the same time. The webcams thing was
an accident at first—I had a long distance relationship going on
with my boyfriend at the time, and we tried talking to each other over
Skype—way cheaper than the phone…

Gingernutz: and one day I walked in on Cherry buck naked, putting
on a show for her boy…

Cherry_ripe: shut up, you wish!

Gingernutz: well, we joked about it. Pepperminty reckoned we could wire up the house for visuals and sound, and charge subscriptions. She was the smart internet person, set up the website and everything.

Cherry_ripe: we figured we'd do it for a month, but we got hooked! We just love getting to talk to you guys all around the world, who tune in to us every day. And it doesn't hurt to not have to worry about the rent thanks to our AMAZEBALLS subscribers. We love you guys so much!

Gingernutz: Pepperminty left us, but we got French_vanilla in to replace her. Now, she *really* thought we were bananas when she met us.

French_vanilla: you are bananas. But I love you.

Gingernutz: *snogs*

Two days after Xanthippe's dinner party with the Gingerbread women, I found a sullen teenager on my doorstep. He was dressed in the usual boy uniform—baggy trousers, sneakers, a band T-shirt in a font too messy to read.

'I'm Shay French,' he said, eyes flickering at me and then lowering.

'I remember you,' I said. Yeah, I remembered him leaning on the convertible and doing his best to chat up Xanthippe. Cocky little bugger who thought he was God's gift. I managed not to say something bitchy now, because I was running through the facts I'd picked up about him from the media coverage of his sister's murder.

Seamus French (17) was Annabeth's younger brother. When I last saw this kid, he was hanging around with Jason Avery. It must suck beyond reason to have your mate arrested for murdering your sister. It had obviously knocked the stuffing out of him—there was none of that flirty over-confidence now.

'You were looking for Anna,' he blurted now. 'That day. I wondered…' He ran out of words, shrugging and lapsing into silence.

I had no idea what Shay wanted from me, but I made it easy for him. 'Want to go for a walk?'

'Yeah,' he said, relaxing a bit around the shoulders.

I locked up the house, and gestured the way. My place is a good ten minutes' walk from the beach. You have to cross suburbia and shopping streets before you get close enough to sniff the salt. But I had a feeling this wasn't going to be one of those chats you got through fast.

Shay didn't seem to mind where we walked. He loped along beside me, hands shoved into pockets. The silence yawned on.

'I wasn't actually looking for Anna,' I said when we were only a street away from the esplanade. 'I mean, I thought I was, but I wasn't. There was this other girl living in Hobart pretending to be her, did you know about that?'

'I read the papers,' Shay said with an 'I'm not stupid' expression on his face. 'That fucken blog too.'

Best not mention that Stewart was a friend of mine.

'Everyone keeps talking about her,' he added impatiently. 'Anna, I mean. I don't give a shit about that other girl, unless she's the one who…' His voice trailed off. 'The police reckon Jase did it. He can't prove he didn't. But he wouldn't do that. He was nuts about her.'

I had once been held at gunpoint by a bloke who claimed to be nuts about me, so I wasn't overly convinced by his argument. 'He doesn't have to prove he didn't,' was all I said, hoping to reassure him. 'They have to prove that he did.'

'Duh,' Shay said. Charming kid. Really.

The street opened up into a burst of sunshine, seagulls and bright colours: the green of the grass strip, the blue of the water, and the yellow and orange of the giant Paddle Pop ads everywhere.

Shay headed for the sand on automatic. I slipped off my sandals and followed him, wriggling the sand between my toes.

'So you didn't actually know her,' he said. 'Anna.'

'No,' I admitted. 'I spoke to her for about five minutes the day she … the day we drove by the vineyard. That's all.'

'This other girl, then,' he said, eyes on the seagulls as they fought over the last chip crumbs in an abandoned paper bag. 'The Vanilla chick. What's she to you?'

'Nothing,' I admitted. 'I don't even know her real name. No one does.' Well, obviously someone knew it. We had to find that someone. Sooner rather than later.

'Huh.'

I waited for Shay to ask why the hell I had been sticking my nose in where it wasn't wanted, or something along those lines, but instead he jabbed the toe of his sneaker in the sand, drawing an unrecognisable shape before he said: 'I reckon it was the other bloke. Has to have been. Not Jase.'

'Other bloke?' I asked, trying not to sound eager.

'Yeah. She was seeing someone else, last summer. Caught her sneaking in one night, and she admitted it. I felt like a real arsehole for not dobbing to Jase that she was messing him around, but she was going off to uni. I figured they'd split up anyway, when she left.'

Don't ask me why people tell me things like this. I've got used to it over the years, running the café. Customers zero in on me, not Lara or Yui or Nin, and I get their life story, romantic dramas, disturbingly detailed medical information, and blow-by-blow accounts of their most embarrassing experiences.

I guess I have one of those sympathetic faces. And right now, Shay French really needed someone sympathetic.

I wanted to take the poor kid home and feed him. Instead I listened as the frustration sparked out of him.

'Didn't break up with him, though, did she? Swanned off to uni, and he kept sending her stupid fucken postcards and texting her, and every time I asked him about it he talked like they had this whole big future together.'

'Why do you think he sent postcards?' I asked, when Shay lapsed into an angry silence. Maybe it was a trivial point, but it was something that had bugged me all along. 'Not exactly private, for love letters. Why not email, or texts?' Bonus points for not using the word 'sext' to the underage boy.

Shay scoffed. 'They weren't love letters. How poncy would that be? I reckon he sent them to remind her of home. They were always Flynn postcards—like a few shots of the scenery were going to drag her back from uni and all her fucken dreams and stuff.'

Uni and all her fucken dreams and stuff. But Annabeth hadn't wanted uni. Or at least, had gone to a lot of trouble to avoid it … so what *had* she been up to? What 'dreams' were so important that they were worth that kind of deception?

'What do you think she was doing this year?' I asked her brother.

Shay shrugged. 'What the hell do I know? Off with that guy, I reckon.'

'Do you know anything about him?'

'Nah, she never told me his name. I thought he was older, though. She said a couple of things that made me think … I know he had money, she was all giggly about that.' For a moment his mouth twisted in typical brotherly fashion, sneering about her giggliness, but then I saw the realisation cross his face all over again that she was dead. In that instant, he closed off from me, from the beach, everything. From reality.

'She was fucken stupid,' he said finally. 'But she was my sister. You know?'

'Yeah,' I said. We both hovered in silence for a few minutes, staring out at the water. 'What's your favourite ice cream?' I asked finally.

Shay looked at me like I was nuts. 'Butterscotch.'

Ooh, butterscotch. I could practically hear the recipe assembling itself in my brain. 'Come on,' I said. 'Let's go back to my place, and I'll see what I can do about that.'

I was tempted to start out by making fresh butterscotch brickle, then smashing it to bits and stirring it into the ice cream, but that felt like cheating. Instead, I made a basic sauce with butter and brown sugar, to stir through par-frozen vanilla custard. Vanilla was good for that, at least. It could provide contrast for the real flavours that deserved to be there. Like the silence between chords.

There was supposed to be vanilla essence in the sauce, but I left it out. Why do so many recipes tell you to add vanilla when they don't want it to taste of vanilla? Anyone would think they were trying to wipe out the world's supply.

Now, there's an idea.

Shay sat on a stool and watched me with a look of bemusement on his face, as if he'd never seen anyone cook before, let alone invent an ice cream recipe right in front of him.

'Tell me about the vineyard,' I suggested as I stirred the slowly thickening butterscotch sauce. Possibly I had overdone the butter. Possibly the sauce needed real scotch to save it. Mmm, scotchy butter. Christmas was coming, and that would be a good time for scotch-related experiments. Rum sauce gelato, brandy butter sorbet... 'Jason's family own it, is that right? You work there, and Annabeth used to as well?'

'Everyone in town works there sooner or later,' said Shay. 'Jase's dad is rolling in it. He's a good bloke, Jase's dad. Anna used to work in the restaurant, but it's closed this year for renovations. That's why she took on shifts at the Scallop when she came back to Flynn in the holidays.'

Jase's dad. That would be Greg Avery (48), local businessman and councillor who had made curt statements about his son's innocence to the papers.

'I don't work there,' Shay added. 'Not really. I help out sometimes. They've got proper contractors in to do the remodelling. Greg's got big plans,' he added, with an odd degree of pride in his voice, for talking about someone else's dad. 'He's taking the town places. Not just Avery Grove, either. Last summer he bought up a whole stretch of shops in town, remodelled them to get decent tenants in. They've been a bit slow to fill, but Greg says by next summer, we'll be a café latté town like Cygnet. Better than them 'cause of not filling every fucken shop with an art gallery.'

'Café latté town' didn't sound like a phrase that a seventeen-year-old kid would come up with on his own.

'Flynn seemed like a nice place,' I said, remembering the friendly ice cream parlour. I wasn't sure I was convinced about the café latté part, though. As far as I could see, everyone in town ate at the pub or the takeaway. They'd need a lot more work before they achieved trendsetter status, and there was a lot of competition for the tourists these days.

'Yeah,' said Shay. 'Greg says it's great that young blokes like me and Jase want to stick around town, help keep the place alive instead of jumping ship to the mainland like everyone else.'

Shay could seriously benefit from jumping ship to the mainland for a few years. Was he really going to spend the rest of his life mooching around Flynn? I was the last person to disparage serving latté as a living, but I wouldn't go around telling a seventeen-year-old it was the pinnacle he could achieve in his life. Not unless he owned the damned coffee machine, anyway.

'What's Jason's Mum doing?' I asked. 'While Greg Avery is transforming Flynn.'

Shay eyed my custard mix like he hadn't eaten in a week, despite the fact that I had thrown two bacon sandwiches and half a cold quiche down his throat since we got back from our beach walk. I found him a spoon so he could taste it.

'Cheers,' he said, digging in. 'Jase's Mum shot through years ago. Greg married Pippa last summer—she's a bit nuts, but cool. Into all this hippie shit, you know, but wicked smart. She's been pushing the council for us to get an online centre, and she did great things with the Avery Grove website.'

'How does Jason get on with Pippa?'

'You mean apart from getting into a fight with two guys who reckoned they saw her sunbathing topless?' Shay had a touch of that spark back, as he grinned. 'Wouldn't have minded seeing that myself. Don't tell Jase, but his stepmum's way hot.'

'No more sugar for you,' I said firmly, confiscating his spoon. 'So how's Jason doing now? With everything that's happened.'

'The police never charged him,' Shay said sourly. 'Held him for questioning as long as they could, but they didn't have enough evidence to arrest him.' That part at least I knew from the newspapers and Stewart. 'I went up there the other day and he couldn't even look me in the eye. Told him I knew he hadn't done it, but...' He shrugged again. Poor kid was all shrug.

'Why did you come to see me?' I asked finally. It was a long way to come for curiosity, for pouring your words out to a stranger.

Shay didn't say anything for a while, watching as I poured the ice cream mix into a metal tub for freezing. 'Want it to make sense, you know? You didn't make sense.'

'I rarely do,' I admitted.

'Nah,' he said with a grin. 'Now I've met you and all. You're all right. Don't know why you care, but it's good someone does, you know?'

I gave him the spoon back, so he could scrape the bowl out. 'Yeah.'

I did care, damn it. That meant it was time to get more involved. And that meant...

Time to square things with the person I couldn't even admit I'd been avoiding.

9

Gingerbread House Forums Q&A, cont.

Vampsparkle8829: French_vanilla, how did you join The Gingerbread House?

French_vanilla: Actually, I answered an ad too—though the one I answered was a bit different, I imagine!

Gingernutz: Wanted, extra person to live inside a web peep show. Must be willing to take top off in front of 50,000 people and do own laundry.

French_vanilla: You know, I remember you being more subtle than that…

Cherry_ripe: hee, it was something like 'broke, need somewhere to live, amazingly open-minded? Call this number, girls only.'

French_vanilla: What can I say, it spoke to me.

Gingerbutz: It was great, we interviewed twelve people, and they all had so many questions. Vanilla just wanted to know—can I keep my cardy on.

Cherry_ripe: We said yes you can, and the rest is history.

✹

At noon the next day, I kidnapped my plain clothed non-boyfriend from under the nose of the entire Hobart police service. No one seemed particularly alarmed. I miss my days of being a suspicious character.

Who am I kidding? I was never all that suspicious. Once you feed a police officer, they're yours for life. In my case, multiply that by several hundred. If I ever wanted to go into organised crime, I could own this town with three dozen peanut butter cookies and a well-timed spit roast.

'You cooked for me?' said Bishop, as I dragged him down on the grass in St David's Park, and repeatedly smacked his hands to keep them away from the picnic basket. 'Usually I'm hard pressed to get a cheese sandwich out of you.'

'Lies, such lies,' I said in my best hard-done by voice, opening the basket and laying out the cloth. We hadn't seen much of each other lately. And it was true that after a long day in the café, I was more likely to beg him to make me an omelette than to produce something awe-inspiringly domestic for him.

It wasn't like I went around demanding he do police work for me on his days off, was it?

Okay, maybe that's a bad example.

I had cooked a chicken stuffed with herbed potatoes, and padded it around in the basket with cheese scones, cold bean salad (for me, since Bishop is as bad as the rest of his police buddies when it comes to greenery) and a bag of fresh cherries from my favourite farm.

Bishop raised his eyes at the spread. 'This is you working up to telling me you murdered someone and hid the body, right?'

I handed him the butter knife, and smiled. 'Just don't ask what's in the gourmet sausage rolls.'

'If there is beer in that basket, I may have to propose.'

I handed him a bottle. 'Don't get grass stains on your knees.'

It's hard to talk to boys when they are eating. Well, not hard if you have something to say and you want to rattle it out while they're chewing. But most of the things I could make conversation about today were … things I wanted to avoid talking about. So mostly I watched him eat.

'You realise how alarming the silence is, right?' he said after a while, eyes dark on mine.

'Maybe I'm enjoying the quiet romantic moment,' I said. Innocent face, innocent face.

He brandished a piece of chicken at me, and then bit into it. 'Tabitha … we're either going to talk about this or we're not. But please don't assume I'm stupid.'

'Honestly not something I ever assumed,' I said wistfully. Oh, for a stupid sexy man in my life. That would be so convenient.

He leaned back, still gnawing on the chicken. 'Let me tell you, then. We can start with how you and my sister got yourself roped in to look for a missing person rather than report said missing person to the police.'

'They did report her,' I said huffily. 'Helping to look was part of convincing the girls at The Gingerbread House to do that. Which they did, thanks to me, you're welcome.'

Bishop grinned and shook his head. 'You do realise that every word you said within that house was recorded, right? I know exactly what happened.'

I stared. 'You watch The Gingerbread House?' My eyes narrowed. 'You're a subscriber? Those girls take their tops off, you know. I don't think I approve.'

'And while we are at it, you can let my sister know that I'd appreciate a heads up next time she's going to flash the internet? So I can leave the country.'

'You can't outrun the internet,' I said sagely, chewing on cold beans. Mmmm. Olive oil dressing. Sesame seeds. Yummy. 'What else have we been up to that you already know about?'

Bishop gave me a look. 'This isn't me lecturing you about getting involved in police business, in case you hadn't noticed. I'm actually impressed at how hard you've been working to avoid it.'

'Which you know because you have been spying on me...'

'I don't have to spy on you. You're Tabitha, and everyone I work with knows you. Regardless of whether or not I get to use the word 'girlfriend', every officer I work with does tend to pass the Tabitha-related gossip in my general direction. I figured out you were involved in this French Vanilla thing pretty early ... though not as involved as Xanthippe.'

'You will note that my boobs did not appear in the footage,' I said with some degree of pride.

'I appreciated that, yes. Very restrained of you.'

Hmm, no mention of Shay French. Did Bishop's all-seeing eyes not extend to my recent entertaining of teenage relatives of murder victims?

'What are your thoughts on butterscotch ice cream?' I asked him now.

Shay had crashed on our couch to the soothing sound of Ceege typing at people about a whole different class of internet smut, but was gone the next morning. That left me with a huge quantity of butterscotch ice cream. I could serve it in the café, of course, but I wasn't one hundred percent happy with the texture.

'I like vanilla,' Bishop reminded me. It was a patient voice, and yet somehow it also silently added that he also likes using the word 'girlfriend' about women he sleeps with and takes out to dinner and all those other things we did together.

'Oh, that's right, I forgot.'

'Also, you are changing the subject.'

'The primary subject was ice cream, you're the one who changed it by bringing in police procedures and missing persons and...'

'Tabitha,' Bishop said quietly. 'Do you think Xanthippe is getting too personally invested in this Annabeth French case?'

What I thought was that it was a little late for him to be

playing the concerned big brother, seeing as he and Xanthippe had ignored each other for most of their adult lives, but that would be possibly less than supportive.

I was never going to make the world's best girlfriend, which was a big part of why I avoided the label. But I could at least be a supportive friend-with-seriously-hot-benefits.

'You should talk to her. Find out for yourself why she's getting so attached to this particular crime scene.'

Bishop laughed. 'From your deep and extensive history with us both, what makes you think my sister and I are capable of a conversation like that?'

'Well,' I said with my best smile as the sister in question approached him stealthily from behind. 'The good news is, now's your chance to find out.'

'Here you are,' Xanthippe announced, throwing herself down on the grass beside the picnic basket and helping herself to a handful of cherries. 'Mmm, well catered, Tish. I've been looking for you all over.' She leaned back on her elbows, looking at Bishop upside down. 'Leo.'

'Xanthippe,' he replied, just as polite.

Those two were impossible. Half siblings, raised in different households, five years apart in age—that was no excuse for being unable to properly tease and beat each other up like real siblings. I don't even have siblings, and I could give them lessons on advanced squabbling.

'So,' Xanthippe said, eyes hard on me. 'Ceege says the French kid came to see you. And you didn't tell me. Spill.'

'Don't mind me,' Bishop said, rolling his eyes.

She waved a hand. 'Don't interrupt official business.'

Like I needed more reasons to want to strangle Xanthippe. To his credit (or something), Bishop just raised his eyebrows and said nothing. Hmm. I find it suspicious when people do not rise to the obvious bait.

I looked from Bishop to Xanthippe, and sighed. 'Shay French, that little charmer who tried to chat you up when we visited Flynn. He's all messed up about what happened to his sister, and he wanted to find out why we were looking for her that day.'

'So you told him we were looking for a different girl and sent him on his way?' Xanthippe asked, batting her eyelashes.

'In a manner of speaking.' Bishop and Xanthippe both gave me an identical expression of impatience, and it struck me for the first time how similar they were. Oh bloody hell, I was sleeping with the male version of Xanthippe. I really did not need to have had that particular train of thought. 'What? The kid needed someone to talk to.'

'I don't know how she does it,' Xanthippe sighed. 'This is why I could never be a private detective. I do all the legwork for days, and people tell me nothing. Tabitha opens her kitchen door and suspects fall over themselves to tell her every secret they ever had.'

'Tell me about it,' agreed Bishop. He frowned. 'You don't actually want to be a private detective, do you?'

'I might have looked into the relevant paperwork.' Xanthippe smiled sweetly. 'Don't you think I'd be good at it?'

'Alarmingly so. That doesn't mean I like the idea.'

'You're just scared people will tease you about having Humphrey Bogart as a sister.' Xanthippe pinched the last cheese scone just as Bishop was reaching for it.

'Yes,' Bishop said dryly. 'That is exactly my fear. Thanks for hitting the nail on the head.'

Xanthippe bit into the scone without buttering it. 'This is kind of doughy.'

'They're perfect,' I said, offended.

'Crumbly, too.'

'It's a *scone*. Crumbly is desirable.'

'Have you considered making these with Romano instead of Parmesan, maybe adding a little tomato paste to give them some colour?'

'You are so not making recipe suggestions to me...'

'I can't have an opinion?' she asked innocently.

I snatched the rest of the scone from her and put it back in the basket. 'No more treats for you. Go away. We're having a romantic moment.'

Xanthippe looked from me to Bishop. 'No you're not. Your hair isn't even mussed, and all your buttons are done up.'

'We were getting there,' I said between gritted teeth.

Bishop looked surprised. 'Were we?'

'Hush.'

'Any more beer in there?' Xanthippe asked, peering at the basket.

'No,' I said, taking the last bottle out and passing it to Bishop, who at least looked pleased as he opened it.

'Mean!' But then a wicked light came into Xanthippe's eyes. Never a good thing. 'So, what are you bringing to the Nikolaidis family Christmas? No pressure or anything, but Nonna Carmella is a bitch queen of the highest order, and significant others bearing dishes are in the main firing line. Last year she made Cousin Tony's girlfriend cry over icing sugar.'

'I'm a professional, I'll have you know,' I said haughtily. As if someone else's evil ethnic grandparent could make me cry by criticising my food. I gave Bishop a look, though. Christmas was about a week away, and he had made no mention of any family gathering to which I might be welcome. Or indeed, unwelcome. 'I wasn't aware I was invited to the Nikolaidis family Christmas.'

'I'm sure I mentioned it,' Bishop said quickly.

Ha.

'No, you really didn't.'

'Well, my work here is done,' Xanthippe said brightly. She grabbed the last of the green bean salad and sauntered away. Wench.

I turned my gaze back on Bishop, a question in my eyes.

'I thought you'd be going away to your Mum's,' he said weakly.

'Maybe I am, maybe I'm not.' It shouldn't be bugging me this much. I hadn't even thought about Christmas, beyond a plan to make plum pudding gelato balls for the café next week, and juggling the holiday schedule with two student waitresses who wanted the maximum amount of skive time.

But of course, being invited to the other person's family Christmas was a girlfriend thing, not a friends-with-benefits thing. Was this Xanthippe's way of telling us it was time to acknowledge we were in a relationship?

My history was full of fun flings that never got very serious. Bishop's history was a long series of sensible girlfriendy girlfriends who did everything in the proper order, and then eventually gave up on him when they realised he really did genuinely love his job more than anything else in the universe.

'Did Helen go to Christmas?'

Bishop blinked. 'I dated Helen two years ago.'

'Did she go to Christmas?'

He frowned. 'Yeah, I think so.'

'You can't remember?'

'Yes, she did,' he sighed. 'She brought moussaka. It was a colossal mistake, because Aunt Sophia always brings moussaka, so Aunt Sophia spent most of Christmas Day announcing loudly how she hoped we didn't have too much. Every five minutes. As if too much moussaka is not the very definition of a first world problem.'

I folded my arms. 'You'd better not have failed to invite me because you think I'm not up to the culinary challenge.'

Bishop winced. 'Actually I'm more worried that one of my elderly relatives will goad you into bitchslapping her. And, you know.'

'The not-a-girlfriend thing.'

'It was your idea.'

'I'm not complaining. I am acknowledging that it is sometimes awkward.'

'Yes,' said Bishop with a sigh, taking a long draw of the beer. 'Thank you.'

I thought about him trying to protect me from his elderly relatives. I smiled at him. 'That's okay, then. Want to make out?'

Bishop blinked. 'Sure?'

'I don't want to rush you and kill the romance or whatever, but I only have another ten minutes before Nin hunts me down with a rolling pin.' My girls take extended lunch breaks very, very seriously.

Bishop put down his beer, and tugged me into his lap. 'I can work to a deadline.'

You have to appreciate that in a man.

10

random_scotsman posts on Sandstone City…

FRENCH VANILLA STILL FLAVOUR OF THE MONTH

As police continue to investigate the mysterious death of Annabeth
French in Flynn a fortnight ago, what of the woman at the centre of
the mystery, who impersonated the victim for ten months and then
disappeared only hours before her violent death?

We've had enthusiastic response to our Find French Vanilla campaign.
Thanks to all Sandstone readers who sent in photos and reports on
the missing webcam star. Our grand prize: a voucher for free ice
cream from Sublime Sundaes goes to Noah Patterson (Glenorchy) for
spotting French Vanilla snacking on hot chips while wearing a tutu
and angel wings at a local soccer match. Best faked picture we've
had submitted to us in months, mate. Good one.

✹

There are ground rules for sneaking up on Stewart McTavish. You are not allowed to enter the Sandstone City office before 10AM. He figured out a long time ago that his boss and co-workers don't drift in until after then, so he arrives early to write his daily 1500 words of whatever steamy romance novel he is working on at the moment.

Yes, the boy writes steamy romance novels. Yes, I've read them.

People who enter the office before 10AM get pencils thrown at them. After that it's pretty safe, unless Stewart has that 'writing's not going well' furrow between his eyebrows.

From the late morning onwards, he's available for coffee, pestering, procrastination excuses, and mad ideas for the Sandstone City blog, a project devoted to making Hobart look more bohemian and interesting than it actually is.

This is how he earns a living. Some people totally suck, don't they?

I wanted to talk to him, and sort out some of the stuff that had been running through my head since my Bishop picnic the day before. Stewart was always good for head clearing. Since I planned to use him shamelessly, I took him a mug of his favourite super strong black coffee from the machine of doom. I timed the thing carefully, dropping in at 9:45—I risked having a stapler thrown at my head, but at least he would be there, and his co-workers wouldn't.

Well, he was pretty much there. He was actually heading out of the office with a guilty look on his face.

'Where are you off to, this bright and sunny morning,' I said, not suspicious at all.

Stewart looked at me, and I could see him trying to think up a cover story. I held out the cup, wafting it under his nose. 'I am a genuinely nice person who brings you coffee. And I only accept the truth.'

'I … hae an appointment with French Vanilla,' he said helplessly.

Hell.

I stared at him. And then I started drinking the coffee. It was hot and stung my mouth, and I didn't care. I didn't want him to have it. He didn't deserve it. 'You weren't going to tell me.'

'Tabitha…'

I swallowed harder, gulping down the coffee so hard it hurt. 'You have a lead and you are going to see her and you weren't going to tell me.'

'Tabitha, stop it!' He disarmed me and held the coffee mug out at arm's length, backing me against the wall of the stairwell. Oh, this was bad. I had a history of snogging inappropriate people in this stairwell. 'She contacted me. Wha' was I supposed tae do?'

I stared him down. Close. He was far too close. 'You were supposed to share.'

Stewart looked uncomfortable, and for one fleeting moment I wondered if he was feeling the stairwell syndrome as strongly as I was right now.

Bishop Bishop Bishop *behave*, Tabitha.

'Will ye please join me tae meet our missing person?' he said finally.

'Why yes,' I said, breathing a little unevenly. From the stress. 'I would like that very much, thank you for asking me.'

'Should we include Xanthippe?'

'Oh, no,' I said quickly. 'Really, she's not that interested in the case.'

I don't share well. Yes, I'm also a hypocrite.

We sat at a café table in Salamanca. 'This makes no sense,' I said, tapping my spoon against the edge of my cappuccino cup. Too much froth, stingy on the chocolate. 'Why would she meet you here? This is Hobart. She'd bump into twelve people who knew her, walking down that street. So much for being missing.'

'Maybe she doesnae want tae be missing any more,' said Stewart, apparently unmoved by the fact that his long black was inferior to anything he could get at Café La Femme.

'How did she get in touch?'

'Email. She says she's been followin' the Sandstone City coverage of her story. She wants everyone tae know she's fine and doesnae want tae be found. So she consented tae an interview.'

I didn't want a three dollar shortbread cookie. I could eat biscuits by the handful when I got back to work. Not that I would. Damn it, I wanted a cookie now! 'You don't think I'd scare her off?'

'If anythin', having a woman here might make her feel more comfortable.' He looked dubious even as he said it.

My spoon tapped more frenetically against the cup. 'She wants to stay hidden?'

'Aye, that's what she said. I dinnae believe it, though. Could ye stop that?'

'Stop what?' Stewart reached out, laid his hand over mine and took the spoon firmly away from me. 'Hey, I need that spoon.'

'Tabitha, if ye cannae sit at the big table with the grown ups...'

I narrowed my eyes at him. 'Buy me a cookie.'

'Fer four dollars? No way. I could get another coffee fer that.'

I pouted at the lack of chivalry, but could not deny his priorities. I checked my watch again. 'She's late.'

Stewart laughed softly. 'Yer so bad at surveillance. Nae patience at all.'

'No patience? Have you ever tried my choux pastry? Or my eight hour goulash?' I didn't know what to think. French Vanilla. The real one. Or the fake one. The one that made no sense at all. She was coming here and I would get to meet her.

What would she be like? I'd been surfing The Gingerbread House site, reading French Vanilla's comments on the forums—she seemed light-hearted enough there, teasing the other girls, messing around. A little more private with her thoughts than either of them, but she had her moments.

I'd watched the highlight archives too, to get a feel for who she was, but it felt weird. Turned out I wasn't quite as nosy a person as I always thought I was. Looking into someone else's private business quite that closely … bothered me.

Not so much Xanthippe. She was tucked up with her laptop most nights, combing through the archives and old forums, almost as bad as Ceege when it came to being glued to the screen. She was seriously obsessed.

Would she be pissed off that I hadn't included her along today, given her a chance to meet the girl who had claimed to be Annabeth French? I told myself it was for the best. Xanthippe was … an intimidating person. Likely to send meek little vanilla girls running for the exit.

Whereas I was me—sipping a bad cappuccino with windblown hair, trying to keep my cute little vintage frock from doing something indecent in the Antarctic breezes that swept hard through Salamanca, even on a sunny day like this one.

It was a week until Christmas, and the weather was stepping up the heat. Most people were out there, sweatily shopping until they dropped. Did French Vanilla have family to shop for?

I didn't, as it happened. My dad was the one with extended family to juggle, and he died a year ago. My mum had quit anything remotely conventional when she ran off to her hippie art colony in the middle of nowhere—she'd had two decades of cooking the perfect dinner with four kinds of roast beast, and these days I would be lucky if we exchanged solstice cards between now and the new year.

Ritual meals bothered me anyway. There were so many nice things you could cook, if you wanted to feed and nurture people. Why did everyone insist on having the same thing every year, whether or not they were any good at preparing it?

Not doing Christmas was fine with me, but now there was this whole Bishop thing hanging over my head. I liked what I knew of his and Xanthippe's family. Zee's mother was one of these dramatic European women who complains if you get too thin. There are never enough of those around when you're an awkward teenager, and I'd enjoyed her company the few times we'd met.

Zee's mother was also Bishop's mother, of course. I'd always known that the disturbingly hot constable that my dad mentored through the Tasmania police service was half brother to the cranky girl I'd been friends with in high school, but I'd never really thought through the ramifications.

Bishop and I had been together for months. Thanks to our agreement that we not label this thing between us, or let it get officially serious, there had been no family visit. Generally speaking, boys like me to meet their mother. I had better relationships with most of my exes' mothers than the exes themselves. Hell, that's where half of my culinary tricks come from.

There was no reason at all to be resentful that Bishop had this whole important relationship with my late dad, and knew my mum's cooking style at forty paces, but I hadn't been included in his family Christmas. Honestly, if anyone should be resenting the whole thing, it should be him.

If I'd let us keep the boyfriend and girlfriend thing when we first tried it on for size, we could be living together by now. I'd know his mother by her first name, and/or her recipe book. Or maybe we'd already have split up and gone our separate ways, because we both spent most of our energy on our work and didn't have time for a real relationship.

'Yer thinking too hard,' said Stewart. It was a fair call.

I looked up in surprise. My coffee was cold. I started choking down the foam. 'She's late.'

'Aye. Probably no' coming.'

'Do you think I scared her off?' I felt a twinge of guilt. Or possibly a reaction to bad foam.

'Maybe she never meant tae come. Maybe she wasnae French Vanilla after all. Just a crank.' Stewart poked me gently with his foot. 'Meanwhile, where were ye?'

'Will you miss your family at Christmas?' I asked abruptly.

Stewart looked taken aback. 'Aye, I suppose so. I havenae been home fer a few years. In Melbourne I had a group of pals—orphans and strays. We'd hang out on Christmas Day, have a barbecue. Better that than the madness back at my mum's in Glasgae. I miss my nan mostly. She'd love the whole prawns on the barbie thing—she sits in the corner at Christmas and bitches about how the food is rubbish and Sharon—my mum—goes tae so much trouble for something naebody actually likes, and we'd be better off gaun fer a curry. Which is true. Then Mum threatens tae strangle her with her knitting, and Da watches the telly and pretends tae be deaf, and the sisters all finally feel guilty enough tae get up off their arses and help peel tatties.'

Wow. Stewart had never said so much about his family in one go before. He had sisters. And a nan. 'Do you help peel tatties?' I asked, which was really the most important question. Also I loved the word 'tatties', even without the Scottish accent.

'Too busy shelling peas,' he said, and grinned at me. 'Maybe I'll gan home for it next year.'

'She's not coming,' I said, because that was … better than anything else I was about to say.

Stewart checked his watch again. 'Half an hour late. Back to the café?'

'Yeah, I really need to.'

He shrugged those bony shoulders of his. 'Go. I'll stick around a bit longer, in case. Have another coffee. Figure out what tae do with my willowy brunette protagonist.'

'Get her laid,' I advised.

Stewart smirked. 'Way ahead of ye.'

The café was in an uproar when I returned, so I didn't have time to give Nin more than a guilty look for being late. It was one of those days where the tables are packed from ten to three, everything goes wrong in the kitchen, and there's a major miscalculation about how much soy milk we ordered. Suddenly the whole world is lactose intolerant.

At least the layers of froth on our cappuccinos aren't too high. Even on our worst days.

Finally things slowed towards 4PM. I emerged from the kitchen to take a few breaths of cool air in our sunny sandstone courtyard out the back. Tea. I needed green tea and a two hour nap, but I would settle for a few gulps of fresh air and a break from the mingled scents of coffee and biscuits and smoked salmon and what on earth had convinced us that it was a good idea to serve all day breakfast? I was so sick of eggs I was ready to start throwing them at the ceiling. A little recipe I like to call pre-scrambled.

A young woman I didn't know was sitting at the staff tea table. Except of course I did know her.

She had a soft face, and curly blonde hair in that bright toddler shade that almost no one actually has without chemical assistance. She wore a light hand knitted cardigan over a flowery sundress, and sandals that had seen better days.

Oh, and she was waiting for me. Her eyes met mine with something like familiarity, though we had never met. Had we? She'd lived in Hobart for nearly a year, if not longer, and I always said I knew everyone.

In any case, I'd seen so many images of her by now, it felt like we'd known each other for years.

French Vanilla.

11

From: Nincakes

tell me you're not planning to deseed those pomegranates that are lurking in the fridge.

From: Darlingtabitha

makes innocent eyes.

From: Nincakes

T, you are your own worst enemy. Consider this a pomegranate intervention

From: Darlingtabitha

hides passionfruit collection

'Tabitha Darling?' she asked in that same quiet, steady voice that I'd heard coming out of Ceege's state of the art speakers when we were raiding The Gingerbread House archives.

'Yes.' She might run, or disappear at any moment, but I risked pulling up a chair, sitting opposite her. 'I don't know your real name.' Only that it wasn't Annabeth French.

'Alice,' she said, though she paused first and I couldn't be sure if it was because she was lying or because she wasn't used to using her own name.

'Weren't you supposed to meet Stewart today?' I asked next, and not only out of loyalty. I was curious—why come out of hiding now, and why on earth approach me?

I had nothing to do with all this. It was getting harder and harder to keep telling myself that.

'I chickened out,' she admitted, and finally that wary look shifted into something a touch more friendly, almost half a smile. 'I don't know whether I can trust him.'

'You can,' I said quickly. 'Hell, anyone can. He won't write shit about you if you don't want him to. He's an appalling journalist that way. Far too nice for his own good.' Why did this Alice person think she could trust me? If that was even the reason she was here.

'I have to talk to someone,' she said finally. 'I can't get involved with the police. But I'm worried about Annabeth.'

Oh hell. Did she not know? 'Annabeth,' I said quietly. 'She's um. Dead. She was killed the day you disappeared.'

French Vanilla—Alice—nodded. Oh, thank goodness. That was probably the worst example of 'breaking it to you gently' anyone had ever done, so I had to be glad she already knew.

'Yes, but I'm worried me being missing might mess things up for the police investigation. Confuse them, so they don't find out who really killed her.'

'Do you know who killed her?' I asked.

Another of those pauses. 'No,' she said finally. 'I … didn't know anyone she was close to. We barely knew each other when we swapped places. But I…' She sighed. 'I've read the newspaper stories and the Sandstone City blog and everything. It seems like the story has become about me, about finding me, and I don't want that. I really don't want anyone to find me.'

'Weren't you worried about coming here?' I said. 'I mean, it's broad daylight. You didn't even come in disguise.'

Alice looked down at her cardigan and smiled helplessly at me. 'This was already my disguise. I don't think I could cope with another one on top of that, my head might explode. Anyway, I won't be here long. I'm leaving soon, and I won't be back.'

'I don't know if I can convince the police to stop looking for you,' I said. Understatement of the year.

Alice gave me a look that was surprisingly hard in her round, sweet-as-pie face. 'Oh, I think you can. I know all about you. You've been involved in this since the beginning. You're dating a police officer, maybe not one who is actually investigating Annabeth's murder, but I'm sure he knows the officers who are. You're friends with everyone. You can let them know that I'm not important.'

Huh. I wasn't seeing much of that meek little bookworm I'd watched on The Gingerbread House archives. Had she been lying to everyone about her personality, as well as her name? Or had recent events toughened her up?

No one was going to stop looking for French Vanilla no matter what she said, because unless they had a cast iron case against Jason Avery (and the investigation wouldn't still be open if they did), she was an obvious murder suspect.

Well, maybe not completely obvious. Not if you looked at her. She still looked like the kind of girl who would help little old ladies do their shopping. The neighbour you would trust with your spare key.

'Can you tell me why you and Annabeth swapped places?' I asked her.

'Is that relevant?' Alice said, looking at her shoes.

'I'm trying to understand what happened. How you got into this situation.'

'I drove,' she said simply.

I blinked. 'You drove?'

Alice nodded. 'At the end of last summer. My boyfriend—well, I was angry at him. Really upset. I took his car and started driving. Didn't take anything with me, just my phone. I didn't turn it on, though. I kept thinking he'd have left lots of messages, and I didn't want to know whether he had or not. I thought … if I stayed away long enough, he'd report me missing or report the car stolen, or something. I kept going through small towns, looking for police cars or police stations, waiting to be noticed. But no one ever did.'

The words were spilling over themselves, like she had been waiting to tell this to someone for a long time. Lucky me.

'Was this here in Tasmania?' I couldn't help asking.

'New South Wales. I'd always wanted to move to the city and he didn't, he liked it in the country, so I headed to Sydney at first. But then I realised he wasn't coming after me, and I got really—I don't know. Freaked out, I suppose. Upset. Numb. He didn't care enough to find me, to look, to report me missing. I didn't have a plan, and I always have a plan. Finally I sold the car—I figured maybe it would be on a register or something and they'd catch me that way, but they didn't.' Her voice cracked a little. 'I wanted him to catch me. I felt like I was doing something wrong the whole time I was leaving, couldn't anyone tell.'

She took a moment, gathering her emotions together, tucking them away for later. 'I bought a new SIM card and junked the other one without even checking my messages.' The frustration dripped from her words. 'If he hadn't even called… I didn't want to know. So I went to Sydney airport. I thought—I'll go somewhere. Start again. I wasn't thinking straight, but that idea stuck with me. I was miserable, but I felt so free, having left all my stuff behind, with him. Everything.'

I didn't want to interrupt her story to skip forward to the present, though I was desperately curious to find out if this was what had happened again, more recently, when she left

The Gingerbread House without a word—without even the phone and purse and car she had taken the first time.

Who was she angry at this time? What was she trying to escape?

'Where were you going to go?' I asked instead.

'Oh, I didn't care. I don't know that I was planning to go anywhere, I just liked the idea. I bought an awful coffee and an expensive croissant and I sat near a window, watching the planes. And that was when I saw the girl.'

I sat still, just listening to her, not interjecting any more, even though part of me wanted to insert commentary along the lines of 'Ah hah, was this when you met Annabeth French?' Or 'What was Annabeth doing at Sydney Airport?'

See, Stewart, I could be patient. Really truly. Even if it made me want to chew through a table leg.

'She was so sad and lost,' said Alice, and her voice cracked a little. 'God, she was nineteen, you know that? I mean, she was younger then. Nineteen when she died. Doesn't that just suck beyond belief? She didn't even make it to *twenty*.'

I knew what she meant. I wasn't quite feeling my thirties bearing down on me yet, but Shay French had made me feel like an elderly schoolmarm. How did you cope with a dead sibling before you were out of your teens? Never mind poor Annabeth herself, who would miss out on so much.

'She was miserable,' Alice said, and her hands kept twisting over like she wished she could keep them busy with something.

She was a knitter, I remembered that from watching the archives. Maybe she'd be more relaxed now if she had needles and yarn in her hands. 'She sat there, looking devastated, her suitcase leaning up against her table, not drinking her coffee. And I thought, wow. There's someone even worse off than me. So I went over and asked if she was okay.'

I heard a movement by the kitchen door and turned my head to see Stewart, with a cup of newly stolen double espresso and a quizzical expression on his face. He gestured for us to keep going.

'That's him, isn't it?' Alice said in a quiet voice. 'Random Scotsman, from Sandstone City.'

How did she know that? Stewart didn't have a picture of himself on the blog. Had she been watching us, or was this all coming from Google?

I gestured him over, and he approached with caution, dropping to the patchy grass at our feet. 'Anything ye say is off the record unless ye dinnae want it tae be.' Like I said, he was about as ruthless as a slice of chocolate cake.

'An interview on Sandstone City would be far more compelling evidence to make the police stop looking for you as a missing person than me putting a word in to my ... friends at the station,' I added. Even now, even under these circumstances, I was not going to bring out the 'boyfriend' word.

Alice hesitated a bit longer, and then nodded. Stewart pulled out his phone and set it recording, placing it up on the table between us. 'Dinnae mind me,' he said. 'I hae coffee.'

Alice looked warily at the phone for a few moments, then continued, still looking at me. Just the two of us. Friendly old Tabitha, you can tell her anything.

'I'm not the sort of person who does that—just goes up to a person and starts talking to them about their life,' Alice said finally, eyes on the phone. 'I don't think Annabeth is ... was that sort of person either. But I surprised her, and she needed someone to talk to. She poured everything out to me—how her family had this idea in their head about how she would go off to uni, because her marks were better than anyone had expected. She would be the first person in her family to get a degree, and they were all so proud of her.

'But she didn't want that. She was obsessed with being an actress, and she had a boyfriend, this older guy who had plenty of money and had bought her the plane ticket to Sydney. He offered to support her while she went to auditions and tried to get into film school. She deferred her uni course and just—went. But she had an hour until her connecting flight, and she had been thinking about how miserable her family would be, how they would freak out when she told them she had given up everything they wanted for her, for this guy, to try for this mad acting thing. And what if it didn't work out? What if he dumped her after a month, how stupid would she look? What if she didn't make it as an actress?'

Alice shrugged uncomfortably. 'I'm a fixing sort of person. I can't sit back and not suggest things when people tell me their problems. And … I didn't have anywhere to go, anywhere to be. We kept talking, and we came up with this mad plan. I would go to Hobart and find somewhere to live, and she could tell everyone back in Flynn that address. I would be her … alibi. She could try out the acting thing, and if it all fell in a heap she could just come back to Hobart and start her degree a semester late.'

I could see Stewart itching to ask questions. I put one in for him, to keep the story going. 'But she stayed the whole year?'

'Yes. The bloke didn't let her down, at least I don't think he did. She didn't get into the school she wanted, but she was taking classes and getting a few auditions, and she wanted to keep going a bit longer. We decided she would tell them at Christmas, and we could stop the charade then. I … hadn't decided what to do about that. I mean, I had friends in Hobart who knew me as Annabeth. I didn't want to slip away from them.'

Stewart met my eyes, and I didn't blame him for being cynical. Alice/Vanilla had done exactly that, and we still didn't know why.

'Is that why ye got in touch now?' he asked in his low burr. 'Ye dinnae want tae leave yer friends not knowing what happened tae ye. So Tabitha and I can tell yer story, and ye can slip off back where ye came from without havin' tae look them in the eye and tell them why ye lied all these months.'

Alice looked taken aback. 'I—I don't know. I didn't want them to think anything bad had happened to me. And I'm not going back where I came from,' she added vehemently. 'I wouldn't … I don't know what I'm going to do, but not that.'

There were so many more questions I wanted to ask. Had she really joined The Gingerbread House on a whim, like she said on the website? Why had she left The Gingerbread House so suddenly? Did she really not know anything about what had happened to Annabeth? It was too much of a coincidence that she was killed at the same time that the girl pretending to be her disappeared. Wasn't it? Did Alice know the name of Annabeth's boyfriend, the mysterious older bloke who had been so generous in setting her up in her dream career?

Why would anyone running away from what sounded like a nasty domestic situation choose to become even slightly internet famous?

One thing I knew for certain, though—it shouldn't be me and Stewart interviewing this girl, it should be the police. Alice had made the wrong decision in coming to me. Xanthippe was the one who could be relied on to go under the radar if you wanted her to. I had learned the hard way that I didn't want to be involved in anything that had 'murder mystery' stamped on it. Not without backup.

Bishop would be furious if he found out I had kept something like this from the official investigation. And he would be right. My rebellious days were over, well and truly.

'Are you okay with answering a few more of Stewart's questions?' I said finally. 'I need tea. Possibly some little cakes.

There's no situation that can't be improved by very tiny food.'

'Tea would be great,' said Alice with that sweet smile of hers.

I brushed Stewart's shoulder with my hand as I left, hoping he wouldn't be too cranky about what I was about to do. It wasn't like he wouldn't have the exclusive anyway.

'A customer was asking about the ladybird biscuits,' Lara said as I came inside.

'We'll get restocked on Friday.' I slid my phone out of my pocket. 'Can you make me a pot of peppermint tea? Plate of little cakes?'

'I suppose I can manage it,' she said, giving me a cheeky look. 'Entertaining in the courtyard, are we?'

'Yep, my life is so very full of excitement.' I waited until Lara disappeared back into the café before I hit my speed dial.

Bishop answered promptly. 'I only saw you a couple of hours ago. Not playing hard to get, are you?'

'I thought you might like to know that French Vanilla is sitting in my courtyard,' I said, without any of the usual banter.

'You're kidding.'

'Bishop, it's me we're talking about. Do you doubt that something this random is happening?'

'Sadly, I can't. Shall I send someone over?'

'Well, you know. She appears to have some information on Annabeth French's death that the police might be interested in, but if you'd rather save on manpower you can always read about it on Stewart's blog later.'

'I'll come over myself.'

'Now who's playing hard to get?'

'Try to resist kissing me when I'm on duty.'

'I'll hold myself back.'

I slipped the phone away and went back outside to find Stewart doing that thing he does where he sits and gazes soulfully at a woman, and she spills her secrets. Or something. He had promoted himself to a chair and was making serious eye contact with Alice, who lapped it all up.

It was his story. The best thing I could do was hang back and try to be unobtrusive. Sadly, I had forgotten one major detail.

The kitchen door opened behind me as Lara brought out a tray that smelled strongly of peppermint. 'One pot of … bloody hell, Annabeth?'

Oh, crap. Seriously. How had Alice not factored in the fact that this city (and this café in particular) was full of people who knew her? Or thought they knew her.

Alice stood up like a frightened animal. She was going to run, and Bishop was going to accuse me of a prank call and one way or another, badness was going to ensue.

'Everyone stay calm,' I said, just as Xanthippe strolled into the courtyard. She took in the scene quickly, and her eyes narrowed as she recognised our guest. 'This is not what it looks like,' I said hastily.

Except it totally was.

Xanthippe stared at Alice. Everyone was staring at Alice. 'It's amazing who'll come out of the woodwork for one of your salad sandwiches,' Xanthippe said finally. 'How did you manage this, then, Tish?' *Why was I not invited,* was implied.

'I don't know,' I said desperately. 'These things happen to me.'

'I need to go,' said Alice, sounding frantic.

'Go?' demanded Lara. 'Melinda and Libby are sick with worry about you. Where have you been?'

'Good question,' Xanthippe agreed. 'Also, where do you think you are going?'

They were both good questions, and I just bet Stewart wished he had asked them earlier. Alice no longer looked like a willing and enthusiastic interviewee.

'You have to tell Libs and Mel you're okay,' Lara persisted. 'They thought you were *dead.*'

French Vanilla burst into tears.

The ultimate girl rule is that when someone starts crying, you stop giving them a hard time.

Xanthippe and Lara looked at each other, equally startled and helpless. Stewart moved into the kill with his nice bloke routine, patting Alice on the arm as she sobbed. 'Tabitha, have ye got any tissues?'

If I went inside, more catastrophes were likely to occur. I'd come back and find that the courtyard was also full of jugglers on unicycles, and Green protestors dressed as giant koalas, and...

A familiar blue light flashed at the entrance of the courtyard, reflecting off the gritty yellow sandstone. Oh boy, this was going to be fun.

Bishop strolled into the courtyard with Constable Heather at his side.

Stewart grabbed his phone, slipping it casually into a pocket of his jeans so it wouldn't be immediately obvious that he had been recording a conversation with the murder suspect. He gave me a reproachful look.

Xanthippe was spittingly furious. 'Tabitha, you arranged a meeting with French Vanilla without telling me *and* you brought in PC Plod?'

'Charming as ever, Xanthippe,' Bishop said mildly, his eyes on French Vanilla. 'You're going to have to tell me your name, miss.'

'Alice,' she said, shaking visibly. Her eyes were wide and frightened. Why was she so afraid of the police?

'Alice what?' Constable Heather asked in her 'I'm so much nicer than Bishop' voice.

My kitchen exploded.

12

TABITHA'S LUSCIOUS LEMON LICK

Ingredients:

1 part Limoncello

3 parts Lemonade (i.e. the clear fizzy commercial stuff, a good way to use up that flat half bottle of S***te left over from last time you ordered a pizza.

Instructions:

Pour 1 part limoncello to 3 parts lemonade into a wine glass. Place glass in freezer. After 30 minutes, remove glass and stir with swizzle stick. Or chopstick, if clean. Rinse, repeat. After about 3-4 hours of this, should be perfect consistency.

Yes, it's a lot of hassle to go to for one cocktail. Yes, it's totally worth it. Yes, you can do a bowlful, to be ladled into several glasses at the end. But where's the romance in doing it that way?

Prep time: 30 seconds, repeated every half hour until you crack and drink it even though it's still a bit runny and not perfect yet.

Suitable for that late, hot evening, a romantic date, or to unwind if you've spent the whole day cleaning up after some ARSEHOLE blew up your kitchen.

No, really. My kitchen exploded.

Bright orange sparks hit the windows in a burst of light and acrid smoke. The windows held. Everyone stared in shock, and then I made a dash in entirely the wrong direction, according to Bishop who grabbed hold of me around the waist, holding me back.

'Tabitha, stay out!' he yelled.

'Nin is in that kitchen, and thousands of dollars of equipment and Lara, get *in* there and see what's going on!' I howled. Lara was closer to the kitchen door than I was, and had the added benefit of not having a large police officer hanging on to her around the waist.

She did what I asked, throwing open the kitchen door and releasing a wave of disgusting smoke. Good waitress. She had her priorities right.

'Goddamn it, Tabitha,' Bishop roared.

I kicked him in the shins hard, which he obviously wasn't expecting, struggled out of his grip, and ran after Lara.

The kitchen looked—okay. Surprisingly okay. The windows over the sink had blown out, and the whole place smelled like burning plastic. Nin stood in the inner doorway between the kitchen and the main café, looking furious.

'What the hell happened?' I demanded.

'There was this *boy*,' she said, in the tone of voice she usually reserved for people who choose prepackaged frozen meals. 'I don't know how he sneaked into the kitchen, he crashed into me when he ran out—' and she threw up her hands, gesturing to a mess of something on the kitchen counter.

Our microwave was toasted. A few charred wires or something lay on the smashed remains of the glass plate. The door had blown off and was lodged in the sink.

I just stared around for a moment, furious. Several glass jars had cracked, and there were scorch marks on my fridge and my ceiling. Not destroyed, but far from okay.

Nin started to cough. I opened windows, trying to air the place out as quickly as I could.

Bishop strode in after me, glaring fit to burst. 'Fireworks,' he said finally. 'Someone set fireworks off in here.' He peered at the microwave. 'In there, rather.'

Steam was practically coming out of Nin's ears. 'I had *cakes* in the oven!' she said between coughs. 'Whatever happened blew a fuse too, there's no power now.' She switched a few things on and off to prove it.

'Where did he go, the kid who did this?' Bishop asked Nin.

She pointed back through the café. 'I threw a rolling pin at him.'

Bishop was caught between disapproving and impressed. 'Did you hit him?'

'Sadly, no.' She went for the back, taking deep breaths of fresh air.

Stewart stood in the doorway, and let out a low whistle. 'This is gonnae tae take some cleaning up.'

'Lara, Nin, can you reassure any customers we have left that this isn't a terrorist attack?' I said, glaring at my usually pristine (ish) kitchen. 'Offer them muffins and takeaway coffee on the house. I'm going to have to close the kitchen—check that nothing electrical has been permanently damaged before we get the power back on. Other than, you know, the *microwave*. Cross everything off the menu that isn't sealed under glass out there.'

Damn it. I hate being a grown up.

'Why would anyone do this?' I demanded the empty air, not expecting an answer. There were bits of charred sparkler embedded in the custard I had been cooling for tomorrow's ice cream experiment. A few hot sparks had turned the cling wrap over the bowl into melted sludge.

Whoever had set off fireworks in my kitchen was going to die slowly, and not by rolling pin. Serrated edges were more what I had in mind.

'I'd think tha' was obvious,' Stewart said dryly. 'A distraction. Anyone notice French Vanilla slipped away in the commotion? Well timed.'

Bishop looked back at the courtyard. 'Did you see her leave?'

'Aye.'

Bishop met Stewart's steady gaze, glaring at him. 'And you let her?'

'I'm nae the police officer around here,' said Stewart. 'Didnae she have the right tae leave? No one placed her under arrest.'

'I'll deal with you later,' Bishop growled, then looked at me. 'You all right?'

'No,' I sulked. 'Go away. Everyone who is not actively mopping or recommending an electrician can leave.'

'I'll question the customers,' said Bishop.

I looked at Constable Heather, who just gave me an uneasy smile and followed him.

That left Stewart and me in the singed kitchen together. 'You called your boyfriend to arrest her?' he said mildly.

'He's not my boyfriend,' I said automatically. 'But, yeah. I did.' I eyed the mess. 'Apparently she has loyal accomplices.'

'I thought…'

'What?' I said, turning on him.

'I thought ye were on her side.' Stewart sounded disappointed in me. If there had been any edible food left in this kitchen, I would have thrown it at him.

I grabbed a mop, and glared at him. 'Either you are helping, or you are leaving.'

Stewart rolled his eyes and his shoulders, and headed for the door. 'I have a story tae write up. Two stories.'

'Make sure you spell my name right,' I snapped as the door crashed behind me.

How was I the bad guy here? I had been doing the right thing. Right?

Sparkler bomb in the microwave. I looked it up, later, and found at least three instructional videos on YouTube that explained how to make one. The internet has a lot to answer for. It took most of the day to fix up the mess that the firework had done to my kitchen. No permanent damage, thank goodness, but it was going to be two days before we could get the building and electrical inspections we needed to reopen.

I was in a filthy mood, but I had grrrlpunk music up at a high volume as I knelt on one of my kitchen counters, wiping black streaks off the ceiling. Seriously, if I found the kid who had done this, I was baking him in the oven.

'You've done a good job,' said Xanthippe, eyeing the space. 'Really. It's all de-terroristed.'

'Thanks for your help,' I grumped.

'Any time.' She didn't sound happy either. Another one. I was so over this. I dropped to sit on the counter. 'What's got your knickers knotted up?'

'You mean apart from the fact that you made an appointment with French Vanilla and left me out…'

'That was Stewart! And then she came to me later on her own, there was no appointment…'

'So you called in Leo to arrest her?'

'Not to arrest her, to question her—why do I even need to justify this? She's involved in a major crime…'

'And you had to be the good girl and get in the police before you even knew the full situation? Since when is that your first response to anything, Tabitha? Oh, right. Since you started dating my brother.'

'This had nothing to do with Bishop,' I said sulkily.

'You mean you're not second guessing every decision you make based on 'what would my boyfriend think'?'

'No!' I was insulted. As if I was that kind of girl. Still, I didn't have the energy to give the 'not my actual boyfriend' line, not this time.

Xanthippe sat at the kitchen table, looking up at me through that shaggy dark fringe of hers. 'This was a sensitive situation. I love my brother, but what on earth made you think he would contribute in any useful way?'

'Bishop isn't the one who set off a handful of fireworks in my kitchen,' I said between gritted teeth.

'True,' Xanthippe agreed. 'And I find that very intriguing. But would someone have been so desperate to cause a distraction to help French Vanilla escape if you hadn't called in the cops?'

'So this is my fault, just because I don't want to run around playing at being a private detective? This is none of our business, Xanthippe. It is a police investigation.'

She looked startled. 'Seriously. What happened to you?'

'Nothing. This is me. Being responsible.'

'Being conventional.'

Okay, that was below the belt. 'I am not conventional!'

Xanthippe shook her head, standing up. 'You say that, Tish, but where's the evidence? I hate to say it, but since you dragged Leo into bed, you've gone kind of … vanilla.'

I stared at her, and the only thing I could think of to say was: 'You like vanilla.'

'In ice cream,' she said with a shrug. 'But on you? It's not a good look. More importantly, it's not your look. You're trying someone else's on for size, and that's kind of sad.'

'Get the hell out of my kitchen,' I snapped. I did not have to take this. Not in my own place, and not from her.

She shrugged, and left. I stood there with a wet rag dripping from my hand. Conventional? I'm not conventional.

And I am so not vanilla.

The next morning found a large-shouldered bloke sitting at the window in my café, a laptop open in front of him and a slice of cranberry treacle tart perching on the edge of his table.

We weren't open, but he was the one customer allowed in to eat up the leftover gateaux. After all, he still owned five percent of Café La Femme.

I took him a pot of earl grey, admiring the outfit he was wearing as I sat opposite. There just aren't that many men who can get away with wearing ruffled shirts and green velvet suits, and I can't think of anyone else who would be insane enough to wear velvet in an Australian December.

Darrow used to own a much larger slice of my business, but had handed over most of his share to Xanthippe in recompense for totalling her previous vintage car. He has a sweet tooth for my cakes in particular, but was not making friends with the treacle tart today, rolling the cranberries around on his teeth and making a thoughtful face. Darrow thinking was rarely a good thing.

'Not a fan?' I said. I wasn't surprised. Treacle was an acquired taste and while he liked his desserts sticky, this was probably a bit beyond him. 'Should have ordered the crunchy lime cheesecake.'

'Sure, you tell me that now.' He poured himself a cup of tea with precise measurements, and added a slice of lemon. 'How's your life, Darling?'

'Found a missing person, Stewart and Xanthippe are both pissed off at me for ratting said missing person out to Bishop, some kid exploded my kitchen and I can't get my muffins to rise.' Not that I needed muffins until we reopened, but I'd put a batch in the oven before I remembered that all over again. Damn it.

'Not a good week.'

'Not especially, no.'

'What's the damage in the kitchen?'

'Nothing expensive except the microwave, and we needed a new one anyway. I sent Nin shopping. How are things with you?' I indicated the laptop. 'Still writing that book of yours?' I tried not to curl my lip. Unlike Stewart's inoffensive romance writing, Darrow's novel had caused me all kinds of problems earlier in the year. Here's a tip—when writing a novel that features inventive crime methods, it's really important to not let it get in the hands of people who want to use it for actual crime.

'Eh, I've gone off the idea,' said Darrow dismissively. 'Rejection letters are terrible, terrible things. I couldn't get out of bed for three days. Who wants to be a writer anyway?'

I was not going to smack him. Not at all. It was for the best if that book never saw the light of day. I might have known he'd never follow through. 'So what are you up to instead?' Darrow was always up to something. He had too much money and no day job, which meant he was constantly teetering between bored and far-too-interesting.

'Thought I'd try my hand at filmmaking,' he said with a wide grin. 'An old girlfriend of mine—remember Cassidy? —is opening an indie cinema bar at New Year's, and she wants a short film for it. Doesn't sound too hard. I've been buying up the equipment, gathering media student volunteers…'

I blinked. 'Writing a script?'

'Nah, I'm going for more of a loose, casual approach. Get some actors who are willing to improvise, turn a camera on them…'

'Let them do your work for you…'

'Exactly.'

'Are we talking a reality TV sort of thing? Contemporary take on something or other?' I couldn't get my head around it.

'Oh no,' Darrow said, ridiculously pleased with himself. 'I'm thinking film noir.'

Improvised film noir featuring a cast of Australians. Someone save us all.

'Sounds fascinating,' I drawled. Oh, it was going to be a cake wreck. Still, hopefully the costumes would be cute.

'Doesn't it though?'

The doorbell jangled and Xanthippe stuck her head in. 'Darrow, move your arse, I'm on a loading zone.'

'Only for you, my sweet.' He started to pack up his laptop.

I looked at Xanthippe in surprise. 'You're involved in his film?'

She gazed coolly back at me. 'Why not?'

Apart from the fact that Darrow was her ex and the two of them could barely spend five minutes in a room together without sniping at each other, I couldn't think of a single reason.

'It just seems sort of...' *Made for failure*. There, I said it. Internally, but it's the thought that counts.

'Fun?' Xanthippe said archly.

'Why don't you join us, Darling?' Darrow asked in that melted toffee voice of his. 'Dressing up, running around a small town playing a femme fatale. Just your sort of thing.'

'I bet you even have the perfect dress,' Xanthippe added. She sounded smug. She was also right. I had the perfect dress, and normally I would completely drop everything for a caper like this. It didn't matter if the end result sucked, the journey would be entertaining and fun. Oh hell, I had the perfect shoes, too.

'Someone has to wait here for the electrician, and the building inspector,' I said pointedly, to my two business partners.

'Very responsible of you,' said Xanthippe with a nod. 'Isn't she being responsible, Darrow? All grown up. I can feel the pride just bursting out of my chest.'

Okay, what exactly had I done to justify Xanthippe being such a dick?

Xanthippe dragged Darrow out the door. 'Stewart, give us a minute!'

'You're taking Stewart?' Talk about rubbing salt into my wound! Stewart was my sidekick, not theirs. At least, he used to be.

'They took a vote and apparently I can't be trusted to point a camera at anyone,' said Darrow. 'I have a sweetarse director's chair, though. And a megaphone!'

The sweetarse director's chair was jammed into the tiny backseat of Xanthippe's Spider, along with Stewart, who gave me a wave.

Of course they were taking Stewart. This sort of quirky adventure was the kind of thing that Sandstone City lived and breathed. I tried not to look bereft as I waved back. 'Have fun, guys.'

Xanthippe shook out her dark hair as she elbowed Darrow in the ribs to stop him getting in the driving seat. 'How can we not?'

13

From: Darlingtabitha

Let's do something this weekend.

From: Bishop

Uh-oh

From: Darlingtabitha

Don't be like that. Adventuuuuures.

From: Bishop

Is it the kind of adventure where you and all your friends end up covered in glitter?

From: Darlingtabitha

THOSE ARE THE BEST ADVENTURES.

From: Bishop

Go ahead without me, I have some report-writing to catch up on.

LIVIA DAY

From: Darlingtabitha

> You're so lucky that you're hot. Want me to drop by later after all the glitter is cleaned up?

From: Bishop

> Now that sounds like a much better plan.

Even my experimentation with sweet potato ice cream (surprisingly yummy, though it needed more cinnamon) didn't cheer me up. I wanted to be racing around a small town with an insane crowd-sourced film noir film crew and my friends. Who wouldn't? The electrician arrived by the end of the day and gave me the all clear, but it turned out the building inspector wouldn't be able to make it until the day after tomorrow. Bloody brilliant.

I mooched home to find Ceege tapping away at his computer, same as usual. Normally I worried about him, but today it was something of a relief. Someone had less of a life than me. Does that make me a bad person?

I would make him steamed chicken dumplings to make up for it. And chocolate mousse. Or I could just lie on the couch and pout.

Pouting won.

'What's wrong with you?' Ceege asked as I collapsed on the couch with my best sulk face.

'Did I get boring?'

'Yes,' he said automatically, and then tried to cover for himself when I let out a yelp of protest. 'Um, I mean—compared to what?'

I glared at the back of his head. 'Compared to how I was before I started going out with Bishop.'

'Oh, well, you know how it is. Girl meets boy, girl likes boy, girl starts thinking that boy is the centre of the universe, girl starts changing herself to suit boy's tastes...'

'That's not me,' I said in absolute horror. 'Stop it. Don't talk. No more talking. I would never ever let that happen in a million years, and you are completely full of shit.'

'I still love you, Tabs.'

'Oh, very comforting, ta for that.' I frowned over at him. That didn't look like *World of Warcraft* or any of his other online gaming thingies. 'What are you doing?'

'I'm designing a set for Darrow's movie, based on a bunch of stuff we've borrowed from some mates in Old Nick.' That was the uni rep theatre club.

'Not you too?' I said, genuinely shocked. I'd been trying to get Ceege to take an interest in something other than his keyboard all month, and Darrow just had to snap his fingers? Or was Xanthippe doing the snapping?

'Sure, it's not like I've got anything better to do over the holidays.' Ceege offered me a sort of grin. 'Want to come along tomorrow? You can bang nails for me.'

'Bang nails?' I said haughtily.

'Okay, make sandwiches.'

Huh.

'C'mon, Tabs,' he wheedled. 'You know it won't be as much fun without you there.'

Well, yes. I do bring the fun. But I wasn't sure how welcome I was with anyone other than Ceege.

'I actually have nowhere I have to be tomorrow,' I admitted reluctantly. 'Thanks to my lazy-arse building inspector.'

'There ya go.'

'Where is it happening? Darrow said something about a small town.' A thought struck me. I stared at Ceege. 'Flynn. It's Flynn, isn't it?' This wasn't Xanthippe switching from one obsession to another. This was Xanthippe sneakily masking her ongoing obsession with Darrow's creative nuttiness. And Stewart was her accomplice.

I was so on to them.

There was no way I was not going down to join them now. 'Okay fine,' I said. 'But I'm going to drive. You've been sitting at that computer or the Playstation for eighteen hours a day for the last month, I don't trust your reflexes in the real world.'

Ceege smiled his almost-charming smile at me. 'Knew I could count on you, Tabs.'

Hmmm. Did my friends really think I'd gone vanilla, or was this all a cunning ruse to get me to come out and play? Only one way to find out.

✳

There's something about driving a ute. It makes me feel like I should be in a flannie and Blundstone boots, hair sprayed up in a mushroom cloud of a fringe, cracking gum.

Instead, I was wearing a glam 1940s navy dress, with vintage red shoes and lipstick to match, my hair tucked back in a crimson snood. Yes, I have a snood. My hair is the wrong shade of blonde for film noir but otherwise I had the look down pretty well.

Ceege was wearing his worst jeans and a faded Lucksmiths T-shirt which he had dragged back from Katie during the awkward 'your stuff in this cardboard box, my stuff in that cardboard box' breakup phase.

More importantly, Ceege was out in daylight. It was a good look on him. He's a stocky guy—a little heavier than he had been a couple of months ago when he had a girlfriend and walked to and from uni every day—with a buzz cut that makes him look more thuggish than he actually is.

The super short hair makes it easier when he puts on his glam wigs and frocks up for a party—when not slouching around in his scungiest attire, Ceege's style of choice is drag queen chic. I was betting he had packed a femme fatale film noir outfit to rival mine.

Pieces of an old *Guys and Dolls* theatre set and a bunch of props rattled away in the tray of the borrowed ute, including the entire makings of a Phillip Marlowe style detective office and a trunk of old costumes.

Anytime I feel that life is getting surreal, along comes Darrow to put things into perspective.

It felt good to be making the wild choice. How long was it since I did something wild? My last road trip to Flynn had been barely a blip. Taking part in Darrow's festival of noir felt more Tabitha than I had felt for ages, and I liked it. We had chosen the road along the river for a bit of variety, and it was one hell of a view.

'You have your thinking face on,' said Ceege, flipping through an issue of *NW* as I drove. 'Should I be worried?'

'Xanthippe said that Bishop is vanilla,' I confessed. 'Or that— me being with him makes me vanilla. Or something like that.'

Ceege wrinkled his nose. 'Should Xanthippe be taking that much interest in her brother's sex life?'

'Ew, not that, gross.' I didn't have anything to throw at him, and I did like keeping my hands on the wheel, so I made a mental note to smack him after I parked. 'There's nothing vanilla about him in bed, as it happens.'

'Way too much information, Tabs.'

'I hope she wasn't talking about sex, anyway.' That was an alarming possibility, best forgotten. 'I think she just meant he's ... you know. Straight. Not as in not gay ... though ha, obviously not.'

'Oh, I don't know, he wouldn't be your first,' Ceege said slyly.

'Shut up. One boyfriend swears off women for life and suddenly the world thinks you're hilarious.'

'Wasn't it three boyfriends? In a row?'

I gave him a very hard look. 'This is on the list of things we do not discuss, Ceege.'

'I don't recall that list.'

'Katie's name is right at the top of it.'

He winced. 'Oh, *that* list. Consider the matter dropped.'

'Thank you,' I said primly, taking the curve a little faster than I should. We were in green mountain and valley territory now, away from the coast. The sets made a noisy clashing sound as the panels bounced under their tarpaulin.

'Y'know, Xanthippe has a point,' Ceege mused as we bounced along.

'About?'

'Bishop. Seriously, Tabs. He's so vanilla it hurts. I bet he's never even returned a library book late.'

Hmmm, library books. What had happened to that stack of books about ice cream making? Possibly they were under that suspiciously high lingerie heap in my bedroom. Time to do some excavation before the fines overtook my weekly business offences.

'That doesn't make him a bad person, Ceege.'

'I never said he's not a top bloke. Just ... you know. Conventional.' He pronounced the last word with several extra vowel sounds. 'Not your usual type.'

'Yeah,' I sighed. I'd had a thing about Bishop for nearly ten years before I finally cornered him into snogging—and more—and at no point had I actually stopped to think about the ramifications of having any kind of romantic relationship with someone who was responsible and dependable and unlikely to drop everything and dash off to take part in an inspired act of bad street theatre in period costumes. I hadn't told him my plans for the day, because I knew exactly what expression he would get on his face. 'Conventional.'

'He's vanilla, and you're ... raspberry vinaigrette sorbet, with a side order of fireworks in the kitchen.'

'Opposites attract, right?' I said, feeling panicky.

'I reckon you're thinking about this way too much, Tabs,' said Ceege, stretching out his legs. 'Just go with it. It's not like the bloke is asking you to marry him. Hell, you don't even let anyone call him your boyfriend. If it doesn't work out ... then so what?'

So what? Really? Was that what they all thought? I knew this whole thing with Bishop hadn't turned into a grand epic romance for the ages, but did my friends really think that what he and I had going was so completely disposable?

Did I think that?

We drove in silence for some time, me muttering away inside my head as I took the several dozen tight corners. The trees were dark and lush around us, casting a deep shade across the road, unlike the rest of Tasmania which was blazing with fierce sunshine today.

Nothing like a looming bit of scenery to make you feel small. This wasn't anywhere near the deepest, darkest, greenest part of Tassie, but it felt like we were buried in the wilderness, far from civilisation.

Eventually my muttering escaped my head, and I started talking under my breath.

'Tabitha,' said Ceege.

We were about fifteen minutes from the turn off to Flynn.

'I mean, it's no one's business but ours, right?' I said.

'Tabs…'

'There's nothing wrong with dependable and reliable. I've had years of blokes who are charming and exciting and trust me, they're not all they're cracked up to be. Hell, Bishop is exciting. He is. And…'

'Tabs, what's going on over there?'

I dragged my attention away from myself and my apparently vanilla non-relationship (what was wrong with vanilla as a flavour, everyone kept telling me how bloody brilliant it was) and noticed what had alarmed Ceege.

There were high rocky precipices on one side of the road and a screamingly steep valley on the other. Up ahead, there was a beaten up old Holden gunning its engine over and over, nose facing over a lookout point with a drop that was … yeah.

Don't ask me how Ceege had spotted it. Chances were I would have just swept past in a haze of my own self-absorption.

But instead I pulled over, and we both jumped out. Stupid, probably. Don't get involved. I'd been working that particular philosophy—or trying to—for weeks now. But I didn't realise how deeply it was ingrained in me until Ceege leaned in over the open window on the driver's side and said 'G'day mate,' in that extra ocker voice that blokes use when they need a layer of emotional protection.

'Piss off,' said the driver, a teenage boy. He sounded tired rather than belligerent.

'We were just passing,' said Ceege. 'Weren't we, Tabs? Couldn't help noticing you looking a bit precarious over here.' He stretched one hand in through the window, and turned off the engine. 'That's better, yeah? Any chance of you putting on the hand brake?'

The driver turned and looked him in the eye—and I recognised him. Here we were, involved all over again.

I couldn't stay away from it, apparently. The driver of the car was Jason Avery. Boyfriend of the murder victim. Author of postcards. Son of the vineyard magnate who had saved the town from financial crisis. Best friend to Shay French.

And, before the charges had been recently dropped, prime suspect in the murder of Annabeth French.

14

Avery Grove Vineyard, 4 Stars ****
Overlooking the quaint Tasmanian village of Flynn, this boutique winery and restaurant is a family business set on a picturesque hillside in the heart of the Huon Valley, with sweeping views to the Wellington Range. Avery Grove's range of crisp wines complement the restaurant's seasonal menu, which features a variety of local specialty produce including organic cheeses, free range game meats and the best Huon Valley mushrooms.
More information at www.averygrove.com.au

There was a long pause. A really long pause, in which I held my breath. Ceege looked weirdly reassuring. You'd never think that an hour earlier he had been swearing at a screen full of pixels as if they were destroying his life.

Jason put the hand brake on, and then we could breathe again.

'Out you come,' Ceege said then, opening the door. 'Tabs, crack open the slab. I reckon this kid needs a beer.'

'I'm not a kid,' Jason muttered, but he stepped out of the car and leaned against it, looking sick.

'Thank fuck for that, or I could be in trouble for giving you beer,' said Ceege with a grin. 'Tabs, are you a girl or what? Beer me.'

Oh, he so hadn't said that. I went back to the ute, pulled three cans off the slab we had bought to donate to the film project, and brought them back. I handed Jason his, and threw Ceege's at his head.

'Ow,' he protested, catching it before it fell. 'Have some respect for the foam, woman.' He opened the beer, and it sprayed noisily out over the grass.

'I respect the beer, I just don't respect you.' There are worse things than drinking slightly warm beer on the side of a road, but it was not my beverage of choice. I drank it anyway, because Ceege had implied women were only good for the fetching of the beer. Unacceptable.

I dropped to the grass, crossing my legs. Jason slid down the side of his car to sit down too, legs stretched out. He looked defeated.

'Where do you live, mate?' Ceege asked.

'Flynn,' said Jason, and there was a world of resentment tied up in just that name.

'Huh, that's a coincidence. We're heading to Flynn.'

'Not that much of a coincidence,' I sighed. Not with Xanthippe involved. Nothing was an accident with her. 'You're Jason, right?'

The kid looked instantly defensive. 'Read that in the papers, did you?'

'Partly,' I admitted. 'Want to tell us what you were doing on that...' Cliff, precipice, which sounded less melodramatic? 'Edge.'

Jason glared at me. 'No.'

'Come on, Tabs, a man's Holden is his castle,' said Ceege reasonably, taking a swig of very beery foam. 'You can't ask questions like that.'

'See, that's the good thing about being a girl. I don't know these mystical Man Rules, so I can ignore them.' Like, why was a nineteen-year-old toying with the idea of driving himself off a cliff? Apart from the fact that he was still a person of interest in a major crime. 'Jason, I thought they dropped the charges against you.'

The papers had been full of the story. First there was the bail hearing, which Dad Avery had dominated. Then the news had hit that the charges had been dropped against Jason pending further evidence. After that, nothing in the way of hard news.

It seemed pretty clear to me that the police were looking for someone else, the obvious suspect being French Vanilla herself.

'Yeah,' Jason said bitterly. 'The police don't have a case against me, and Dad's lawyer got them to admit it. Doesn't mean anyone else thinks I'm innocent. I live in a small town. You know what that means?'

Oh, hell. 'I think I have some idea.'

'My dad is somebody in Flynn,' Jason said, setting his chin. 'People used to look at me like I was somebody too. Girls liked me, and their parents smiled at me in the street. Now suddenly they all believe I killed Anna. They look at me like I'm shit on their shoe, or worse, like I'm going to hurt someone else...' He trailed off, then looked at me suspiciously. 'Who are you? You're not a fucken journo, are you?'

'No,' I assured him. 'I'm not involved, I'm just...' Hmm. 'A friend.' Nicely non-committal. He didn't ask whose friend I was.

'I didn't,' Jason said, and broke off, looking around at the car. 'I wasn't... I'm just sick of it. Everyone looks at me all the time, no one talks to me. Even my mates just...'

Mates. Well, maybe that part I could help with. 'Shay French came to see me, a little while ago,' I said in a low voice. 'He's broken up about all this too, you know.'

'Yeah, I bet. What am I supposed to say to him? Sorry your sister's dead, mate, I didn't do it?'

'Probably couldn't hurt,' Ceege said in that reasonable voice.

Jason gave him a wounded look.

'Shay doesn't think you did it,' I said helpfully. 'He said that, when we talked.'

Jason looked thoughtful. 'Huh.' He drank some beer.

'Seems to me you have two choices,' I said. 'You can suck it up and wait for them to start talking crap about someone else, hope the police arrest someone soon so everyone knows you didn't do it.' Unless of course he had done it. I didn't used to be such a suspicious person. Jason's boyish face and big eyes would have been enough to convince me, once upon a time. His mate's loyalty for him and belief in him would count for something too.

But I'd been stung by a boyish face before. I didn't believe in them anymore.

'Or?' Jason said, sticking his chin out.

'Or you leave town, go somewhere else. The world is your oyster.' French Vanilla Alice had done that, once upon a time. Twice, maybe. I wondered where she was now. I wanted to find her, if only to catch her accomplice and shake him until his teeth rattled for setting off that bloody firework in my kitchen.

I looked pointedly at Jason's Holden. 'Those aren't great options, but they're both … reasonable, yeah? You don't need to go looking for any other alternatives. If you need to escape next time, leave town until you can get your head clear. And um. Tell someone where you're going.'

Jason looked at me. 'For someone who's not involved, you talk a lot.'

Ceege snickered, and I smacked him. 'Hush, you.'

The kid shrugged and wrapped his arms around his knees. 'I want to wake up and have it all be okay, you know? I really want Anna not to be dead.'

That, I believed. But would a nineteen-year-old really consider driving himself off a cliff because the town thought he killed his girlfriend? Or was there something else going on here?

'How about we take you back into Flynn,' I suggested. 'Ceege could drive your car back, and I'll drop you home.'

'I don't want to see my dad,' Jason said quickly. 'I don't…' His shoulders dropped. 'I thought he believed me,' he said finally. 'He's been standing up for me in front of everyone. But he got pissed off this morning and started yelling and … yeah, he's covering for me. But he still thinks I did it. He thinks I'm capable of hitting her, holding her underwater, I mean what the hell? How could anyone who knows me think I could do that? How could my dad defend me to everyone in town when he thinks I'm some psycho murderer?'

Jason raised his eyes, meeting mine, so earnest it hurt. 'Annabeth was a real cow sometimes,' he said clearly. 'If I was going to lose it and kill her, it would have been when we were first going out. Maybe even in the first few months after she left. But I was … basically immune by the time she came home.'

I should pack this boy up and get him to someone motherly who could feed him soup and make him feel better. There had to be someone other than his dad.

Meanwhile, my inner Xanthippe wanted to know more. Much more. 'Tell me about when Annabeth came home.'

Jason gave me a look, a darting 'you're not fooling anyone' kind of look. Ceege gave me one to match his, and I shrugged.

'You don't have to.'

'It was about a month ago,' Jason said, wiping his nose on his sleeve. 'She turned up and acted like nothing was different. Like I should be grateful. Or something. Because here she was, back for good.'

'For good?' I said in surprise. 'Not just for the holidays?'

'Nope.' His voice was dry, and he peered into the bottom of his can. 'Got another of these?'

I passed him mine, which I'd barely started on. Jason shrugged and knocked some more beer back down his throat.

'Can I ask a question?' Ceege asked.

Jason shrugged and opened his arms in one of those whole body shrugs that teenage boys are so good at. 'Go for it.'

'Why did the police reckon you did it, when they arrested you?'

'Apparently breaking up with someone an hour before they get murdered is really suspicious. We had a row—a big one, in the bloody Main Street. About fifty people saw me yelling at her. Everyone knows Anna hangs out at the lake when she's pissed off, she's been doing that since she was twelve.' His face shifted slightly, hollowing out. 'Only, you know. Past tense.'

I nodded. 'And why don't the police think you did it now?'

'Oh, they do,' he said sourly. 'But they don't have any evidence to pin on me. They can't link me to the scene. And they can't find my fucking alibi. Until she turns up, I'm in … limbo.'

I blinked. 'You have an alibi?'

'Not if I can't find her. And because I was a moron I didn't tell them the first day, not until they started making noise about not letting my dad bail me out. So yeah. Suspicious behavior.'

'Jason, who's your alibi?' I asked him.

He wiped hair out of his eyes, looking exhausted. 'Alice. I was with Alice.'

I rocked back on my heels, staring at him in shock. 'Alice? How can you possibly have been with *Alice?*'

'Who's Alice?' asked Ceege, leaning back on the grass.

'Alice is French Vanilla,' I said, staring at Jason. 'The other Annabeth. What the hell?'

Jason was looking … guilty. Supremely guilty. Not of killing anyone, perhaps, but something else. It was all over his face.

'You knew,' I said quietly. 'You knew about the switch with Alice? Is that why you and Annabeth fought, because you'd found out?'

'Kind of,' he said, leaning back against the warm metal of the car. 'Only I hadn't just found out. I was angry she was still pretending, like … like I was stupid. I found out back in March.'

'March?' I repeated. 'March? But … how did you find out?' And, more importantly, why had Alice left that part out of her story? Why on earth hadn't she given Jason his alibi? Especially since it gave her one too.

'I went to see her. Because I'm an idiot. Annabeth was acting weird, but she kept assuring me she didn't want to break up. That I could come visit her, or she'd come home a lot. But then she called and she sounded … different. Put me off from visiting, said she was still trying to find a place, then that her flatmates didn't want male visitors, but wouldn't explain why. I figured—okay, this is it. I can't go all year without seeing her, either we're together or we're not, so I drove up to Hobart to tell her that—either we'd see each other regularly or I was breaking up with her. And she wasn't there. Some other girl answered the door, pretending to be Anna.'

'Alice.' I stared at him. 'But you sent those postcards. Like—you still thought Anna was there.'

Jason blushed. I mean, actually blushed, all over his face. 'They weren't for Anna, they were for Alice. It was kind of our inside joke. We, um, got to know each other. After a while. She took me for coffee, explained to me what was going on … well, she didn't tell me the part about Anna's other bloke, not at first. I figured it out later. But thing is, I got to know Alice, and…' He looked supremely embarrassed. 'She was easy to talk to.'

You wouldn't read about it. Seriously. Well, you would. There are magazines for this sort of story: 'I fell for my fake girlfriend'.

'So the girl you were texting all the time and sending flirty postcards to all year—you knew you were romancing Alice, not Annabeth.'

Jason had a look on his face, that was … sheepish and embarrassed and so adorable I wanted to eat him up with a spoon. 'Yeah,' he said, fast like he wanted to get it over with.

'Boys are dumb,' I told him, just in case he needed a reminder. 'And this is making my head hurt.'

'I was mad at Annabeth for lying to me, still trying to make out like we had something,' Jason said. 'I mean, what the hell? I didn't say anything when she first came back, pretending she was on uni holidays and maybe she was going to come back to Flynn for good, but she just kept lying. Finally I lost it—on the Main Street—and you know the rest. But I was irritated, not homicidal. I'd had months to get over it, and I'm kind of into someone else now. Anna didn't like that. She flounced off and someone else killed her, and I don't reckon the police are looking for anyone else, they just want to find Alice because they think she won't be my alibi.'

I was not going to be the one to break it to him that Alice had had a recent opportunity to clear his name, and hadn't even mentioned him. 'Come on, let's get you home,' I said finally.

Jason tossed his keys to Ceege, and came to sit in the passenger seat of our borrowed ute without too much argument. He looked exhausted. 'I didn't kill Anna,' he said as he strapped himself in.

'Yeah, I know,' I said.

The weird thing was, I did. I totally believed him. I've been suckered before—suckered beautifully, by someone I'd known a lot longer than this kid. But I believed in Jason Avery's innocence.

I wasn't so sure I believed in Alice's any more. But if Jason said they were together, that meant she had an alibi too. Right?

15

random_scotsman posts in Sandstone City:

FILM NOIR IN DOWNTOWN FLYNN

A horde of detectives, murderers, blackmailers, hoodlums and dames converged on the small Tasmanian town of Flynn today, shooting an improvised and crowd-sourced film noir short.

Producer Xanthippe Carides (26) told Sandstone City: 'Darrow's insane, but I think he might have something here. The resulting film will be short, effective, and unlike anything you've ever seen before.'

Director Darrow (31) said: 'We're going for style over realism, which is what film noir is all about. I think we're really going to surprise people.'

The volunteers for *Flynn By Night* are Hobart film and media students, as well the townsfolk themselves. Greg Avery (52), local mayor and the owner of the Avery Grove vineyard and restaurant, as well as several other local businesses said: 'It's about time that the people of Hobart realised that there is so much to see and do beyond the more familiar outskirts. Flynn has a lot to offer as a community, and we're glad to host such an exciting creative project.'

'So what's all that shit?' Jason asked, jerking a thumb towards the clattering mess of props and boards in the flat tray as I drove us along the winding road. 'You guys a theatre company?'

'It's for a film,' I told him as I made the turn off to Flynn, approaching the town.

'They're making a film in Flynn?'

'I think it's more of a flashmob with pretensions of grandeur.' And, holy hell. They'd already started. I slowed as we drew up the Main Street, and found it blocked off.

When Darrow wants something done, it gets done.

'What the fuck?' Jason said, mouth hanging open. The boy had a point.

The Main Street of Flynn had been transformed into something that … well, it wasn't like any film noir set I'd ever seen. It was more like something out of a wacked-out western. People in 1940s costumes ran back and forth across the street, mostly around the Scallop, which had been transformed into The Swell Dame Hotel. The takeaway was now Joe's Liquor, and the newsagency was Bettie's House of Sin. The ice cream parlour was Florian's Dime and Dice. Classy.

There were notices everywhere, addressed to the 'cast' and 'crew' (and yes I was using those terms pretty damn loosely).

'Please don costume before entering filming area.
Guys wear hats at all time. Dolls, no bare arms or
skirts above the knee.'

'The director reserves the right to mock
all fake American accents. Dinkum Aussie is
just fine, ta very much.'

'Are you a private dick, femme fatale, gangster
or murder victim? Ask Ms Carides (producer) to
make a judgement call, then costume up!'

'What the hell is going on?' demanded Jason, stunned at
the sight of his town transformed into a bizarre amalgam of
Bogart films, possibly constructed by people who had never
actually watched one.

'I think it's art,' I said knowledgeably.

Jason muttered some words that I'm pretty sure I didn't
know when I was nineteen.

A gang of media students pounced on the ute almost as soon
as I parked, carting away the costumes in one direction, props
in another. A couple of blokes in goatees started to unload
the set panels.

'Oi, careful with those,' said Ceege, who had parked behind
me in Jason's Holden.

'Yeah, who the hell are you?' said one of them in a snotty
voice.

'You're looking at our stage manager,' said Xanthippe, slapping Ceege's hand in a matey sort of way as she passed him. 'Listen to everything he says—unlike the rest of you, I trust him to put up a structure that won't collapse and kill half our talent. Dude, we need a casino over by the ice cream parlour.'

'No probs,' said Ceege. 'Going to crack out the good hammers for this one.'

I hadn't seen Ceege looking so animated in a long time. Whatever hijinks Xanthippe and Darrow were up to, it was worth it to see my friend back in his element again.

Xanthippe loped up to me and Jason. 'Not that I'd mind us losing half our cast to accident or injury,' she added confidentially. 'But the way we're going, it would be the wrong half. Good to see you, Tish, about time you figured out you wanted to be here.' She looked me up and down. 'Nice outfit. We'll have to get you front and centre.' She eyed Jason speculatively. 'Excellent shoulders. Ever considered wearing a trench coat?'

'Are you completely nuts?' he demanded.

'You kind of have to be to do this,' Xanthippe said, dragging him away. 'Don't worry, you'll get the hang of it.'

'Should I feel bad about letting her do that to him?' I asked aloud, but Ceege was already busy talking about flats and squares to film students with bemused expressions on their faces. And hey, at least it would get Jason's mind off his troubles.

I leaned against the ute and watched the beautiful chaos.

A couple of cops ran across the street, demanding that a glamorous girl in pearls and heels 'stick em up'. The lack of guns was a touch on the unrealistic side. They had rallied to the lack of props by pointing their fingers at her.

No, seriously. Their fingers.

'Cut, brilliant!' yelled Darrow the director, emerging from a side street in a flappy striped suit and ... yes, a beret. He saw me, and his face lit up. 'Darling. Knew you couldn't stay away.'

'I brought sandwiches and beer and your stage manager,' I said, shading my eyes from the sun. 'Do they call it a stage manager in films? Isn't he supposed to be a Best Boy or a Key Grip or...'

Darrow was eyeing me with a definite gleam in his eye. I felt a rising urge to slap him around the chops and call him a cad. I always knew my love for old movies would be the death of me. Or something. 'Good outfit, Tish. Very authentic.'

'Thanks. Darrow ... what are you doing here? Your actors don't even have guns.'

'It's metaphorical,' he told me with a nod. 'No use of any prop resembling a gun was one of the stipulations of filming on the streets here. Do you think the fingers work? My other option is bananas.'

Metaphorical. Okay then. 'Where do you want me?'

The ridiculously bereted director dived into the nearest pile of props and produced a heavy brown paper parcel, about the size of a garden gnome. 'Need you to deliver this to McTavish over in the alley by Joe's Liquor. They have this metal staircase that almost looks like a fire escape,' he added proudly. 'Also, a fog machine.'

I looked at the parcel. 'Video equipment?'

'Just deliver it. Try to stay in character.'

I looked around at Darrow's guerrilla team of film students, many of whom were eyeing me through their iPhones. 'You're all going to be filming me?'

'What?' Darrow grinned. 'Can't you handle the pressure?'

I gave him a cool look. 'Give me the damn package. Am I a femme fatale or a good girl?'

'Entirely up to you. Just as long as it looks right from above—I have a couple of film students hanging from the rooftops who know no fear.'

My eyes narrowed. 'Repeat after me, Darrow. You are not Orson Welles.' I hefted the package (it felt as heavy as a garden gnome too, it better bloody not be) and walked up the Main Street of Flynn.

My heels made a trip-trapping sound. The street was oddly still. Except for the various people watching/listening/filming me. I lifted my chin, arched my back a little and kept walking.

At least I knew I looked good in the dress.

I walked under the Joe's Liquor sign and found Stewart sitting on a flight of steps that in no way looked like an American fire escape. He was in an oversized dark suit, a trilby pulled down over his face as he examined some footage on a fancy looking digital camera. When he saw me, he hit a dial on a small mechanical device on the steps above him, and dry ice vapour flooded slowly along the lower half of the fake alley.

I leaned a hip against the brick wall. 'Here's looking at you, kid.' Wow, it was hard to say old movie quotes with an Australian accent.

Stewart looked up at me, and grinned slowly. 'She gae me a smile I could feel in my hip pocket.' Heh, possibly it was just as difficult in Scottish.

I arched my eyebrows in true Lauren Bacall fashion. 'Not very tall, are you?' Damn, wait. That wasn't Lauren Bacall. Right film, wrong dame.

'I try tae be,' Stewart drawled, still very much Scottish. Somehow the dialogue worked better in his accent than mine. 'If they hang ye, I'll always remember ye.'

Ooh, *Maltese Falcon* now. I could *Maltese Falcon*. 'I haven't lived a good life. I've been bad, worse than you know.'

'Yer a bitter little lady.'

'It's a bitter little world.'

Okay, we needed to quit while I was ahead. Every other film noir quote I could think of was about kissing, cheating on your lover, or policemen. None of which seemed appropriate. Or safe. I held out the package. 'You'd better take this before someone shoots me for it.'

Stewart stood up, taking the brown paper parcel off me. 'I wouldnae worry too much about the dialogue. Sound quality's not gonnae be usable. Besides, I think Darrow has something else in mind for the audio track.'

'So why all the signs about not using fake American accents?'

'Fake American accents really, really annoy him. Did I see Jason Avery come in wi' ye?'

I nodded. 'We found him on our way into town—gunning his engine on the edge of a precipice. And get this ... he has a thing for the other Annabeth. Alice. French Vanilla. He knew all along that his Annabeth wasn't living in that house. And *Alice* is his alibi for Annabeth's murder.'

Stewart tilted his head. 'Xanthippe has been trying tae get residents of Flynn to tell her their side of the Annabeth French story for two days, and Tabitha Darling breezes in and get a random confession on the side of the road. How do ye do that?'

'People like to talk to me,' I said defensively. 'There's something about the hope of getting fed that brings out the spirit of confession.'

'Aye,' Stewart said, giving me an odd look. 'There's something, all right.'

Oh, awkward pause, just what we needed.

'Alice never mentioned Jason,' Stewart said finally.

'Nope.'

'So whatever reason she had fer telling us her story ... it wasnae getting him off the hook with the police.'

'No, it wasn't.' I was starting to have a funny feeling about Alice.

'Shouldae let Bishop arrest her after all,' he muttered.

I looked at him in surprise. Was he actually suggesting I had made the right call? 'Not that we had much choice in the matter. But she might have told us the truth if I hadn't dragged him into it.'

Stewart laughed. 'Ye admitting ye were wrong?'

'Not in this lifetime.'

We shared a look that said that neither of us was going to apologise, but we weren't cranky at each other any more.

I sighed, and moved to sit on the steps. Stewart sat beside me, the brown paper parcel between us. Like a little Great Wall of China tied up with string. 'I don't know what's wrong with me lately,' I confessed. 'I used to have a sense of adventure, but now—it feels like I'm playing everything safe.'

'Nae one could taste yer ice cream experiments and doubt ye have a sense of adventure,' Stewart assured me.

'Have I changed?' I blurted out. 'I mean—' How weird was it to talk about this with him? But he wasn't just the boy who kissed me an hour before Bishop finally figured out that he liked me back. He was my friend. Stewart and I had clicked the first time I saw him, and we'd never been short of things to talk about. He'd been gone for months, travelling around Tasmania as part of some stupid experiment to see if Sandstone City could branch out to cover the whole island (the correct answer to that was no, not if it meant being deprived of my Stewart).

Still, he was looking at me right now in a way that didn't make me feel stupid, and that was one hell of a good start. 'Changed how?' Stewart asked me.

'Xanthippe and Ceege think I've got boring since I started going out with Bishop,' I said, and yes, I was sulking. 'Well, they said conventional. And vanilla. But they meant boring.'

To his credit, Stewart thought about it seriously. 'I havenae seen as much of ye lately,' he said finally. 'And that's my fault, I know. But it seems like yer more cautious. Ye work harder and party less. Nae as likely tae drop everything for some frivolous reason … though yer here today, so…'

'The café is closed, I had literally nothing else to do, and Ceege guilted me into it,' I muttered.

'Heh. There ye are then. Also,' Stewart said pointedly. 'I couldnae help noticing yer more inclined to call the police when people on the wrong side of the law cross yer path.'

'Sense of civic responsibility,' I muttered, and felt embarrassed even saying the words aloud.

'Aye, right. My point is—I don't think this has anything tae do with yer boyfriend.'

He's not my boyfriend, I didn't say aloud.

'You don't?' I blinked at him. If he thought I had changed like the rest of them (and why would it be more alarming hearing it from Stewart than anyone else) then how could it be anything other than the huge big thing that had changed in my life, namely that I had a tall, dark, gorgeous drink of police officer I was sleeping with.

'Tabitha,' Stewart said patiently. 'Some pretty bad stuff happened earlier this year. Someone ye cared about turned out to be a murderer. Ye were stalked and abducted, and ye couldae died. It'd be odd if that didnae hae an effect on how ye see the world.'

Don't ask me why it was such a relief, but it was. Also how weird that I had known Zee since high school, and lived with Ceege for three years, but Stewart knew me better than either of them. 'So you do think I've got boring and conventional … but not because of my boyfriend.'

'In a nutshell.' He was teasing, though. 'Either that or yer finally becomin' a grown up, and what are the odds?'

'Pretty slim,' I grinned back, feeling ridiculously happy. A weight had been lifted from my shoulders. Post traumatic stress made so much more sense than 'your relationship makes you boring' syndrome. 'Stewart, can I ask you a really important question?'

'Why yes ye can, Tabitha.'

I poked the parcel. 'What's in this damn thing?'

'The Maltese Wombat.'

I stared at him. 'Tell me you're kidding.

'Wish I was.'

'Wish I hadn't asked.' Maybe all this was my fault. Darrow and I shared a love of old movies, but I'd never noticed that his interest in them was, um, a touch on the pathological side. 'You know,' I said, looking sideways at Stewart. 'You could have agreed with everyone that Bishop was a bad influence on me. Turning me vanilla. I'd have listened to you.'

He gave me a slow, incredulous look that made me blush to my toes for even thinking for a minute that something like that was a possibility. 'I'm not tha' fellow.'

'I know that,' I said quickly.

'Dae ye?' He shook his head, eyes on me. 'I've done this before, Tabitha. I fell for my best friend, and she fell for someone else, and I didnae—seduce her away from him, or make up stories tae make her like him less. I didnae make any grand gesture tae make her choose me. I let her go.'

I didn't know anything about Dinah Leiber apart from what Stewart had told me, but I kind of hated her for breaking his heart. He was a sweetie, and he was funny, and he was seriously cute despite (okay, maybe because of) dressing like a broke band groupie who couldn't afford new T-shirts. He was always up for an adventure.

I'd hardly known him any time at all, and he was one of my best friends.

How could she have chosen someone else over him? My stomach went kind of queasy at that point, though. Because she wasn't the only one.

'I like the suit,' I said helplessly. He looked horribly good in the 40s gear. I'd always been impressed by how well he rocked fancy dress when he had to.

'It's just a costume.' Stewart sounded annoyed with me again.

Impatient. I couldn't blame him, really. 'Dinnae look at me like ye ran over my puppy, Tabitha. I'm no' drinking cheap whiskey and dreaming what might hae been, because ye decided to give it a go with Bishop instead of me. Di was the most important person in my life from my eighth birthday onwards, and I got over her. Yer really no' that special.'

I laughed, because that was good. It was a good thing. I didn't want to make him miserable, he was my *Stewart*. I wanted him in one piece. 'So I'm going to go now, and we can work on pretending we didn't have this conversation.'

I got four steps down the alley before he caught my arm, pulling me around to face him. 'Tabitha, yer an Australian, do ye no' recognise bullshit when ye hear it?'

'Apparently not,' was all I got out before he kissed me, and oh bloody hell. It wasn't a friendly kiss. It wasn't light and teasing and not quite there, like the last time we did this. It definitely wasn't drunken and sleepy like the one before that.

It was clear cut, sober, and in blazing daylight. Stewart kissed me hard and searching, walking me backwards until I hit that brick wall, and he kept after me. I let him. I kissed him back. I opened his mouth with mine and dug my hands into his hair so hard that his ridiculous trilby fell off, and I gave him everything I had.

16

SANDSTONE CITY: So what kind of movie are you shooting here? Film noir covers a lot of ground. Are we talking a crime caper, tragedy, romance, spies, mobsters?

DARROW: All of the above. To be honest I won't know what kind of story it's going to be until I get into the editing suite, but based on some of the footage we've manage to get today, it's going to be a story of love and betrayal, with lots of red herrings and complicated plot twists.

SC: You don't think it's a bad idea, to be shooting a film without any idea what's going to happen in it?

DARROW: Completely bonkers, I know. That's the joy of it.

SC: Pippa Avery, local mayor's wife and freelance web designer, is here with me now. Pippa, tell me about the character you constructed for *Flynn By Night*.

PIPPA: Oh, her name is Tippi Godspeed, and she's a femme fatale—a bad girl, of course! I'm ridiculously well behaved in real life, so it's lovely to cut loose and pretend to be evil. I'm hiding the Maltese

Wombat from my husband, small town cop Charles Danger, and we just had a lovely scene where he flashed a light in my eyes and tried to get me to crack under the pressure.

SC: Charles Danger was played by your real life husband, local mayor Greg Avery. Do you think he found it difficult to get so hard with you in the scene you improvised?

PIPPA: Not at all, actually. (laughs) That's a little scary, isn't it? We were just so into it, it felt like being Bogart and Bacall. Though I always had more of a thing for Rita Hayworth, actually.

SC: Didn't we all...

Breathing was a problem, apparently. Eventually we had to breathe, and that meant we had to look each other in the eye. Bad form, Tabitha. Really bad form.

Handy guide to kissing someone other than the person you're regularly sleeping with: once you make eye contact, that's when the guilt sets in.

Tabitha Darling, this is why you can't have nice things.

I stared at him, letting my hands fall to my sides, feeling ridiculous. When in doubt, movie quotes, but the only one that swum up to the surface of my mind through all the *Stewart kissing, OMG, Stewart kissing!* was from *Murder My Sweet.* 'You shouldn't kiss a girl when you're wearing that gun,' I said quietly. 'Leaves a bruise.'

Stewart gave a wan sort of smile. 'I killed him fer money and fer a woman,' he said quietly. 'I didnae get the money. And I didnae get the woman.' He let go of me, which felt belated. 'Sorry.'

'Don't do that,' I blurted. 'Don't pretend it was only you.' It was an equal opportunity kiss if ever there was one.

The awkward silence stretched out before us. It practically walked off into the sunset and then returned, circling us like a vulture.

'Is it me,' I said finally, 'or is film noir really depressing?'

'Ha,' said Stewart, shoving his hands deep into his pockets. 'Take it up wi' the director.'

After the day of chaotic shooting (with cameras and fingers but so far no bananas) Darrow's cast and crew took over the weatherboard town hall for a wrap party.

I couldn't understand how one day of mad semi-filming a bunch of people improvising bad film noir vignettes could possibly produce a satisfactory result or anything resembling a coherent movie, but Darrow was happy enough.

Any party I don't have to cater is an awesome party (obviously the ones I cater are better, but a whole lot less relaxing for me personally). Darrow was doing his bit to bribe the town for their approval, and had bought out the contents of the local ice cream parlour, along with what looked like half the cellar of Avery Grove. A barbecue was set up outside with a couple of organic free-range goats turning on a rotisserie. The local berry and honey farms had been raided too.

There was dancing, and laughing, and drinking, and an altogether happy glowing kind of vibe. I dragged Darrow up to dance with me, and thank goodness he hadn't extended the historical theme to the music, because I never did learn to foxtrot.

He'd done it all with a community that was mourning the death of one of their own. Did that make him like one of those clowns that goes into hospitals to entertain the sick people?

'You did good,' I said, still a little bewildered by the whole thing. 'I'm still not sure what you did, or why, but … it was a fun adventure.'

'Adventures never need a reason why,' Darrow said firmly. 'They simply are.'

I needed more of that. Simply being. I used to be good at letting go and throwing myself into the universe, but lately—and Stewart was right, it was post-stalker, not post-Bishop—I'd been so damned careful about everything.

'I'm getting the hang of days off,' I told him proudly. I'd even texted Nin to ask her to wait for the building inspector in the morning—she was on the payroll anyway, and it only needed one of us. I'd stay the night in Xanthippe's room here and drive back tomorrow to take the afternoon shift.

'Good to know.' Darrow glanced at something behind me. 'Looks like the playing hard to get thing is working for you too. Someone's come looking.'

I turned my head and my stomach hit my vintage pumps like it was weighed down with the Maltese Wombat as I recognised the man in the doorway of the hall. Leo Bishop, with a warm and relaxed smile as he surveyed the room, looking for me. When had he got here?

'Shouldn't you be happier to see your sweetie?' Darrow said into my ear.

I didn't say 'he's not my...' because really if I couldn't cope with 'sweetie' I shouldn't be sleeping with anyone. Or kissing anyone, come to that. What I said instead was: 'Hide me.'

The thing about Darrow is, when the shit hits the fan you can rely on him to rescue you without question. He swung me around and through the crowd, one arm slung over my shoulder. 'Someday you can tell me the story.'

I nodded enthusiastically. 'Or not.' And I fled through the back door.

Away from Bishop. The man who shared my bed and gave me footrubs and had been incredibly, stupidly patient about the fact that I wasn't willing to play girlfriend. Or, more importantly, to actually be his girlfriend.

I wasn't used to sleeping with someone who was so genuinely stable and commitment-worthy. I was used to flings with men who talked a good game but got easily distracted, or cheated on me while their mothers taught me to cook, or decided they fancied other girls more. Or I found someone I liked better, before it all went too far.

Almost every relationship in my life had ended with the words 'no hard feelings'.

So basically my issue was, I had finally developed a better taste in men. #firstworldproblems eat your heart out.

I didn't know how to have the conversation where I told Bishop I was ready to move forward like a proper grown up, or the one where I told him it was time to call it quits. Maybe it would be better not to have any conversation with him ever again. Or maybe all this was in my head, and that one random kiss with Stewart had been a symptom of me freaking out about nothing.

If it was really so random, I shouldn't still be feeling it on my mouth.

It wasn't properly dark yet. The best thing about a Tasmanian summer is the long late days. That, and the ice cream. The town hall backed on to a green oval, and in the interest of getting as far from the wrap party as possible, I sashayed (you can't do an ordinary walk in shoes like this) across the grass.

Two lads looked up as I approached, and tried to conceal the fact that they were smoking something Unofficial. 'Nah, it's all right,' said Shay French, relaxing. 'Tabitha's cool.'

Ha, I was cool enough for teenagers to smoke weed in front of. Who said I was a grown up?

I sat down on the grass with them, and swallowed down any comments about how nice it was to see that the two of them were talking again, or at least hanging out in the same general vicinity. Because I was not a maiden aunt.

Jason held the joint out to me with a question in his eyes and I laughed. 'Thanks, but I don't think that will make my night any less confusing. I'll have some of what you're drinking, though.'

They had a bottle of Coke, a bottle of Bundaberg rum and a stack of plastic cups. It really was like reliving my youth.

Shay mixed me a drink and passed it over. I swallowed it down. Sweet. Sticky. Perfect.

'So what sordid tales of teenage iniquity have I interrupted?' I asked.

Both boys shrugged. Stunning conversationalists.

'You know that ice cream you made,' said Shay. 'Can you make ice cream out of, like, anything?'

'That's basically my mission in life,' I confessed, then took another mouthful of the sticky drink. 'I could make one of this. Well, not an ice cream. A sorbet, maybe. Or a granita.'

Shay was grinning, much closer to the cocky kid I remembered from our first meeting. 'What about beer?'

'I could do it,' I assured him. 'It would be revolting, though. I'd have to add sugar for the freezing to work right, and it's unlikely I'd end up with anything that actual beer drinkers would like. Or non beer drinkers, come to that. There have been some experiments with Guinness. I can see one of those micro-brew chocolate beers becoming something ice cream worthy.'

'You cook, right?' said Jason, inhaling deeply. 'Shay reckons you cook.'

'I've been known to scramble the odd egg. Also, I make the best minestrone soup known to man, woman or beast.'

'I thought about doing that,' Jason said thoughtfully. 'I like to cook. We have a restaurant at the vineyard. I'd have to go away to do an apprenticeship. Do it properly, get the piece of paper and all.'

Shay looked away, as if they'd had this conversation many times before.

'Your dad wouldn't let you go?' I asked. Couldn't be many nineteen-year-olds who actually wanted to step into the family business.

'Dad reckons if I leave town I'll just keep on going,' Jason shrugged. 'That's what happens around here. The kids leave.'

'I'm leaving,' Shay said abruptly. 'Soon as I save up enough. This place is dead.'

'It could be amazing if people stayed,' Jason argued. 'Put in the effort, build the community into the next generation.'

Shay rolled his eyes. 'No one wants to make the effort, mate. No one except your dad. The most exciting thing that happened around here in the last three months was when Burgers McCall figured out how to make caltraps with his dad's welding equipment and covered Main Street in them, ripping up half the town's tyres. You could Dark MoFo the crap out of this town, and there would still be no jobs on Monday.'

I opened my mouth to suggest that a film crew had taken over their main street today, and the recent murder also had to count as something out of the ordinary. Then I decided that was really, really tactless and shut my mouth again.

More people were wandering out from the party. Shay and Jason exchanged a look and quietly stubbed out the joint, tucking the remainder of it in to Shay's backpack.

'My lips are sealed,' I said firmly, refilling my cup. 'I almost never tell things to police officers. At least, I'm trying to give it up as a bad habit.'

'Taaaabitha,' came a cry from one of the meandering groups of party escapees. Xanthippe made a good attempt at crossing the oval in her high heels, then collapsed at the last minute and put her head in my lap. 'Are you hiding?'

'Yes,' I said truthfully.

'Good for you. Should be more of it.' She grinned up at me. 'We made a movie!'

'I'm very proud.'

'Also, your hair looks excellent.'

Oh, I was so behind on the recreational drinking. I made 'gimme' sign language to Jason, who filled up my cup again. 'I'm impressed that Darrow hasn't got himself run out of town yet. Surely his powers to irritate and offend can't have entirely abandoned him.'

'Are you kidding?' said Jason as he settled the bottle of Bundaberg back on the grass. 'Greg Avery said yes to letting the circus come to town, and no one says no if Greg Avery wants something. Greg Avery was pleased as punch to get the chance to whack on a fedora and pretend to be a mafia boss—it's like his wet dream.' There was something creepy and disturbing about the fact that he was saying the full 'Greg Avery' instead of, you know, 'Dad'.

'Ha,' said Shay, taking the bottle back. 'Mrs Avery is my wet dream.'

Jason leaned over and smacked him. 'No perving on the stepmother, you wanker.'

A few town girls in borrowed glam dresses and very non-period lipsticks walked past, keeping a distance between us. They glanced over at us a lot and whispered to themselves in between checking their glittery candy-coloured phones, and it was pretty certain that Jason was the centre of their attention.

He scowled and looked at his feet.

Shay glared after the girls. 'Snobs,' he muttered. 'A month ago they were climbing over themselves to make you notice them.'

'That was before I was a murderer, right?' Jason said flatly, no trace of humour.

Xanthippe raised her eyebrows at him and then at me. 'You know what I feel like, Tish? Walking. Let's walk.'

'You have to take your head out of my lap first,' I told her.

'That shows a lack of imagination,' she said, but rolled her weight off me. 'How about you fellas show us that lake of yours?'

I shot her a look because really, asking to see the place where their sister/girlfriend was found dead was beyond rude, even for Xanthippe.

The boys didn't seem to be bothered, though. 'It's not far,' said Shay.

'Awesome. Bring the bottles.' She took off ahead of us, walking unsteadily. And that was the point at which I realised she was faking it. Zee is not an unsteady drunk. The more she drinks, the stiller and calmer and more watchful she gets. It's eerie.

Okay, then. She wanted to see the scene of the crime. Avoiding the girl detective game hadn't been doing me any favours. I could play along. Or at the very least, keep an eye out for the boys who were in no way prepared to deal with the wiles of Ms Xanthippe Carides.

Plus it allowed me to avoid the adorable, delicious man in my life, and the conversation I had to have with him.

We weren't the only ones heading across the oval in the direction of the lake. A few straggler kids and film students meandered in that general direction, or were already making themselves comfortable on the grassy bank when we arrived.

'Popular hangout?' Xanthippe asked.

'Yeah,' said Shay. 'It's somewhere to go.'

'Hmm,' she said, still unconsciously swaying on her heels as her sharp and suspiciously incisive gaze swept the lake. 'Not for privacy, obviously.'

'Depends,' said Jason, looking around uncomfortably. I didn't blame him. The place had a sinister vibe to it now. 'It's a big lake.'

Xanthippe swung around, almost giving the game away as she looked at him with a firm, unblinking stare. 'So this isn't where...'

'No,' Jason said sharply. 'You have to walk about ten minutes that way, around the curve and beyond those gum trees. Can't miss the spot, there's a shitload of flowers and junk set up there. Cards. People pretending to care.' He dug his hands in the pockets of his jeans. 'Go see for yourself if you want to.'

'Okay then,' said Xanthippe, and swayed for effect.

'I'll show you,' said Shay, giving Jason a weird look. 'Don't want you to fall in or anything.' How sweet. He actually believed Xanthippe was off her face. Either he was being protective or he reckoned he could cop a feel, but either way he was in for a surprise.

Jason just shrugged, dropping down by the lake's edge and setting up the plastic cups again. It was probably my job to stick around here and make sure he didn't drown or give himself alcohol poisoning. I gave Xanthippe a finger wave and watched her totter deliberately away with Shay sticking close to her.

I accepted another eye-wateringly strong Bundy and Coke from Jason. 'So your dad liked the idea of Darrow's film?'

Jason shrugged, the cynicism apparently worn away. 'He likes anything that distracts from newspaper articles about me and Annabeth or our families. So yeah. Your bloke Darrow turned up a couple of days ago, and got Dad on side by talking up the positive press for Flynn. Worked like a charm.'

'Darrow is so not my bloke,' I said quickly.

Jason looked mildly interested. 'Which one's yours, then?'

'That is a complicated question.'

'You're talking to someone who had two girlfriends at the same time who were pretending to be each other,' said Jason with a welcome flash of humour.

'This is true,' I agreed. 'I can't beat you at complicated.' I wasn't sure I bought the idea of Darrow charming Daddy Avery and the town of Flynn into this chaotic madness. There had to be more to it than that. I mean, he's good, of course he's good. Darrow could talk a cup of coffee into believing it was dandelion and burdock. But conservative middle-aged businessmen are not his target audience, and they don't tend to fall for his charming wiles the way the rest of us do.

The gaggle of girls further down the shore of the lake were doing that giggly screechy thing that signals the beginnings of group hysteria. It made me feel old. They were looking over at us again, and at their phones, and it made me feel oddly protective of Jason. Poor kid. Last thing he needed was his misery showing up on Instagram.

I wriggled my toes inside my vintage pumps. It was one of those rare hot summer days in Tasmania where the heat still lingers into the evening. I wanted to dip my feet in the lake to cool off. I'd have to take the authentic 1940s style stockings off to do that, though, and Jason had probably been traumatised enough for one day without getting a flash of my garter belt. 'It's cool that your dad was willing to costume up with the group. My father would never have loosened up enough to do something like that.'

'Eh,' said Jason. 'I reckon Pippa pushed him into it. She's all about bringing Flynn kicking and screaming into the twenty-first century.' He laughed unexpectedly, eyeing my costume. 'Well. You know what I mean.'

I had seen Jason's stepmother in passing throughout the day, dressed up in black and white movie vamp style, her dark hair in starchy ringlets, and stocking lines pencilled up the backs of her bare legs. She couldn't be more than twenty-five, and seemed pretty tech savvy. She was the one who had been helping everyone upload their smartphone footage to Darrow's computer, and making sure they all used the right hashtags to document the day via Twitter. 'She's younger than your dad, yeah? How long have they been married?'

'Not even a year. He's scared she'll get bored of lamington drives and Friday Night bingo and run back to the big city. Between them they're all about the idea of turning Flynn into one of those shiny cappuccino tourist towns. Dad is obsessed with Cygnet and how wicked trendy they are now. Cygnet has like Bollywood festivals and major events every other weekend. Every time he drives through that town you can hear his teeth grind about how full the cafés are. The other day I actually heard him muttering 'ten art galleries, ten art galleries' under his breath.'

The girls peeled off their faux film noir outfits now, jumping and splashing their way through the water, laughing as if this was the funniest, most original thing they had ever done.

Hell, they were babies. It could be true.

Not just stockings now, dresses were coming off, and there was more splashing. Also some whirling. Surely this had to cheer Jason up? But no, he looked as grim as ever, and barely seemed to have noticed the semi-naked young ladies.

'I wish I knew where Alice was,' Jason said finally. 'Not just—you know, to help with my case. The alibi thing. But I miss talking to her. She hasn't been responding to my texts since the day she disappeared.'

It didn't seem to occur to him something bad might have happened to her. 'She left her phone at the house when she disappeared,' I said. That was a point. How had the police not seen evidence of Alice and Jason madly texting each other, if she had left her phone at the house on the day she left?

Maybe they did know the connection. Maybe I was reinventing the wheel, wasting my brain energy even thinking about this stuff. The police were on the case, probably five steps ahead of me and Xanthippe. Leave it to them. Have another drink.

'We might be able to find Alice,' I suggested, out of nowhere.

Jason gave me an odd look. 'You'd do that?'

'She's your alibi. Someone has to find her. I don't suppose your dad would help?'

'He might make a financial contribution,' said Jason. 'Pippa's good with computer stuff, she might be more use.'

'Also, we have Xanthippe on our side, with her wily wiles,' I told him. 'That's practically a team of crack troops, you know.'

'I thought you didn't want to get involved.'

'I tried not being involved. Someone blew up my kitchen, my friends all stopped speaking to me, and I ended up snogging someone who is not only not my boyfriend, but also not the person who is specifically not my boyfriend.' I took a deep swallow of Bundy and Coke. Gah, it tasted like sweet fermented tar. 'Not being involved is not working for me.'

The girls were screaming again, and it took me more than a few moments to realise that it wasn't the shrieky 'ooh aren't we daring, semi-skinny dipping on a hot evening with a boy in the vicinity' screams of earlier, but something entirely different.

Jason went after them first, splashing through the water to where two or three of them screamed and grabbed at each other, setting the others off, crying as much as laughing and screaming, and doing their best to get the hell out of the lake even if it meant climbing over each other to get there.

I stood on the sidelines, and it was only when Jason turned to me with a sick expression on his face that I realised what that bobbing shape in the water actually was.

There was another corpse floating in Lake Serenity.

17

BUTTERSCOTCH FOR SHAY

(COMFORT ICE CREAM FOR STRESSFUL SITUATIONS)

Custard:

6 egg yolks, beaten

1 cup cream

1 cup whole milk

1 cup thickened cream

2/3 cup sugar

1 tablespoon (REAL) vanilla extract

Sauce:

125g butter

1/2 cup brown sugar

2 tablespoons golden syrup

1/2 cup cream

CUSTARDY BIT:

You're going to need a double boiler for this. Trust me, no other way. Also you need a tin or pan of cold water standing by, big enough to rest the top part of the double boiler in it after the cooking part.

Pour the pouring cream and milk into the top part, and let the water underneath simmer slowly. While that is happening (don't let it go too long, you want it just hot), whisk the sugar into the egg yolks. Then take a good big spoonful (big cooking spoon not teeny eating spoon) of the hot cream and whisk it into the eggy mix. Seriously. Not scary. You can do this. Pour it all into the pan and stir constantly while it all cooks. You know it's done when you stick a spoon in and the custard coats it in a nice surface. Take the pan off heat and pop it straight in that pan of cold water. Remember it? Yep, that's the one.

Stir in the thickened cream and vanilla. You're done. Look at you, you just made custard from scratch! You ROCK.

Cover and chill in fridge for 2 to 3 hours, or until, you know. Cold.

SAUCY BIT:

Ever wondered what you put in butterscotch? Turns out it's lots and lots of butter. Combine the butter and sugar in a small pan and heat until butter has melted and sugar has dissolved. Bring to the boil, then reduce heat and add golden syrup and cream. Keep on low heat for 5-10 minutes or until sauce has thickened, then remove from heat and chill until lukewarm (not completely cold).

AND NOW IT GETS INTERESTING:

When the ice cream is part frozen but still soft, pour lukewarm *sauce over it, stirring with slow and meaningful strokes until it is swirly but not melted.*

Freeze. Eat. Yum. Feel better.

What can one say about a corpse? Especially one that has been submerged in water for … let's say more than a couple of days. It's not pretty.

Oh, and throwing up Bundy and Coke into a nearby bush was one nostalgic teen moment too many for me. I think I'll stick to champagne and margaritas in future.

The party was over. While the police dealt with the crime scene, those of us who had witnessed the uninvited guest's arrival all waited in the back room of the deserted town hall to be questioned.

Xanthippe and Shay were with us—they had returned a few minutes after the screaming started. The no-longer-giggling girls were keeping their distance, shooting odd looks at Jason. I texted Nin to let her know I would need her, Lara or Yui to hang around the closed café waiting for the building inspector tomorrow afternoon as well as morning. At this rate I would be sleeping until midday, if not later. I was so tired my stomach hurt.

I walked around the room once, because I couldn't sit still any longer.

One of the gang of girls tilted her head at me as I passed her, as if she knew me and meant to say something. I kept going. On my second lap of the hall, she looked at me again. I stopped.

'What?' All my usual warmth at getting information out of strangers had melted away, leaving me belligerent and edgy.

The girl nibbled her lip, and showed me her phone. 'I just wanted to—this is you, right? It's got more hits than any of the others. You're up to a thousand.'

It was a YouTube video, on pause, so all you could see was blurred brick and half an arm. But it was my arm. And oh fuck, it was the brick pattern from that alley, which had apparently seared itself on my memory.

'This is so completely what I don't need right now,' I said to no one in particular, and pressed play.

Filmed from above, I saw Stewart and me talk, flirt, quote movies at each other and then kiss each other up against a wall like our lives depended on it.

I didn't feel anything. That was probably the shock. I mean, the dead body shock, not the 'oh look there's you kissing the wrong boy on the internet' shock. I couldn't even feel embarrassed about it. Looked at from a purely artistic angle, it was a good piece of footage. I could see completely why it had attracted more hits than the other #flynnbynight vids, which were mostly people mucking around with fake gunfights and props.

'Thanks,' I said finally, handing her back the phone. 'I didn't know.'

I did, though, didn't I. Darrow even told me that they were filming from above. I hadn't looked. I'd just been swanning around with no thought of consequences, again.

For the first time, I felt completely calm about the fact that I hadn't let Bishop call me his girlfriend. It might save him some embarrassment when this particular bit of footage went around the station, as it inevitably would.

'Can I get a selfie with you?' asked the girl, waving her phone at me.

'Um, no, sorry.' The thought of it made me want to throw up. 'Any other day, sure.'

'No, right, I get it. Another time.'

'Sure.'

The awkwardness of the recently discovered dead body rose between us, bobbing. I turned around abruptly, and walked back to where Xanthippe was lying full length across a row of chairs. Jason and Shay sat near her, talking quietly together. She was close enough to hear them if they said anything incriminating, and feigning sleep to lull them into a false sense of security.

That's my girl.

We could hear talking outside, and then Darrow came marching in with Stewart and Ceege on one side, and Detective Sergeant Leo Bishop on the other.

All the men in my life. Oh, joy.

I stood awkwardly in the middle of the room for a moment, waiting for Bishop to check on Xanthippe first. He glanced over in her direction, obviously taking her fake sleep as genuine, and then headed right for me and gave me the world's biggest hug.

The first word that floated into my brain was *safe*. I don't know if that's a good thing or a bad thing.

'You all right?' he asked.

'Tired,' I said. True. That was a good start.

'So,' he said, letting me go. His business-like, police voice was back. 'You and Xanthippe on a double date with a pair of teenage boys?'

'Because that's a logical interpretation of events,' I said, rolling my eyes.

'I was looking for you earlier,' he said lightly. 'Came down to see how you were all getting along.'

'We were getting along fine until the surprising dead bloke turned up,' I said, more sharply than I meant to. Ceege, Stewart and Darrow were all keeping their distance, giving us space. 'Do you know who he was?'

'We have some ideas,' Bishop said. 'A name, anyway. Malcolm Drake, lives in New South Wales. He had his wallet still on him, driver's licence and everything. Whoever dumped his body wasn't too good with details. Still don't know why he's dead in a Tasmanian lake, but a name is a good start.'

'Annabeth had a rich older boyfriend,' I said quietly. 'He set her up at an acting school on the mainland this year, that's where she was when Alice was playing French Vanilla.'

'See,' Bishop said after a pause. 'I could ask how you know that, but I don't think I want to know.'

'People tell me things.' I wanted to curl up in bed and pull the covers over my head and not get up in a week.

'I remember.' Bishop pulled a notebook out, and scribbled a few things down. 'They want a Hobart liaison to work with the locals on this one, and it's probably going to be me. Any more evidence to add, that I can share with my colleagues?' He gave me a slightly more intense look. 'Any reason for me to declare conflict of interest and make sure I'm nowhere near this case?'

'Not that I can think of,' I said, honestly.

Bishop blew out a long breath. 'Whoever this bloke turns out to be, it looks like he's been underwater for a couple of weeks—can't know for sure, but that puts his death close to Annabeth's. His girlfriend and her other boyfriend dead at the same time ... it's not looking good for young Mr Avery.' He looked across the hall to Jason and Shay. They weren't talking any more, but looking at Bishop with matching expressions of worry. Plain clothes was one thing, but no one looked more like a police officer than he did.

'Don't you dare,' I said furiously.

Bishop was taken aback. 'Tabitha...'

'No, I mean it. Don't you even think about accusing that poor kid of anything else. He already has to deal with the whole town thinking he committed some kind of weird crime of passion. And now he's going to have her boyfriend's death pinned on him too? He really wasn't that into her.'

Bishop's facial expression was one I knew well—where the police officer took over from the human being. 'I have to do my job, Tabitha. You can't take it personally.'

'You can't, I can,' I muttered. 'The police ruined his life by accusing him the first time, and they couldn't make a case stick. No evidence.'

His face went all stormy. 'You know how this works, Tish.' Well, yeah. When your dad is a police superintendent, you understand the 'police work and integrity comes before every-thing, even friends and family' philosophy loud and clear. I know completely how this works. I always understand, and yet he always treats me like I'm this irrational child who doesn't get the more complex ethical issues of his job. But then the next thing out of his mouth was: 'Why are you trying to pick a fight with me?'

Oh, fuck. Was that was I was doing? Was I really such a terrible person that I would fight with him deliberately to distract him from the fact that a thousand people on the internet had watched me kissing Stewart today? 'Dead bodies bring out the worst in me,' I said quietly.

Bishop patted my arm. He didn't look stern any more, he looked kind and forgiving, which was completely and totally worse. 'I know. You should be able to go home soon.' And he left, crossing the hall toward Jason Avery.

I went to join my friends. Xanthippe was no longer pretending to be asleep. Ceege budged along the bench to make room for me to sit next to him. 'How you doing, Tabs?'

'Trying to set fire to Bishop with my mental powers,' I said. 'How am I doing?'

'His collar isn't even smoking.'

'Damn.'

I couldn't stop this. I couldn't make it unhappen. And I wanted to cry, because it felt more wrong than anything else that had happened lately.

Jason looked like he was about to bolt, staring at Bishop like he expected to be hit, or arrested, or both. Shay stood at his side, so defensive and scowly that I would put money on him assaulting a police officer before the night was over.

'He didn't do anything,' I said in a fierce whisper, and my friends all glanced at me, then back to Jason. Except Stewart, who didn't move. I looked closer and saw that, yes, he was discreetly filming Bishop and Jason with a very small video camera that would get him much better quality footage than all the smartphones people had been flinging around today.

The doors swung open and a self-important older man in a pristine 1940s style suit and hat strode in as if he owned this town. His pretty brunette wife, *femme-fataled* up from her cute vintage shoes to her heavily made up face, walked along beside him.

Stewart swung the camera in their direction, capturing their dramatic entrance.

'Detective, I trust you are not attempting to interview my son without his lawyer present?' boomed Greg Avery, Mayor and entrepreneur.

'We're taking witness statements right now, sir,' Bishop said mildly.

'Forgive me, but that's less than convincing,' Greg Avery replied, staring Bishop down. 'Jason will not be a scapegoat. No one in town even knows who this latest dead man is.'

'In which case, Jason has nothing to worry about,' said Bishop. 'Jason is of age, Mr Avery. We do not need your permission to interview him either here or at the nearest station.'

'Just get it over with,' Jason said abruptly, standing up like a string puppet, all jerky and sudden. 'Can't be worse than last time.'

'Jason, our lawyer,' Greg Avery reminded him. 'There is a procedure for these things, for your own protection.' He placed a hand on his son's arm. It looked more controlling than comforting.

Jason shook his father off. 'I don't care about that. I haven't done anything wrong.'

'Of course you haven't,' said Pippa Avery, stepping forward to hug Jason. He let her do that, though he stood awkwardly in the circle of her arms until she let go. 'Everything's going to be okay,' she promised him.

I was glad someone thought so.

✱

I crashed that night in the tidy twin bedroom over the Scallop that Xanthippe had booked for the night, and woke up with a crunching, thudding, deeply painful reminder of why drinking like you're seventeen is not a good look on someone who is officially past her mid-twenties.

I buried my head under the pillow and moaned until a persistent beeping sound alerted me to the fact that Bishop was awake, bright eyed and bushy tailed, and wanted to have breakfast with me.

What my body wanted me to do was climb back under the covers and sleep the day away until my skin felt like it was the right way around, but I knew a flag of relationship truce when I saw one.

My only consolation was that Bishop almost certainly didn't know what YouTube was. The man barely thinks he needs email on his phone. He couldn't know yet.

But it was only a matter of time. Damn the information age.

Half an hour later, I sat in a candy yellow booth in the Flynn ice cream parlour, nursing an atrocious cup of coffee while Bishop attacked a high stack of pancakes with apple slices and bacon.

'We're inside now, you can take the Audrey Hepburn sunglasses off,' he suggested.

'Have you seen the decor in this place? Believe me, it's best I keep them on.' That, and it hid from him how bad I look with a hangover. I was wearing a borrowed T-shirt from Xanthippe, and the underskirt of my 1940s dress from yesterday. I was too wiped to care whether it looked like I was wearing underwear in a public place or not.

'Okay then,' Bishop said. 'How are you feeling this morning?'

The giant sunglasses and greenish hue to my skin didn't tip him off? 'Marginally worse than last night. I'm surprised you're so perky—how do you manage to put in a full night's policing and still get a good night's sleep?'

'Hard drugs,' he said with a straight face.

'As long as someone enjoyed themselves last night.'

'Not my idea of fun, interviewing a bunch of teenagers about their possible role in a murder,' he said, more sharp than he usually was with me.

Well, that wasn't true. But since regular sex entered the equation, he has done his best not to lose his temper with me the way he used to on a regular basis. I'm not sure if this is a positive sign for our relationship. I knew where I was when we were shouting. Plus it was kind of hot. This restrained control thing was ... uncomfortable.

'Sorry,' I said in a low voice. 'I was—not particularly nice to you yesterday.'

'You were having a rough night,' he replied.

'Just a bit.' I took a deep breath. Keeping secrets was not one of my specialties. Time to blurt the truth and find out for certain how much damage I had done with that badly-timed snog I had shared with Stewart yesterday. 'So I have something to tell you.'

My phone beeped with a message.

'You check that,' said Bishop, getting to his feet, eyes on me. 'I'll get more coffees—if you think this is going to be a long conversation?'

'Long enough for coffee,' I said. It wasn't so much the part where I had to confess I'd been smooching someone else. It was the horrible but inevitable relationship conversation that almost certainly had to follow. Unless he walked away once we got past the first bit.

Bishop went in search of coffee, and I called up my message. It was from Shay French. I'd put my number in his phone back during the Great Butterscotch Bonding Moment, in case he needed to get in touch again.

The message was simple: Jase has done a runner. I stared at it for some time.

'I have to go,' I told Bishop, not even waiting for him to return from the counter. 'I'm sorry. It's an—emergency.'

'Darrow's having a fashion crisis?' he said, more resigned than surprised.

'Xanthippe *is* a fashion crisis. I have to go talk to her right now.' That part wasn't a lie. If I was going to get Jason out of this unholy mess he had brought upon himself, I was going to need her. And every other dodgy resource at my disposal.

Bishop couldn't know.

Stupid, stupid kid. I still didn't believe that Jason was guilty. Well, obviously this was a sign of guilt, it was a bloody big billboard advert saying 'arrest me, I'm guilty as hell' but it never occurred to me that he actually was.

Apparently I was still capable of belief in people. That was good, right? It meant I hadn't changed as much as people kept saying I had. The horrible experience I'd had earlier in the year hadn't completely broken me—or if it had, I was mending at a reasonable speed.

'We can meet up tonight?' Bishop suggested. 'I'll be around Flynn most of the day. We could grab an early dinner before you head home—or catch up back in Hobart, if you prefer.'

'Tonight,' I agreed and kissed him fast before the guilt set in.

Never mind the YouTube thing. I was now keeping a secret from him that he would find completely unforgivable. The worst part was, it almost felt like a relief. When he found out I had covered for Jason, he would probably dump me. And that meant I didn't have to make any decisions at all.

I ran for it.

18

From: Darlingtabitha

There is nothing that can't be fixed with ice cream.

From: Nincakes

That is an opinion. That you have. I could provide a list to the contrary, but I know it's not worth arguing with you on these points.

From: Darlingtabitha

Liquorice ice cream, for instance. If they'd had that at the early twentieth century, there would have been way fewer wars.

From: Nincakes

I'm pretty sure they had both ice cream and liquorice, so chances are…

From: Darlingtabitha

NO WARS. I wish liquorice ice cream was as black as real liquorice.

LIVIA DAY

From: Nincakes

I really hope this isn't a natural extension to your war theme. Just say no to replacing the world's weaponry with candy substitutes, Tabitha.

From: Darlingtabitha

If you could get liquorice ice cream to actually look like liquorice then you could create the world's biggest and most spectacular liquorice allsort, formed entirely from ice cream.

From: Nincakes

well OBVIOUSLY what you need is giant squares of actual liquorice, which you can use as wafers to spread thick slabs of orange, pink and green ice cream on, and then you have your giant ice cream liquorice allsort.

From: Darlingtabitha

have I ever told you how much I love you?

From: Nincakes

Which you could send back in time to all world leaders, distracting them at various moments of crucial decision…

From: Darlingtabitha

Peace in our time.

✸

Shay was waiting for me back at the pub, lingering near Jase's Holden, which was still where Ceege had parked it. 'So,' I said in a crisp voice. 'As the kids say, WTF?' Also OMFG, but we'd work up to that.

'I didn't know he was going to bolt,' Shay said, looking almost as pissed off as I was. 'He texted me just now that he was on his way and could I try to stop people figuring out he'd left town.'

'Don't you dare,' I said quickly. 'That's what we call accessory after the fact. Bad enough that you know about this, but if you do anything to actively help his escape, you're screwed.' I had already deleted the message off my phone. 'First things first. He didn't take his car, so he would have needed a vehicle. Something people wouldn't associate with him.'

I stared for a minute at the blank space beside the Holden. And then its significance hit me between the eyes. 'That little rat. He took my ute!' Well, Ceege's mate's dad's ute. But still.

I glared at the Holden, and kicked one of the tyres. 'Now I'm an accessory too. Fucking brilliant. Cheers, Jason, way to make me that *little* bit more invested in your problems.'

Well, let's face it. I was always invested.

I flipped out my phone and called Xanthippe. 'I need you. And your Spider. And a cricket bat.' I was mostly kidding about the cricket bat.

She was fast, I'll give her that. It was four minutes between hanging up, and Xanthippe loping out of the pub with her car keys, hair still wet from the shower. She also brought Stewart with her, his camera case slung over one arm. Had I mentioned that other people were invited? I don't think so.

'Couldn't find a cricket bat, so I brought Stewart,' Xanthippe said cheerfully. 'He's bendy in the middle, but otherwise sturdy enough to be used as a blunt instrument.'

I folded my arms. 'I'm not sure if you want to get involved in this, Stewart.' I tried to use my eyebrows to make expressive 'go away' signals, but I think I just ended up looking like I had indigestion.

Stewart just raised his eyebrows at me. 'Is that yer way of saying 'blog about this and I kill ye'?'

'Basically.'

'I can live wi' that.' We locked eyes. He's so much harder to fight with than Bishop, because nothing ever seems to get to him.

'If you two are finished flirting?' said Xanthippe. 'I got the impression this was an urgent situation.'

Shay was starting to panic. 'How do I know you lot won't just run off and tell stuff to the police?'

Xanthippe rolled her eyes, and hopped into the front seat of the Spider. 'Explain to the little boy how this works.'

'She lives on the edge, and she laughs in the face of authority figures,' I told Shay. 'If anyone's going to call the police on Jason, it would be me. Only I won't, because there's a very particular police officer that I really don't want to know about all this. You can trust us to help track Jason down, and kick his butt all the way back to Flynn, hopefully before the police figure out that he tried to skip town. That's the plan.'

Shay considered this. 'Can I call shotgun?'

'No,' Xanthippe and I said in unison.

Crammed into the tiny backseat of the Spider with the teenager, Stewart took on the responsibility of interrogating him. 'So can ye think of anywhere Jason might go? Anyone he might ask fer help?'

Shay looked completely lost. 'Me,' he said flatly. 'He should have asked me. Dunno why he didn't.' He kicked the back of the seat. 'What's the point of telling me after he's gone? I could help. I can do more than cover his arse.'

'Apart from ye. Who else might he contact?'

'Alice,' I said from the front seat. 'They had a thing. But she hadn't been in touch lately.'

Stewart laughed. 'Yer kidding me. Jason was cheating on Annabeth wi' the girl pretending tae be her? Tha's impressive.'

'It's fucken stupid is what it is,' said Shay. 'No way. I don't believe it.'

'I'm pretty sure they're just friends,' said Xanthippe, tapping her fingers on the steering wheel. We still had yet to go anywhere. 'He trusts her, though. If he has any way of contacting her, I'm sure he'd go to her. Trouble is, we don't know where she is either. It's not entirely helpful.'

Okay, I was feeling ganged up on. This was the one vital clue I had gleaned in recent days, and none of them believed me. 'I got my info from Jason directly. He and Alice were on together. What's *your* source?'

'I can't tell you that,' said Xanthippe.

'Oh, I really think you can.'

Xanthippe eyed the boys in the back. 'Maybe later.' Hmm, was this a genuine promise to tell me later or just putting me off? I might have to pull out all the stops to drag it out of her. 'Where are we heading first?'

Oh, this conversation was so not over. 'Shay, do you have his number? We could try to get him to meet us somewhere close, before he gets too far away.'

'Reckon he's going to trust you?' Shay said, not sounding convinced.

'No, but he'll trust you,' I decided. 'In the meantime, let's go visit his dad and stepmum. They're bound to notice Jason is gone, and we don't want them to freak out.'

'You're going to tell his parents?' Shay said in horror. 'What the hell kind of help is that?'

It's so annoying being the only responsible adult in a car of four. 'If they call the police to find out where their son is, it's all going to kick off. But if we can talk Jason into coming back himself before the police realise he skipped town, he might not get into so much trouble. Not having his parents raise the alarm has to be a priority until we find him. We can make them understand that—and they can help us buy time to bring him back.'

'Unless, ye know,' Stewart said in a low voice.

'Shut up,' I flung back at him.

'Just sayin'.'

'Well, don't.'

What if Jason was running because he was guilty? The longer we went without saying that sort of thing aloud, the better we would be.

Avery Grove was deserted as we approached, the Spider's tyres crunching over designer gravel. The renovations on the restaurant at the front of the house had been left unfinished, which was hardly surprising considering half the town were busy shooting a film noir epic on the streets of Flynn, not to mention the second dead body in a week.

A door slammed, and a tall woman with short red hair strode out of the house and got into her car, driving past us quickly in a slew of gravel.

'Hey!' Xanthippe yelled, thinking of her paintwork.

'That was Ginger,' I said in surprise. 'Wasn't it? Libby, I mean.' From The Gingerbread House.

Xanthippe parked the Spider smoothly. 'Oh yes it was.'

'How does she know the Averys?'

'I don't know.'

When we rang the bell, Jason's stepmother Pippa answered the door too quickly, wearing a Greenpeace T-shirt and jeans, with giant daisies in her hair. She looked flustered, which I assumed was for some reason other than 'OMG I have daisies in my hair, what was I thinking?' though you never can tell. Pippa passed her eye over all of us and landed on Shay. 'Seamus? What's going on?'

'We need to see Jase,' he said, hands in pockets. Everything normal here, yeah.

'He can't see anyone today,' she said, and you could tell there was lying going on behind the bright blue eyes, because her whole face shifted as she tried to look normal.

'We know he shot through,' said Xanthippe, in one of her more brusque voices.

Pippa tensed. 'What do you want from me?' she asked, looking from one to the other of us. Her tone wasn't angry so much as ... resigned.

Interesting. She was expecting blackmailers.

'We want to make sure he doesn't do anything stupid,' I said in a firm voice. 'Also, we wouldn't say no to a cup of tea.'

'My husband isn't home.'

'That's a shame. He'll miss out on the tea.'

Pippa paused for a minute or two as if about to slam the door in our faces. Then she turned and went inside, leaving us to follow her. We traipsed through a high, wide corridor lined with the kind of scenic art photography that costs more than paintings. All of the pictures depicted the Huon area in general, and Flynn in particular.

She led us to a bright, homey kitchen at the back of the house, and put the industrial chrome computerised kettle on as if she had a grudge against it, all thumps and rattles.

'I'm Tabitha, by the way,' I said brightly. 'I don't think we met properly yesterday. The stern lady in black is Xanthippe, and the laidback Scotsman is Stewart.'

Pippa barely reacted. 'Greg is out looking for Jason. He will bring him home and it will all be fine. He won't have gone far, he's not that stupid.'

'He texted me,' Shay said in a low voice. 'Sounds like he's serious about getting out of here.'

'But he can't,' Pippa said, banging the mugs against the shiny basalt counter and pulling out a range of organic herbal tea bags that smelled like Xanthippe's ridiculous taste in perfume. 'They'll think he's guilty. They'll catch him and…'

'Nineteen-year-olds,' I said with a sympathetic smile. 'Not big on the sensible decision making. Apparently the brain doesn't properly develop until the mid-twenties.' So what was my excuse for anything?

'I'm going to kill him when I find him,' Pippa muttered.

'We'll help,' Xanthippe volunteered. 'Well, with the finding. Not the killing. Best to keep that in the family.'

'Good to know,' Pippa said dryly. She started to make the tea, less aggressively than before. 'How do you think you can help Jase?'

Shay's phone beeped at him, and he read the message with all of our eyes on him. 'He won't meet me,' he said finally. 'Says it's better I don't get involved.'

'Oh, but asking you to deliberately hide his disappearance from the police, that's okay?' I held out my phone. 'Give.'

Shay recovered a bit more of the confidence I'd seen in him before his sister died. 'No,' he said, holding the phone away from me.

'How can me talking to him make this situation worse?' I demanded.

'Ye'll find a way,' said Stewart in an undertone.

'Have faith,' I ground between my teeth, but I was looking at Shay and not Stewart.

Shay put the phone in my hand. I tapped the number, and waited for Jason to pick up.

'Shay,' Jason said after three rings. 'Look mate, I can't—'

'It's Tabitha.'

Silence, in which I used all my mental powers to beg him not to hang up.

'I don't want to talk to you,' he said finally.

'Don't you think it's time you talked to someone?'

I heard him snort faintly over the phone. 'You're such a girl.'

'You know that's not an insult, right?' I paused. 'Are you with Alice?'

'No way.' That sounded honest, at least.

'Just because she's managed to stay off the radar for a few

weeks—it doesn't mean anyone can do it. Or that she'll be able to keep it up forever. Sooner or later, the police will get hold of her. You too. Do you have any idea how difficult it's going to be, trying to keep out of sight? And how badly the police will take it when they find out?'

'I don't have any better options,' he muttered.

'Of course you do. You can come home and ride this out. If there isn't any evidence, they will *not* arrest you. They can't. I know the people running this investigation, and they are good blokes. They want the real killer, and as soon as they realise it isn't you, everything will be fine.'

'What kind of evidence would they need?' he said hollowly. 'To be sure I'm the real killer?'

I think my feet went cold at that point. 'Jason...'

'Tabitha, thanks and everything, but believe me when I say I can't come back.' And this time he did hang up.

19

From: Darlingtabitha

I'm thinking of inventing some kind of calming draught sorbet for times of high stress in the middle of summer. Maybe a chamomile tea granita?

From: Nincakes

I suppose it's possible. Green tea ice cream is pretty good.

From: Darlingtabitha

How about a delicious cocktail of green, chamomile, peppermint and liquorice tea, for the ultimate relaxing experience in your mouth.

From: Nincakes

T, that sounds gross. With our customers, you'd have way more luck with a quadruple shot espresso sorbet.

From: Darlingtabitha

have you been talking to Stewart? *is suspicious.*

✴

Shay glared at me as the call ended and I handed back his phone. 'What did he say?'

'He's scared,' I said. 'It's okay. We'll find him. We'll have a cuppa first and we'll come up with a plan, and we'll find him by lunchtime. No worries.'

Pippa offered me a choice of hot water that smelled like lemons and hot water that smelled like vanilla and cinnamon. I went for the lemon. Vanilla gave me a headache these days. 'Why am I not convinced?' she said.

'It will all be fine,' I said, meaning it as much as I could.

Stewart took the vanilla tea, and Xanthippe chose a virulent pink one that smelled of mangoes and coconut.

Mmm, mangoes and coconut would make a great gelato ... no, bad Tabitha. Focus!

'How exactly is the tea going to make things better?' Xanthippe asked.

'Tea makes us calm,' said Pippa, swallowing down the contents of her own near-scalding cup. Mint, I thought. 'So how are we going to find Jason?'

We all looked at Shay.

Shay was still glaring at me. 'You were supposed to help. You're supposed to be cool. This is all—tea and parents? What the hell?'

'I'm not a miracle worker,' I snapped back. 'I make good ice cream and people confess their intimate secrets to me over coffee and cake. What exactly made you think that I was qualified for superhero duty?'

'I don't know where he is,' Shay said grouchily. 'And I wouldn't tell you if I did.' He stood up and stomped out of the kitchen.

I looked at Stewart, meaningfully. Stewart looked alarmed. 'Wha-at?' he asked warily.

'You're a bloke.'

'Aye, I'd heard a rumour to that effect. What d'ye want me tae do, chase the kid out there and grunt at him in a manly fashion until he spills his secrets?'

I nodded earnestly. 'Our only other option is Xanthippe taking her clothes off in front of him, and frankly that seems inappropriate.'

'Fair call,' Xanthippe agreed, and we clanked teacups together.

Stewart left the room, muttering something about the unrealistic expectations of women.

Xanthippe turned to Pippa. 'Give us fifteen minutes to look through Jason's room. We might spot something you missed, something to tell us where he is.'

'Speed is of the essence,' I agreed solemnly. 'The bad news is that Bishop's on the case now, and he's kind of good at his job. It sucks, I know.'

✹

Jason's room held few surprises considering we knew going in that he was a nineteen-year-old male. There was a distinct odour of boy, lingering mustily in the air. The room was a mess, with used clothes and crockery packing just about every surface.

'This should be a drinking game,' I observed. 'One shot for every car or sports magazine, two for every depiction of a naked woman…'

Xanthippe was already booting up his computer. 'Or we could search the place for more useful data.'

'Well, if you're going to be pragmatic…'

I rifled through Jason's drawers, looking for a mysterious scrap of paper with a diagram of his planned place of hiding. Preferably with an address and some nice handy arrows.

There were no mysterious notes.

'Ha,' Xanthippe said with more than a trace of smug in her voice. 'Does the phrase "browser history" mean anything to you?'

'I thought you weren't interested in porn.'

'The boy is far too vanilla for that, apparently,' said Xanthippe, scanning his history.

'No teenage boy is too vanilla to look for internet porn.'

'Heh, well I'm just looking at the last forty-eight hours.' Xanthippe pressed her lips together, tapping her foot thoughtfully. 'No Google Maps. Not the White Pages, either. That could mean that he knew exactly where he was going.'

'Or he was so panicked he just drove without thinking or

planning,' I pointed out. 'Or he used his phone to look stuff up on, like a real teenager.'

'Yeah, yeah, poor chicken. You're too nice for your own good, Tish. Has it occurred to you that Jason Avery is acting guilty as hell?'

'Wash your mouth out.' But yes, I had that prickly uncomfortable feeling again. Once someone you have fed and smiled at and given romantic advice to turns out to be a killer, it's kind of hard to think of people being universally good and innocent and honest.

Of course we were snooping around a teenage boy's bedroom without his permission so moral high ground was somewhere in the far distance.

'He's been peering into The Gingerbread House recently,' said Xanthippe.

'Tell me he hasn't bookmarked the night when you took your top off. Apparently it's a popular one.'

'They put it up as an archive highlight,' Xanthippe said proudly. She tapped a bit and looked thoughtful. 'Interesting. Jason's been trying to access the archives from before French Vanilla joined the merry band. But they're locked. I guess when Pepperminty left, she really left. Ginger said they had to take all the material with her offline.'

'Why would Jason care who was there before Annabeth?' I asked. 'I mean, Alice.' Hmm. 'You know, Stewart has Alice's email address. Maybe we could ask if she knows where Jason is. It couldn't hurt.'

'I'm not convinced she has Jason's best interests at heart,' said Xanthippe.

I could go along with that. 'Me neither.'

A sound of car on gravel sent me to the window. 'Oh, holy crap,' I said looking out the window.

'Who is it, Daddy Warbucks?' said Xanthippe.

'Um, no,' I said. 'No one arriving. Someone leaving. Two someones.' I winced as I turned to break the news to her. 'Stewart and Shay just stole your Spider.'

I don't think I've ever seen Xanthippe go quite that colour. She's always cool and collected: gorgeous hair, immaculate clothes. She wears black every single day, and fluff never clings to her. Her boots are eternally shiny, and her nail polish never chips.

Seriously. I thought she was about to stop breathing she was so angry. Her skin went all splotchy. 'They stole my *car*?' She pulled out her phone.

I took it off her, for safety's sake. 'Are you calling the police or an assassin?'

'My brother,' she hissed. Oh boy. If Xanthippe was actually turning to a) the police and b) Leo Bishop in her hour of need, then things were dire.

'He can't know what we're doing, and he really can't know Jason has shot through yet,' I said desperately. 'He will be mad at me and Jason will get *arrested*.'

Xanthippe just stared at me with cold, reptilian eyes. 'Your

Scotsman took my *car*, Tish. Do you know how many hours I put into the Spider?'

Why yes I did. I also knew she was still mourning the Lotus that had met an unfortunate end at the hands of Darrow and the Richmond Bridge. This was her rebound car. She had spent many hours a week on its restoration over the last several months, and she loved it with a passion greater even than my attachment to the Collette Dinnigan handbag that I found for five dollars in the local Salvos.

'Even so,' I said weakly. '*Our* Scotsman has to have had a reason.'

'Besides,' Xanthippe said, tilting her head at me. 'If we're talking about things you've done lately that will make my brother mad at you, I don't think protecting Jason Avery will be top of the list. Will it?'

Oh, double crap on a stick. She knew about the kiss. How did she know about the kiss?

She read the question in my eyes. 'There's a hashtag, Tish. Every piece of footage that has already gone up on YouTube gets announced all over the place, and everyone involved in the film has been following it. Your little performance piece was retweeted many, many times.'

Now it was me who was having trouble breathing. 'I'll get the car back for you,' I promised. 'And—I'll tell Bishop about the other thing. After all this has calmed down.'

Xanthippe put her phone in her jeans, still scowling at me. 'You'd better.'

✹

Ten minutes later, Ceege pulled up in front of the Avery house, in Jason's Holden. Luckily he still had the keys. 'What's the emergency? I'm supposed to be taking down the sets to stop Flynn looking like 1940s San Francisco.'

'Hate to break it to you,' I said, sliding into the backseat. 'Flynn never looked like 1940s San Francisco.'

'You wound me, babes. Where are we going?'

'To kill Stewart,' said Xanthippe, taking the front passenger seat. We were slow enough off the mark that Pippa Avery made it to the car too, strapping herself into the back beside me and silently daring us to challenge her presence.

'Excellent,' said Ceege. 'More the merrier. Where to, dollfaces?'

That was the million dollar question, now wasn't it? I tried texting Stewart again. WHERE ARE U????

Of course, since he was the one at the wheel of the Spider, I had to hope that he wasn't going to text back anytime soon. Damn him for being a responsible driver.

'Head into Flynn,' I ordered Ceege. 'We'll figure out something from there.'

When all else fails, call Darrow.

'Darling,' he said into the phone, sounding as luscious as ever. Did everyone feel the need for a cold shower after a conversation with that voice of his, or was it just me?

'Turn right!' Xanthippe snapped as the Holden reached the foot of the hill.

'You said back to town,' Ceege complained. 'Make up your mind, sweetcheeks.'

'Logic says back to town, but those tyre marks say the other way,' she said. 'They also justify why we never ever let Stewart do the driving. That fucking Scotsman is going to total my precious, precious Spider. Do they even drive on the left side of the road in his country? Does he have a licence?'

'He will be careful,' I assured her. 'He knows it's more than his life is worth and he is very, very afraid of you. It's all good.'

Darrow coughed, still waiting on the line. 'Fascinating though this is, it's not about me. Did you want me for something, Darling?'

'I was going to ask you if Xanthippe's runaway Spider had buzzed through Flynn, but we're heading the other way now,' I told Darrow. 'Um, if Bishop asks where we all are, can you pretend we're doing another scene for you?'

'Easily done,' said Darrow. 'Who's we?'

'Me, Zee, Stewart, Jason and Pippa Avery and Shay French.'

'Darling,' he said in a pained voice. 'You're doing something stupid, yeah?'

'Even by your standards,' I agreed, and flipped the phone shut. 'So what's along this way? Where could they be going?'

We were heading into greenery and wilderness from what I could make out—deep mountainous bush with no noticeable destination. There were a few other towns further south of us, but nothing that leaped out at me as an obvious destination. Surely fugitives from justice should be heading towards Hobart, where there was an airport and highways with occasional straight bits that might be suitable for proper car chases.

'I think I know where to try,' said Pippa quietly. 'You—you're really not going to call the police about Jason?'

I rolled my eyes. 'Believe me, we'd have done it long before now. And Xanthippe doesn't want anyone finding out about her imminent murder of Stewart, so we're good.'

'My husband owns a property about forty kilometres south,' Pippa said. 'There isn't much on it—an old house, barely habitable. He's planning to build a holiday resort.'

'Does Shay know about the place?' I asked.

She nodded. 'He and Jason helped to survey the property when Greg bought it.'

Worth a try.

'Can I put on the radio?' Ceege asked, some time later. 'Or do you want to chime in with a hundred green bottles hanging on the wall? Much though I love how you're all working this awkward silence well beyond its use by date.'

'I'd rather we used the time constructively,' I said. 'Zee, what did you mean when you said you didn't think Jason and Alice were an item?'

'Jason and Alice?' said Pippa, folding her arms. 'Who is Alice?'

Xanthippe smirked, meeting Pippa's eyes in the mirror. 'Oh, you know exactly who Alice is. Don't think I haven't figured out who you are.'

'I'm Mrs Greg Avery,' said Pippa in an extreme 'don't mess with me' ice queen voice.

'The digital world is a wonderful place,' Xanthippe replied. 'Once you're on there, it's very hard to erase yourself completely. You've done well—I mean, you deleted the archives, and it was all under pseudonyms. You even dyed your hair to conceal the resemblance. But if you think a dedicated person can't find archival Gingerbread House footage of Pepperminty on Youtube, you have a very strange idea of how the internet works.'

I stared at Xanthippe, and then at Pippa Avery, whose hair had always been that bit too dark and glossy to be natural, especially for someone who dressed like such a hippie. 'Oh, you are freaking kidding me.'

Pepperminty. Who was good with computers, and set up The Gingerbread House website, and whose overprotective bloke didn't like the idea of her staying in the webcam house...

'You're from The Gingerbread House,' I said softly. 'That can't be a coincidence. I mean, I know this is Hobart, but still...'

'Believe me, I didn't want him to get mixed up with all that,' Pippa said angrily. 'Jason's dad was furious when Annabeth's death connected our family to The Gingerbread House after I have worked so hard to keep my past hidden.'

'Why was Ginger at the house today?' I asked.

'Another one who can't leave the past behind,' Pippa said bitterly. 'She kept prodding me about Alice—like I was supposed to know where she was. I never even met the bloody woman. She replaced me as the token blonde in the house, and that's the only connection between us.'

'That and she was hooking up with your stepson on a regular basis,' I said. The look of horror that crossed Pippa's face was actually kind of funny. I'm a bad person. 'You didn't know?'

'No,' Pippa said, sounding stunned. 'That can't be right. Are you sure?'

'No, actually,' said Xanthippe. 'Seriously, Tish. People may tell you all their secrets, but I make the better private detective.'

'Oh really?' I shot back. 'Jason told me himself that they had a thing together.'

'Yeah, but he was lying,' said Ceege, piping up from behind the wheel.

'What? No he wasn't. He has a very honest face.'

'I was there too, babe. He said he was texting the Alice chick all the time, and sending those postcards. You assumed they were all smoochy for each other,' said Ceege. 'He leaped on that idea of *yours* like a surfer on a six-pack. Doesn't mean it was true. All he actually said was that she was easy to talk to, and he was into someone other than Annabeth.'

Did this mean everyone in the car had greater romantic insight than me? Including *Ceege*? The world was topsy turvy. In my defence, I had been distracted lately. Just a bit.

20

BITTER LEMON GELATO

Ingredients:

1 cup of water

2/3 cup caster sugar (no, not nearly enough, that's kind of the point)

1 cup freshly squeezed lemon juice (use squishy ones—barely ripe new lemons will break your heart, they take so much squeezing for such little result—you'll probably need somewhere between 4-8 lemons depending on squishiness)

2/3 cup thickened cream (or for low fat option, 125g cream cheese, but why even do that to yourself?)

Instructions:

Place water, sugar and juice in small saucepan. Stir over low heat until sugar dissolves. Chill in fridge—the colder the better.

Whisk/blend cream and lemon mixture (if cream cheese you will so need to use machinery of some kind).

Freeze-stir-freeze method, or throw in your handy ice cream maker.

Like revenge, best served cold.

I could see why Greg Avery had this property earmarked for holiday cottages or whatever. It was deep in a valley so green that it hurt the eyes, with a view overlooking two small lakes.

'Am I the only one who finds lakes ominous now?' I said aloud.

'Nope,' said Xanthippe as we drove up the dirt road to the falling-down shack. Three cars were parked haphazardly outside it—a shiny Mazda, the borrowed (and stolen) ute, and Xanthippe's Spider. 'It's ominous for McTavish. He may not be leaving here alive.'

There was a crunch under the vehicle, and we bumped the last few metres to stop near the other parked cars. 'What the hell was that?'

'Wow,' said Ceege, opening the door to lean out. 'Bloody hell. Medieval warfare!'

I got out gingerly, and only just avoided having my sandals pierced by some very nasty hardware. They were little four-pronged spikes of metal, nastily designed so that one spike was always sticking straight up. 'Thank you, Burgers McCall,' I said under my breath.

'How did the other cars get past this?' Pippa Avery asked.

I had a horrible thought, and checked the other cars. There was a reason they weren't parked neatly. They all had ripped tyres.

Xanthippe let out a low cry and flew to check her precious Spider for other damage. There didn't seem to be any bumps or scrapes, which was good, because I liked Stewart in one piece. Not for any particular reason or anything, just for the sake of humanity.

We could hear shouting from the far side of the shack. 'Save him from this lot first, kill him later?' I suggested.

'That does seem wise,' Xanthippe agreed, straightening up. 'We won't want witnesses.'

We came around to a crumbling patio at the back, made from bricks and old mortar. Greg Avery stood there yelling at the top of his voice at his son Jason. Stewart was hanging on to Shay French to stop him leaping in to defend his mate. Shay was scowling and furious.

'Well,' I said brightly. 'Isn't this nice?'

'You must be wondering why I summoned you all here,' Xanthippe added in an undertone.

'Yes, yes, best private detective ever,' I said tiredly. 'Should we applaud before or after we fix everyone's tyres?'

'Of all the ridiculous, selfish, stupid stunts to pull,' Greg Avery roared.

Jason looked angry and defensive, as if he was about to cut and run for it. When he saw us, he became even more panicky.

'What do you expect me to do?' he shouted finally, standing up to his dad. 'They're going to *arrest me*.'

'*You* are going to return to Flynn as if nothing has happened, you little shit, and stay calm,' said Greg Avery, his large physical presence dominating his skinnier son. 'The police have no evidence against you, it's all circumstantial. You didn't kill that little slut, so stop behaving like you did.' Greg turned finally, seeing the new arrivals. 'What the hell are you—' He was momentarily sapped of bluster. 'Pippa, what have you said to these people?'

'These people want to help Jason,' Pippa said calmly. 'I do too. Don't you think maybe listening to him would be a good start?'

Couldn't have said it better myself.

Jason folded his arms. 'I don't have anything to say.' He glared at his father. 'Really think I'm innocent, do you? Then why were you asking the lawyer about plea-bargaining? I'm not stupid. You think I did it. That I killed Annabeth.'

'I don't think anything of the sort,' said Avery, in an entirely unconvincing show of paternal trust. 'I think you are acting like a guilty man, and that if we are not very careful, the police will take you at your word.'

Shay finally shook Stewart off him, but had the sense to stay back from the Averys. 'Your dad has a point, Jase. You're being a tool.'

Caught off guard, Jason laughed. 'Thanks, French.'

'Anytime, mate.'

Greg Avery looked at Stewart, and then at me and Xanthippe. Trying to figure out how we all fit into the very complicated picture. Ceege leaned against the shack, in a way that he probably thought was casual and 'so not involved,' though he's a solid enough mass of person that there was an implied threat there.

I didn't have a problem with that.

'So,' said Avery in a calm voice. 'What is it going to take for you all to stay quiet about my son's loss of nerves?'

Jason rolled his eyes at his dad. 'I'm going to call the RACT and wait by the cars.'

'I'll come with you,' Shay said quickly, and the two boys made a fast exit. I'm surprised there wasn't a screeching sound as they rounded the corner together.

Seriously, was no one asking the question of why Jason (or someone) had deliberately set up a trap to strand us all here? I had a nervous tic when it came to traps.

'We're no' gonnae tell anyone, Mr Avery,' said Stewart, the first of us to speak. 'It might make an interesting story for a day, but no one here wants tae mess things up for Jason, legally speaking.'

'Story,' Avery repeated in alarm. 'Are you from the fucking papers? Is that what this is about?'

'We're trying to help, actually,' I said, folding my arms.

'Some more than others,' said Xanthippe with a pointed

look at Stewart who might as well have Doomed Spider Thief tattooed on his forehead.

'You don't have to worry about bribes or rewards or anything like that,' I added firmly.

'Speak for yourself,' chimed in Ceege. I leaned over and hit him on the arm.

'Let's go, Greg,' Pippa Avery said in a firm voice. 'Jason's willing to come home. I think we should check that the RACT is on their way, so we can get him home as soon as possible.'

Greg Avery stared at all of us, opening his mouth as if to start shouting again, and then turned and marched off after the boys.

Pippa hesitated. 'When you say you won't say anything … can I assume you mean about the other thing too?'

'We'll try to restrain ourselves,' said Xanthippe. If I were Pippa I'd worry about the levels of sarcasm in her tone, but the other woman seemed to take it at face value.

Pippa followed her husband out of the courtyard.

Stewart raised his eyebrows at us both. 'There's an other thing? Is it scandalous?'

'It's been a busy morning,' said Xanthippe. 'I don't even remember what her scandalous secret is.' She smiled so harshly you'd swear her teeth were fanged. 'And now you die.'

Stewart held up his hands. 'In my defence, I didnae get a scratch on her.'

Ceege scoffed. 'That's why she hasn't killed you *already*.'

I stood next to Xanthippe, supporting her glare at Stewart with my own. 'I think I'd rather talk about the gratuitous hoarding of information, actually. And the kidnapping of witnesses?'

'Hey, I'm the innocent party here,' Stewart insisted. 'The lad Shay slipped off and was tryin' tae make away with the Spider all by himself. I couldnae let him go alone.'

'My hero,' Xanthippe said sarcastically, but she hadn't strangled him yet. Obviously going soft.

My phone started ringing, which was a surprise—the mobile coverage was better out here than I had thought. I excused myself to take it. 'If you're going to kill him in an entertaining way, Zee, wait until I come back, yeah?'

'Hey Tish,' said Bishop, sounding tired. 'Where are you?'

'With Xanthippe and Ceege and Stewart,' I said, which was true if lacking in essentials. 'I'm heading back to Hobart soon, though.' That was completely the truth. I was tired. Jason had two caring (if shouty) parents protecting him. He had lawyers. Hell, if Greg Avery really wanted to do something to improve the town, he could hire a team of therapists. Psychoanalysis for everyone!

They didn't need me.

'You know, we got a search warrant to go over the Avery house,' Bishop said conversationally. 'It was strangely empty of Averys.'

'Um,' I said as the word 'busted' scrolled across my vision.

'I think they had car trouble. But they'll be home soon. For a given definition of soon.'

'Good to know. Might be a bit late, though. What was that noise?'

I glanced over to where my friends were negotiating terms with each other. 'Xanthippe wrestled Stewart to the driveway and is trying to make him eat his own shoe.'

'Sorry to miss that,' said Bishop.

'It's quite a show.' I frowned. 'What do you mean, a bit late?'

I could hear more yelling from the other side of the house, and a vehicle. I hoped they had warned the RACT that there were siege devices in play, or cleared the damn things from the driveway. Wouldn't do to strand the bloke with the tow truck. I hurried around, to see Jason and his dad going at it again, while Shay and Pippa avoided making eye contact with each other.

I was just in time to see the police car, with Constable Heather driving and Bishop in the passenger seat, come up the driveway and over the caltraps. They jolted to a stop, looking around in surprise. And then Bishop saw me.

To wave, or not to wave? I settled for an innocent, apologetic smile. I suspect it was less than convincing.

Bust-ed.

Greg Avery reacted to the police presence by smoothing his jacket lapels, transitioning from angry father to shiny civic leader in just a moment or two. 'Officers,' he said, all tension disappearing from his voice.

'Mr Avery,' said Bishop as Constable Heather walked around her car, distracted by the damage. 'We met last night, I'm Detective Sergeant Bishop of the Special Crimes Unit.'

'I remember,' said Avery, trying to smile. 'Can we help at all? My family is about to return home. I'm afraid we got caught by the same prank as you did—local kids messing around, I expect.'

'Effective kids,' Heather muttered, eyeing the collection of sabotaged cars. 'Didn't any of you think of clearing the bloody things off the driveway?'

A fair question. We had been distracted.

'We've been looking for you, Mr Avery,' said Bishop, calmly avoiding the issue of the cars. How was he doing this super calm thing? He never used to be this calm, even on the job. Maybe it was the promotion. 'We have warrants to search all of your properties, including this one.'

He might not have been looking directly at Jason when he said that, but I sure as hell was. I saw panic cross the kid's face, and he shifted slightly as if—I don't know, to bolt back to the house, or down the driveway. Shay latched on to his sleeve, not letting him budge. I met Shay's eyes and nodded approvingly. No matter what had happened, no matter what it was that had put that look on Jason's face, if he ran now it was all over.

Though, admittedly the police wouldn't be able to pursue him in their vehicle immediately. It would still be a terrible idea.

Xanthippe sidled around the side of the building, followed

by Ceege and a limping Stewart, who still had not retrieved one of his shoes.

'Of course,' said Greg Avery. 'We have nothing to hide, Sergeant.'

Oh, I think you do. Avery was sweating in the searing sunlight, which was a perfectly good excuse. But still, there was something very non-innocent about him. I didn't know if it was his lack of faith in Jason, or something else.

'We've been following some leads based on your financial records,' Bishop said pleasantly. 'Were you aware that regular instalments of cash have been made from one of your household accounts into a bank account owned by Annabeth French, beginning January of this year?'

Greg Avery looked at his wife. Just a flicker of uncertainty, which she reflected right back at him. Jason looked genuinely astonished, for once.

'Phillipa Avery,' Bishop said formally. 'We would like to question you about the death of Annabeth French.'

'Me?' said Pippa, eyes wide.

'This is ridiculous,' Greg blustered.

Shay had dropped Jason's arm.

'I don't understand,' said Pippa, looking from her husband to Bishop and Constable Heather. 'What money?'

'The payments indicate a pattern of blackmail,' Heather said to Pippa, sounding genuinely regretful. 'We're going to need an explanation that fits with the relevant dates, or this can be counted as evidence that you had a reason to do harm to Ms French. The final payment was very large, and made only a few hours before she was killed.'

'Blackmail,' Pippa repeated, and either she really was surprised, or she was one hell of an actress. Sadly, I had no doubt about the latter. 'What on earth could Annabeth have been able to blackmail me about...' And then she went white, looking at Greg. 'My husband knows about my past,' she added fiercely. 'I have nothing to hide from him.'

'We'll be wanting to question Mr Avery as well, of course,' Bishop said politely.

'Are you suggesting the ... young lady was blackmailing me about Pippa's lack of judgement in her chosen lifestyle before our wedding?' Greg said dangerously.

'Don't talk about it in front of Jason,' Pippa said quickly, and then bit her lip as she realised that gave lie to her pretending she had nothing to conceal from the world.

I didn't have the heart to tell her that Jason probably knew of her past as a Gingerbread cookie, given the detective work he had been attempting on his desktop. None of my business.

'I don't want to be interviewed here,' Pippa said sharply. 'Can we go to the police station?'

Constable Heather looked at the torn remains of her tyres and made a small noise.

'Of course,' Bishop said calmly. 'We'll call for a couple of cars.' He nodded to Heather who walked away muttering, but pulled out her phone and looked around for the best place to get a signal. 'When you've done that, start searching the shack,' he called after her, and she nodded.

Bishop turned his attention back to Mr and Mrs Avery, the perfect gentleman. 'We can drive you both to the local station at Huonville, and conduct formal interviews there. I'm sure Jason and his friend can get a lift home, unless you'd rather he joined us?' Bishop glanced over at me for a moment, and I tried to look like the trustworthy type you would totally let your nineteen-year-old son drive home with while you were questioned about being blackmailed by a woman who had pretended to be his dead ex-girlfriend.

It was a tricky expression to pull off.

'Interviewing my wife is completely unnecessary,' said Greg Avery, stepping forward. 'I authorised those payments to Annabeth French.'

'What the hell?' Jason demanded. 'She was blackmailing *you*?' He looked at his father with genuine fear.

'Don't be more of a dickhead than you can help, Jason,' his father said impatiently. He set his chin, meeting Bishop's gaze. 'It had nothing to do with blackmail. I paid the girl to leave the state. I believe she spent most of the cash on acting school. She received regular instalments to cover her tuition, rent and expenses. No threats or extortion were involved. It was a gift.'

The words hung in the air for just a moment, and then Jason

lunged for his father. Shay reacted a moment too late, and I ran over to join him, dragging back on Jason's other arm.

'Let me go,' the boy roared. 'You?' he demanded of his father. 'You were the other bloke? Like marrying someone barely older than me wasn't bad enough, you had to fuck my girlfriend too?'

'He didn't say that,' I hissed in Jason's ear, dragging him back. Indeed, Greg Avery looked taken aback at his son's assumption. Pippa was veiling whatever thoughts she had on the subject.

'Yes he bloody did,' Jason snarled.

'No, he said he *paid* her to go to acting school. He didn't say he was the boyfriend.' I looked at Shay, who looked just as bemused as the rest of us. Then back at Greg Avery. 'There never was a rich older boyfriend, was there? She just said that in case anyone asked where the money came from. You gave her the money.'

'Not—blackmail,' Greg Avery said again, disgust evident in his tone. 'If the little bitch had tried something like that, I would have turned her straight over to the police.'

'Indeed,' said Bishop. 'So the payments were for…'

Greg folded his arms, and looked mutinous. 'For her to leave, of course. To get her the hell away from my son.'

'What?' Jason said, and the anger had been replaced by something numb that prevented him from trying to act like someone in a mobster movie. I didn't let go of his T-shirt, though, and neither did Shay. 'But she was always going to leave. That was her plan.'

'Not far enough,' Avery said in a clipped voice. 'That girl was never going to stick to university, anyone could see that. She would have dragged you with her wherever she went. Off to the mainland, chasing her flighty little dreams. I need you here. I have plans for this town, and my son is part of that. So I gave her the opportunity, and she jumped at the chance.' There was a note of pride in his voice now. 'I told you she wasn't serious about you. She didn't even think the offer over—she took the money in an instant.'

Jason was staring with his mouth open. Possibly I was too. 'You paid off my girlfriend so I wouldn't leave town? That's—sick.'

On the bright side, it looked like Avery Senior hadn't been sleeping with her. Possibly that was little comfort to Jason right now.

'She was more than happy to take the money,' Greg sneered. 'Which only goes to show what kind of girl she was.' He turned away from Jason, addressing his remarks to Bishop. 'I had expected her to release my son from their relationship long before she returned to Flynn for the holidays, but she did not. That final payment was given on the understanding she would end what remained of their arrangement.'

'She picked a fight with me,' Jason said, wondering. 'That day. She checked her bank balance at the ATM, and then she turned around and picked a fight with me for no reason, and I got mad and yelled at her about lying about where she was living, and the other bloke … but that wasn't true? None of it was true?' He shook his head, looking gutted. 'The last thing I said to her was that I couldn't stand to look at her. She was dead a couple of hours later, and that's the last thing she ever heard me say. Because of *you*, Dad.' His whole year was unravelling, making less sense the more closely he looked at it.

I knew what it was like, to have everything you thought you knew come apart. To find out something you valued was based on a lie. And, oh bloody hell, I was doing the same to Bishop. Wasn't I? Pretending everything was okay, that we were okay, that I hadn't been freaking out about whether or not we were getting too serious, or not serious enough. And the second I wasn't with him I had thrown myself at one of my best friends.

'I have a question,' said Shay French in a quiet voice. 'If my sister didn't have an older boyfriend on the side, then who was the bloke in the lake?'

Good question, Shay. Excellent question. 'I have a theory,' I said, but no one heard me because Constable Heather came marching back out of the house, looking even more pissed off than when her tyres were torn out. 'You know that search you wanted me to do?' she said.

'Yes, that would be good,' Bishop said impatiently. 'Any time now.'

'No, I've done it.'

He didn't look around. 'You were only gone five minutes. Do it properly.'

'Well, I already found the spade used to inflict head wounds on Annabeth French and Malcolm Drake before they died, a set of clothes with bloodstains, and this.' She held up an evidence bag containing a gun. 'Not that I'm not willing to look for more evidence, but I think that makes a good start, don't you?'

21

From: Darlingtabitha

Would it be possible to create a scone with jam and cream entirely out of ICE CREAM?

From: Nincakes

Why are you planning ice cream catastrophes at four in the morning?

From: Darlingtabitha

It's when I get some of my best inspiration.

From: Nincakes

GO TO SLEEP I HATE YOU

Bishop turned very slowly, and stared at Constable Heather. I'd never realised before that she had such a dark sense of humour, but it didn't surprise him.

Of course, just because she saw the humour in the situation didn't mean she was actually joking.

'The spade and clothes are still in the shack?' Bishop said finally. Heather nodded.

'I have a call to make,' he said.

'Yes, Sarge. Thought you might.'

It was still a shock to the system, hearing Bishop called Sarge. There was a small quiet hurt inside me that my dad hadn't lived to see his protegé finally get that promotion he'd been working for.

My dad really loved Bishop. I don't know if that helped or hindered us getting together in the first place, knowing how much he would have approved (probably) of us being together. It was definitely a factor in me keeping my crush good and (mostly) hidden for the first decade we knew each other.

I can't help thinking that either Dad or Bishop or both of them would have pushed me a lot harder to resolve the 'girlfriend' question, in that particular alternate reality. But maybe that wasn't being fair to either of them.

Jason Avery's life was falling apart in front of my eyes, and I was wrapped up in thoughts about my love life. Way to go, Tabitha.

Bishop moved away and punched numbers into his phone, speaking in a low voice. Heather, caught between a desire to supervise us, and her duty to protect the evidence inside the house, hovered in the space in between.

'Excellent searching,' Xanthippe said cheerfully.

'I thought so,' said Heather with a hint of smug.

'Do they send you on a special course for that?'

There was a crash inside the shack. Heather swore, and ran back into the house. Xanthippe ran after her, and after a moment's hesitation, I followed. I heard Bishop giving strict orders for the others to stay where they were, before he came after us.

We entered a main rumpus-style room. There was an old couch there, but it was obvious no one house proud had been living here for some time.

There was a hole in the ceiling, and French Vanilla lay crumpled on the floor, her skin bone white. She wasn't blonde any more, her hair a more natural looking brown, though it had to be a dye job—you don't lose blonde that fast. Also, she had possibly broken her leg.

'Hiding in the crawl space in the roof,' Xanthippe said knowledgeably. 'Don't blame yourself for missing her, Heather. All that evidence at once would distract anyone.'

'It did make me kind of giddy,' said Heather. 'Alice Conway?'

She had a last name. And the police knew what it was. How could I not be impressed?

'Yes?' Alice said in a small voice, her whole body shaking. 'Yes, I am.'

'You're wanted for questioning in regard to the deaths of Annabeth French and Malcolm Drake,' Heather said gently. 'Are you hurt?'

'I don't know,' said Alice. Xanthippe came over to hold out an arm, and Alice managed to stand. 'I think I'm okay. Ow!'

'If we were to ask you why you were hiding in the roof,' said Bishop, behind me. I respected the fact that he wasn't taking over Heather's arrest, but standing back and letting her take point. 'Would we like the answer?'

Alice pulled one hand through her curly brown hair. 'I don't know. What do you want me to say?'

'Leave the difficult questions until later,' I suggested. 'She's shaken up and has a distinct lack of lawyer.'

Bishop frowned, but he allowed Xanthippe and Heather to help Alice limp outside. Alice had tears streaming down her face, and by the time she stepped out on the gravel driveway she only had eyes for one person. 'Jason, I'm so sorry,' she said.

Jason sat on the ground, head in his hands, and I saw it, finally. The reason a kid of nineteen sits at the edge of a steep drop, gunning his engine and thinking about letting everything go.

There had never been any mystery here, and I was just too wrapped up to see it. The evidence only pointed one way.

'I didn't mean to do it,' Jason said quietly, looking utterly hollow.

Shay stepped away from his mate so fast he almost tripped over his own feet. Stewart went to Shay, hand on his arm, talking in a quiet voice.

'Don't say a word, Jason,' said Greg Avery. 'Our lawyers...'

'Did you kill Anna?' Shay asked, his voice ragged, shaking with disbelief. He stared down at his mate as if he was looking at a stranger. 'Jase, did you drown my sister?'

Jason looked up, eyes wide. 'No. No way. I never—I would never.'

'That's what I thought,' Shay muttered, more to himself than to Jason or the rest of us.

'He did it,' said Jason. 'That bloke. Drake. He killed her.'

'Why the hell didn't you tell anyone that?' Shay demanded. 'You knew what happened to her, and you never … were you *there*?'

'I killed him,' Jason said in a whisper. 'I didn't mean to … but I did.' He made a noise that was almost a laugh. 'Can't take it back.'

Greg Avery turned on Bishop now, howling and blustering about how he couldn't possibly take this admission as evidence. The boy was upset and confused.

I let go of Alice's arm. Let Xanthippe support her, if that was what she needed. Stewart was looking after Shay. I crossed the driveway toward Jason, knelt down on the gravel and hugged him, because no one else was doing it. He grabbed on to me like I was a lifeline, and I hugged him harder.

Maybe it wasn't just for his benefit.

✹

There was a long wait, for Bishop's backup officers and cars to arrive. He wasn't keen to let us all inside, though the evidence had already been well and truly disturbed.

Instead, we all sat out on the sunken patio at the back, which was in rather better condition than the house itself. Jason sat on the steps, Pippa sitting deliberately close to him on one side, and me on the other. Tellingly, his father kept his distance, pacing back and forth.

Alice and Xanthippe sat on the steps opposite Jason. Alice looked utterly broken, her hands constantly squeezing together in her lap. Ceege had chosen a step near Xanthippe, but I suspect that was more about symmetry than actual allegiance.

Stewart stuck with Shay like I was sticking with Jason. They sat up on the shady wooden deck, looking down at the rest of us. For a long time, no one spoke.

'You said you had a theory, Tish,' Xanthippe said, speaking across the patio as if she and I were the only ones here. 'About the bloke in the lake? Malcolm Drake.'

I resisted the urge to point out that Drake rhymed with lake, because no one wanted jokes right now. 'You remember that?'

'I pay attention to the things you say. Never know when it's going to turn out to be interesting.'

'Please don't discuss the case,' Bishop said flatly. 'The cars will be here soon, and we can get this sorted out at the station.'

Xanthippe gave him a withering look. 'Just killing time, Leo. Don't mind us. Pretend we're not here.'

'Okay, my theory,' I said, because I would rather talk to Xanthippe right now than endure another minute of the police-appointed awkward silence. 'He can't have been Anna's rich boyfriend, because she didn't have one. She told Shay—and Alice—there was a rich boyfriend because it was her cover story for where the money came from. But I was thinking, there's one other bloke in the story that we didn't have a name for. Someone from the mainland.'

Stewart made a small noise of recognition, then smiled and shook his head. 'Nice.'

'Like Zee said,' I told him. 'You never know something's going to be interesting. So it's worth paying attention to details.'

Stewart nodded, and despite the crowd it felt like it really was just the three of us. 'Alice was tryin' tae get away from something bad at the start of it all. I thought there had tae be more there.'

'There was,' I agreed. 'Alice, why don't you tell it?'

'Tabitha,' Bishop warned in a low growl.

I felt more myself than I had in months, and I wasn't going to stop now. 'Don't pretend like you're not as keen to know as the rest of us. Alice? Was Malcolm Drake *your* boyfriend?'

Alice hesitated and then nodded. More tears blobbed down her nose. 'I was scared of him,' she said in a low voice. 'I was … I ran away from him. I kept running. I became Annabeth to get away from him completely, as completely as I could.'

'And then you went intae a house full of webcams?' Stewart said dubiously.

Alice looked surprised. 'Of course. I had to be Annabeth, not Alice. Alice would never do something like that. Malcolm would never look for Alice in a place like that. I didn't just dye my hair blonde and start wearing cardigans. I turned myself into a completely different person. It worked, too. It wasn't The Gingerbread House that led him to me. He had no idea.'

'Then how did he find you?' Xanthippe asked.

'Annabeth,' Alice said quietly. 'I didn't realise—it never occurred to me that she would use *my* name, when she went to drama school. She used her own name for all the formal stuff, applications etc. But she chose Alice Conway as her stage name. She didn't even tell me, or I would have warned her.'

'What would you have warned her about?' I pressed, ignoring the look Bishop shot me. He wasn't in control here. Hell, no one was in control. Until the cars arrived (and Heather had already enlisted Ceege to clear the driveway of the evil little caltraps, so hopefully these mythical police cars would get here unscathed) we were all stuck here together. Might as well find out something about the events that had led us to this particular place and time.

'That he was dangerous,' Alice said quietly. 'That he wouldn't stop looking for me. That performing under my name was a way to make herself vulnerable. It wasn't much, maybe a review or two online of a couple of plays. Enough to come up in a Google search.' She shook her head. 'She was the only one who knew where I was, and he must have got the information out of her somehow. I don't know if he threatened her, or just tricked her. But that day, the power went out at The Gingerbread House, and I went to check the fuse box, and he was *there*.'

One mystery cleared up, at least. 'What did he do?' I asked in a low voice, my eyes on her. I was a step or two above Jason, and couldn't see the look on his face. I wasn't sure I wanted to. But I reached out, and patted his shoulder so he'd know there was someone there.

Alice swallowed, looking miserable. 'He grabbed for me, and I ran. I couldn't think, I couldn't breathe. I made it to the garden shed, grabbed the first thing I found, and when he came for me again, I hit him with it. And I kept hitting. I wanted him to leave me alone, I wanted him...' She swallowed again, darting a look at Bishop, who had a blank expression on his face.

'I thought I'd killed him,' she said finally. 'I wish I had. Then no one else would have ever got involved.'

'So wha' happened next?' It was Stewart who prompted her that time. I couldn't get a read on whether he believed her or not. Maybe neither. Maybe he was just unbiased and non-judgemental, like a journalist was supposed to be.

'He was so ... still, on the concrete,' Alice said, speaking slowly as if the words physically pained her. 'Lying there. I didn't know what to do. It was the middle of the day, it was sunny. I waited for someone to find me, to come and find out what the noise was. But no one did. His car was in the driveway. I dragged him over, and it was difficult, he was heavy. I got him into the boot instead, covered him with a blanket, and I just started driving.'

Alice shook her head. 'I was so angry at Annabeth. She'd given the person who hated me most in the world my address, and she hadn't even let me know or checked whether it was a good idea. I called her—I knew she was back in Flynn for the summer, we had agreed that would work if she stayed away from Hobart—and I yelled at her, crying, scared. She said I should come to meet her, we'd figure something out. She didn't know what the hell I was talking about, but she was sure it wasn't all that bad.'

Alice took a deep breath, looking around and her eye falling on Jason. 'She was like that, yeah? I mean, she was always trying to find the upbeat answer to anything. No worries, she'll be right.'

'Yeah,' Jason said with a hollow laugh. 'She'll be right. Whatever.'

'I drove all the way to Flynn,' Alice said finally. 'Only I hadn't been there before, and I got turned around at Huonville, and then I was low on petrol and…' She took a deep breath. 'I didn't get to Flynn until after dark. Waited by the lake, up by the trees, where no one could see the car. Called Annabeth, and she came to find me. I was a wreck.' Tears dribbled down her face again. 'She was so kind. So encouraging. When I told her—what I had done, she was completely calm. Said it was self-defence, and no one would blame me, though the driving around all day with him in the car thing wouldn't go down too well, but we could totally come up with a good story to explain that.'

'Not that we're not enjoying the narrative,' Xanthippe said dryly. 'But at what point did the body in the boot manage to get himself shot?'

'What, you can spend two hours a day practising taekwondo or whatever the hell it is you do in those white pyjamas, and you can't wait ten minutes so the girl can tell her story in the proper order?' said Ceege. 'Suck it up.'

'Blow me,' she advised him.

'In your dreams.'

'Children, please?' I interjected. Alice looked like she was about to clam up for good, and we were on a deadline. Once Bishop's buddies turned up, the police would shut down the situation completely, and we might never hear the whole story.

'I don't understand how you got involved, Jason,' Pippa said quietly.

'Alice called me—' and his words got caught in his throat. 'Just listen, okay?'

'He wasn't dead,' said Alice, picking at one end of her cardigan. The stray thread of yarn had come loose, and she was well on her way to unravelling her sleeve. 'I hadn't killed him at all.' That was an important detail, surely. 'When we went to look in the boot for him, he was gone. We both panicked, and then he leaped out at us from the trees, tried to grab us. We ran…'

She was shaking now, and Xanthippe got up without a word and went off to her car. When she came back, she had a soft throw rug with her, to put around Alice's shoulders. Okay, when Xanthippe felt sorry about you, it meant you were in pretty bad shape.

'I heard Anna scream,' said Alice after a moment of rough, panicked breathing. 'I was hiding in the trees. We'd got separated, but even when she screamed, I didn't dare come out of hiding. Jason was the only other person I knew in Flynn. So I called him, told him we were both in danger.'

'You didn't think of calling the police?' asked Bishop.

Jason made a noise of disgust and looked at him sideways, pulling his hand through his hair. It was the first sign of life we had seen from him in some time. 'Nearest police are what—half an hour away? Forty minutes?'

'He's right,' Alice said flatly. 'I should have called the police. I didn't even think of that. It was like my brain had shut down, and I was inside one of those horror movies where everyone dies.'

'She didn't make much sense on the phone,' Jason said, staring at his feet as he took up the story. 'But I knew about Alice's boyfriend, the way he treated her. She said she thought he was going to kill her. And when I got there, the first thing I saw was Anna … lying in the water.'

He clenched his fists.

'Where did the gun come from?' Constable Heather asked.

'Is this an official interview, officer?' Greg Avery snapped in return.

Jason rolled his eyes. 'So you have an unregistered gun, Dad. Big deal. Do you even get what kind of trouble I'm in?'

'I know that you should have a lawyer before you make any admissions,' his father hurled at him.

'How's this for an admission?' Jason yelled back. 'I killed Malcolm Drake. He killed Anna, and I found her lying in the fucking lake, and I shot him to stop him doing the same to Alice. Lawyer *that*.'

Silence stretched from one end of the patio to the other. Alice buried her head in her hands. Pippa just closed her eyes. Greg Avery had no expression at all.

There was the sound of cars pulling up on the gravel on the far side of the shack. The reinforcements had arrived. They weren't so melodramatic as to have their sirens on, but we could see a flash or two of blue lights.

Jason pushed himself up and walked over to Bishop. 'I think this is the part where you arrest me, yeah?'

'That's usually how these things go,' Bishop said gravely.

The boy nodded, setting his chin. 'I'm ready.'

After that it was all procedure. Greg and Pippa went in one of the police cars, with Jason. Alice went in another, huddled up under the blanket. Her leg wasn't broken, but they were going to take her to get it looked at. Before or after they arrested her, I guess? I wasn't sure of the order of events.

For a moment, in the middle of organising the witnesses and evidence and everything else, Bishop looked over at me, to check I was all right. I lied to him with a brave smile, because what was one more lie? He turned away, and got on with his job.

Ceege and Xanthippe had taken over the task of keeping Shay in one piece, which was good because I had nothing left. I walked away from the shack, away from all of them, down to the line of gum trees and the view of the hills and mountains and lakes. For a moment there was nothing but calm scenery and the sound of my own breathing.

Arms wrapped around me, a familiar scent of coffee and boy. It was Stewart, but that was okay. More than okay. He was exactly what I needed right now.

'Give me a minute, and I'll be fine,' I said in a shaky voice. It was dumb to feel this involved. It wasn't about me, not this time. But every time I thought about Jason Avery, I wanted to cry. There were no bad guys walking around here. Just people who had fucked up their lives. I leaned back into Stewart's arms and breathed.

'Ye know what I feel like?' Stewart said after a long moment.

'If you say ice cream, I'm going to bitch-slap you,' I warned him.

He leaned in, his mouth tickling my ear. 'Ice cream.'

Then he took off, laughing, and let me catch up easily and pummel him. As friends do.

22

THE MORTICIA ADDAMS SUPER SPECIAL SUMMER WAKE UP PUNCH

(CAN WAKE THE DEAD, ESPECIALLY IF THE DEAD HAVE A HANGOVER)

Ingredients:

1 litre commercial lemonade

8 lemons, juiced

4 oranges, juiced

2 limes, juiced

500g strawberries

500g watermelon

500g pineapple

1 handful of garden mint, finely chopped

As much finely smashed ice as you can fit in the bowl.

Puree the fruit and lemon juice until fine and frothy. Pour over bowlful of smashed ice (meat tenderisers are good for smashing purposes). Pour lemonade over entire glorious mess.

Obviously the recipe can be much improved by the addition of a bottle of gin, a bottle of champagne, or both. But its finest application is to serve it mocktail style the morning after a big night. That way, no one ends the weekend with scurvy. It's especially useful if the morning after doesn't get started until after lunch…

Life went back to normal. For me, anyway. I gave Nin an extra day off to make up for the whole building inspector thing, reopened the café once we had the all clear, and buried myself in my kitchen. I experimented with four different kinds of affogato and tested them on various willing subjects, I finally decided to retire panini in favour of tremazzini (who has the time to wait for cheese to melt?) and I juiced so many lemons for my special summer Wake Up Punch that my cuticles swelled to twice their usual size.

It was nearly Christmas, and I wasn't ready for it. No one seemed to be, this year. I declared Café La Femme a Christmas free zone, set a blackboard on the pavement outside that declared 'Guaranteed No Merry Jingle Bells Music!' and saw my numbers for coffee-between-shopping customers soar.

It was hot in that week before Christmas, the kind of hot that makes Hobart natives stare in confusion at each other because we're never, ever prepared for it. I stepped up the ice cream production—sometimes offering two or three flavours a day. Sure, it meant staying up later at night to get the batches going, but that worked for me.

I hadn't been sleeping great. Only work made me feel like that was halfway normal.

Things between me and Bishop were … well. We'd had a talk. The talk. It went something like this:

BISHOP: Why does this coffee have ice cream in it?

TABITHA: It's an affogato, which is basically what coffee was invented for.

BISHOP: The coffee is melting the ice cream really fast. Hard to see how there's going to be a happy ending for any of the ingredients.

TABITHA: To be fair, I think that's true of all food.

BISHOP: Are you absolutely sure you meant the ice cream to be pink?

TABITHA: I'm trying to prove that the perfect affogato can be made without the use of vanilla. It's chef science.

BISHOP: For the sake of our relationship, I will pretend that everything you just said makes sense and is no way a mutual waste of our time and energy.

(long pause)

BISHOP: And I know that I breached some kind of clause by using the word 'relationship' but I think I should be allowed that one given that, you know.

TABITHA: That I kissed someone else on the internet?

BISHOP: Which I got to find out about thanks to a hashtag my junior colleague was reviewing for work purposes.

TABITHA: Awkward.

BISHOP: Yes. Though not in the top five of awkward work related circumstances in which you have somehow been involved.

TABITHA: Wow, really?

BISHOP: There's a pie chart in the break room.

TABITHA: Why do you put up with me?

(long pause)

BISHOP: That is a surprisingly difficult question to answer.

TABITHA: Thought it might be.

BISHOP: Not—I didn't mean that in a bad way. You are basically wonderful. I'm not ready to give up on figuring out how to combine—you know.

TABITHA: Hot coffee and cherry coconut gelato?

BISHOP: Bad example. Considering the mess in this cup right now.

TABITHA: I was trying not to look too closely.

BISHOP: Do we need to bury it in the back yard?

TABITHA: Can the bad affogato please stop being a metaphor for our relationship?

BISHOP: You used the 'r' word.

TABITHA: I didn't mean to.

(long pause)

TABITHA: Invite me to Christmas.

BISHOP: What? That is so not where I thought you were going with this.

TABITHA: Me either. Apparently the part of me that talks

is not connected to the rest of my brain. I'm not saying that I want to girlfriend up or anything, just…

(pause in which Bishop reminds me that he is also most excellent at kissing)

TABITHA: Huh.

I also had a talk with Stewart. It went a bit like this:

STEWART: Why is there ice cream in my coffee cup?

TABITHA: It is double espresso flavoured ice cream.

STEWART: Keep talkin'.

TABITHA: And I'm now going to pour a shot of hot espresso over it.

STEWART: Yer ideas are intriguing tae me and I subscribe tae yer newsletter.

(long pause, for pouring and tasting)

STEWART: Tabitha.

TABITHA: Stewart.

STEWART: Ye cannae do this. Taste it.

TABITHA: Ugh. Omigod it's horrible!

STEWART: Ye know what would work, though?

TABITHA: It has to be vanilla.

STEWART: Damn straight it has tae be vanilla.

TABITHA: Fucking affogato.

STEWART: Never mess with a classic. (long pause, slightly awkward) So. Four thousand hits.

TABITHA: I knooow. We're practically internet famous.

STEWART: Some of us were already internet quite-well-known-ish.

TABITHA: Still.

STEWART: Aye. Hell of a kiss, Tabitha.

TABITHA: Yes. It was.

STEWART: Did you tell…

TABITHA: He already knew thanks to the unfortunate invention of Google Alerts and the equally unfortunate invention of hashtags. But yes. I told my boyfriend about kissing someone else on YouTube. And for the sake of my honour I would add that I would have told him even without the YouTube evidence. Eventually.

STEWART: And calling him yer boyfriend now basically answers all my other questions.

TABITHA: It's a work in progress. I'm… (for the record the next word was totally going to be sorry but someone totally didn't let me say it.)

STEWART: Nae, what we're goin' tae do here is take some genuine vanilla ice cream and heat up the espresso, and make some fucking affogatos like God and Thomas Jefferson intended. Aye?

TABITHA: Right.

STEWART: Never mess with a classic.

Three days after both of my awkward affogato-relationship-metaphor conversations, neither of which quite turned out how I expected, Xanthippe breezed into the café an hour after closing. For a business partner, she was pretty good at avoiding anything that involved sterilisation or a mop.

'Ready to go?'

'I'll give this one a miss,' I said. 'I was going to give cassata a chance tonight. Maybe pistachio.'

I was lying. I had three trays of vanilla bean gelato to make before I officially added affogato to the Café La Femme menu. Vanilla and I were still processing this change in our relationship status and we chose not to share it with others.

'Tish,' Xanthippe said in a stern voice. 'There is more to life than ice cream. We were invited to go, and we are going. That's all there is to it.'

I glared. 'You're the one who made friends with them.'

'They asked us both,' she replied, beating me down with the truth. Wench.

'I don't want to go. I need to keep Ceege company.'

'As we speak, Ceege is introducing Darrow to the wonders of a vintage Hollywood online RPG. He found a website where you can pretend to be golden age film idols, and I don't think either of them will surface for some time. Ceege said, and I quote, "tell Tabs if she comes home before 9PM I will make her wear the I Have No Social Life hat for a week. Also, bring back milk and beer".'

'Finally they find an RPG worthy of my time and they kick me out of the house? Is Ceege worried I'll steal Grace Kelly before he gets the chance?'

'They're fighting over who gets to be Ginger Rogers.'

'Fine, I'll come,' I said reluctantly. 'But I reserve the right to get a headache at 8:55.'

'I'll make a note of that,' Xanthippe agreed.

'You're here!' Melinda crowed as we arrived at The Gingerbread House. I wore a black and white houndstooth-patterned frock cut off at the knee, with matching sandals and a handbag that had been repurposed from a vintage Sherlock Holmes hardcover. Xanthippe wore a real tuxedo. Rare for her to be more dressed up than me. 'Perfect. Xanthippe, want to do the honours? We're taking the last of them down.'

'I'm up for anything,' Xanthippe said cheerfully. 'What am I taking down?'

'The cameras,' Melinda said, as if it should be obvious. 'Come on, help me with the one in the living room. I can't stand on a chair.'

'Chairs I can do,' said Xanthippe, and abandoned me. I hoisted my bottle of sparkling white and my two litres of raspberry crunch gelato (crunch is what happens when you forget to strain the seeds out) and pushed my way through the crowd, making for the kitchen. I'm always more comfortable in kitchens. Well, within reason. Alice 'French Vanilla' Conway was standing in this particular kitchen, which severely limited how comfortable I was going to feel.

'Hi,' she said, looking startled to see me. She was in her usual cardigan and sundress combination, her hurt leg wrapped in bandages that had been decorated by one of her arty roommates, with biro doodles and paper roses.

'Hi,' I said back, and lodged the ice cream in the freezer, the bottle in the fridge. No, the hell with it. I took the bottle back, and opened it. 'Must be good to be home.'

'Strange, is what it is,' she said, with that little bashful smile that made me want to like her all over again. 'I'm glad Cherry and Ginger—I mean, Mel and Libby took me back, I wouldn't have blamed them for cutting me off altogether.'

'They're good people,' I said. 'You're family to them. They were miserable when you disappeared.'

Alice nodded quickly. 'That's why they decided to close The Gingerbread House. They say it's because Libby's graduating soon, and Mel wants some privacy for when the baby comes. But I don't think they would have taken it all apart so quickly if I hadn't told them that I can't live with cameras any more.'

'I don't blame you for that,' I said. 'A day in Flynn with cameras all over the place was enough for me.' I hesitated. 'Have you heard anything from Jason?'

'No,' Alice said, and sighed. 'I don't expect to. I know his dad paid his bail, but … he's not supposed to make contact with me before the trial. And I don't think he'd want to speak to me even if he was allowed to. He was such a good friend to me, and look what I did to him.'

I could have said that Jason was nineteen, not twelve. He knew that taking his dad's gun was a stupid thing to do. Even if he thought he was protecting his friends. Life is not a slasher movie, and he had to know that pointing a gun at someone was going to have consequences. Those are all things that I would have said, if I wanted to put her at her ease. But I wasn't entirely sure that I wanted to. The whole thing still had a wrong feeling about it.

What I said was: 'Quite a party you have going on here.' I'd spotted Lara and Yui on my way in, and a few other mates from around the city. I wouldn't be bored.

'We've never been able to have people over before,' Alice said with a wan smile. 'We had the rule for The Gingerbread House—no men at all, and the only time we invited friends here was when we knew we could trust them about keeping our privacy rules. And signing waivers, of course, since everything that happened here was broadcast live.'

I nodded. 'It's a shame you never wired up cameras in the driveway, really. It might have helped corroborate your story to the police.'

She gave me a wary look. 'I suppose so.'

'Or Vanilla here could have strapped a camera to her head and filmed everything just in case she needed to prove her innocence,' put in Ginger—Libby, coming into the kitchen. She stood beside Alice, and even though it was casual, I knew a protective instinct when I saw one.

'See,' I said, matching her fake flippant tone. 'The perfect solution. Constant CCTV coverage everywhere.'

'Sounds like a terrible idea to me,' said Libby, which only went to show that she was incapable of spotting irony. She opened another packet of corn chips and filled the empty bowl she had brought in with her. 'Speaking as a film student—anything can be faked. If we relied on film footage for everything, a lot of innocent people would end up in jail.'

'Interesting,' I said, pouring myself a glass of the sparkling white and offering it to them both. Alice shook her head, while Libby reached for a new beer from the fridge. 'I'd forgotten you were a film student,' I added. 'You didn't take part in *Flynn by Night*?'

Libby wrinkled her nose at me. 'Some random improvisation project produced and directed by a team with no training? Xanthippe's a sweetheart, but I take my work a bit more seriously than that.'

'That's a shame,' I said. 'We had a lot of fun. You were there, though, weren't you? At Flynn that day. You went to visit Pepperminty—I mean, Pippa.'

Libby's face went from neutral to downright resentful. 'Vanilla,' she said. 'Take these chips out, yeah? There are a few engie students eyeing the furniture hungrily.'

Alice gave her a wary look, but went. Obviously she'd been playing the meek and accommodating flatmate for so long, it was deeply ingrained.

Libby leaned in towards me, hissing her words. 'I don't know what you're getting at here, or why you think you're entitled to know our business. Pippa had been hassling Mel for months to close the website down and pretend it had never existed, because she didn't have to worry about money any more and didn't give a damn about the rest of us. Mel was half sick with stress about it, so I went down to give our so-called friend a piece of my mind. Vanilla doesn't need to know that we were still trying to keep the site going a week ago—the last thing we want is her going all noble on us.'

She folded her arms and glared at me. For someone who didn't think I was entitled to know her business, she was certainly being more than forthcoming.

I opened my mouth to ask another cheeky question, but Xanthippe interrupted us. 'Sorry, Libs. Can I borrow Tabitha for a minute?' She wound her arm in mine and dragged me off before I could express a say in the matter. She led me out the back, where the city's last remaining smokers were gathered around a small glass jar. We kept going until we stood on the very driveway where French Vanilla had been jumped by her abusive ex. 'Forgive me for asking, Tish, but didn't we close this case?' Xanthippe asked lightly when she was sure there was no one in earshot. 'The police are pretty sure they matched the right people to the right dead bodies. Can't you be satisfied with that and, you know, leave it at home where the party isn't?'

'Can you?' I shot back. 'The story doesn't make sense, Zee. How did a small woman like Alice manage to lift a guy the size of Malcolm Drake into that car boot? I tried to raise it with Constable Heather and she gave me some bullshit about how mothers lift cars off their children in time of great emergency. It makes a lot more sense if the others helped her.'

'So?' Xanthippe said. 'If they did, so what? It doesn't make any difference to the final result of what happened that night. I know you want Jason to not be in trouble—to not have shot that bastard Drake—but you can't hunt around for a different solution because you don't like the real one.'

I leaned my head back against the wall, sighing. She was right. I knew she was right. The reason I was having this conversation with her and not with Bishop was because I knew he'd say the same thing, and I wasn't ready to have a conversation about how much more he knew about police work than me, when we were still having tentative conversations using ice cream metaphors for our relationship.

'I still feel like there's a piece missing,' I grumbled. 'How did you know Jason and Alice didn't have a romantic relationship? I mean, you were so sure about it.'

Xanthippe shrugged. 'I read their texts. Well, not all of them. Memory only saves so many messages. But it was a very different story to what the postcards told us. She spent her whole time talking to him about the bad relationship that messed her up for anyone new, and he talked about the person he thought he was falling for, after Annabeth left.'

I stared at her. Because hello, completely missing piece right there. 'You read her texts? You had Alice's phone? The one she left behind that night?'

'Not exactly,' said Zee. 'But I found a memory card in the pot plant in her room, when we were searching it.'

'You didn't tell me.' I had no way of knowing how to deal with this. What the HELL?

'Xanthippe shrugged. 'I was going to, but there wasn't anything useful there, just squishy feelings. Plus other people were always around. Why do we never hang out, just the two of us?'

'Greater temptation for me to strangle you.'

'You make a reasonable point.'

I wasn't comfortable with this. 'So Alice just made a habit of hiding her memory card in her room?'

'Hmm,' said Xanthippe, which was her way of saying 'you said something stupid there'. 'Except it turns out the phone Alice left in the living room had a blank message history.'

'They swapped it,' I said immediately. 'Libby and Melinda. Or one of them.'

'We don't know that,' said Xanthippe.

'It's a logical suggestion.'

'Mmm, are you sure you thought of it?'

'Don't tell me you haven't.'

'Okay,' Xanthippe sighed. 'So one or both of them hid her message history, and one or both of them helped her lift a body into a boot. That doesn't mean anything. Not what you want it to mean.'

'And what do you think I want it to mean?' I demanded.

'That Jason is innocent. Which, by the way, he's not. Because evidence. And confession.'

'Oh, whatever,' I sulked, and swallowed half my drink. Sensibly I'd brought it with me when she hustled me out of the kitchen. 'Don't you think it's strange that they are dismantling the cameras now?'

'No, I really don't. I think it stopped being fun, and they're ready to move on.'

'Do you know what else is not fun?' I said. 'This party.'

Xanthippe reached out, and took the glass from me. 'So go home.'

'What about Ceege and his hat?'

Xanthippe just grinned. 'Kick his arse from me. If you want to mooch around and brood, then go for it. You've earned the right.'

Why yes, I had.

When I got home Ceege and Darrow were deep in an argument as to whether Katharine Hepburn and Cary Grant would ever have hooked up in real life. They didn't notice me sneaking in. I went straight up to my room. My bed was an island surrounded by discarded frocks and other items of clothing.

The little black dress was still hanging up in the empty wardrobe, taunting me with how mainstream and ordinary it was. Vanilla. I pulled it out, smoothing it out, looking at it. So not me. At all.

I think what Bishop was trying to say, in between all the awkwardness and ice cream mutilation, was that he'd rather have me in his life than someone who suited a dress like this. Which was good to know.

Unfortunately, this revelation had gone so much to my head that before I knew what I was doing, I had talked him into taking me to the family Christmas.

The phone and I stared at each other. I almost reached out and picked it up. It rang before I could touch it.

'So I'm trapped in my room, with several days of no' writing to catch up on,' said Stewart in that voice that always made my skin warm. 'Tell me yer having more fun.'

I relaxed, all the stress melting out of me, and lay back on the pillows. Stewart not being weird about me and Bishop failing to break up was one of the best things that had happened to me all week. 'I'm hiding from Darrow and Ceege while they arm wrestle to decide which 1940s actress they would most like to shag.'

'Those two really know how tae party.'

'Tell me about your latest book,' I said. 'What's the theme this time? Hot chef falls for restaurant owner? Journalist and photographer playing cat and mouse with each other? Foreign millionaire shags the nanny?'

'Amateur detective falls fer murderer.'

Caught off guard, I glared down the phone at him. 'Really?'

'Nae, no' really. That would be a good'un, though. This one's about a film director who falls fer her leading man.'

'Does he have rippling muscles?'

'I never understood why they say that. Wha' makes muscles ripple? Would anyone really want muscles tae ripple? Sounds painful.'

'You're just saying that because you don't have any.'

'Ha, I flex my puny muscles at ye.'

'I would swoon at your puny flexing muscles but I can't even see them…'

We went on like that for the rest of the evening, chatting about nothing important. I forgot what I'd been planning to do before he called, but I didn't mind at all.

Nothing had been broken, this time around, and he showed no signs of getting so annoyed at me that he had to leave town for half a year or more. So that was progress.

23

From: Darlingtabitha

you know about ice cream Christmas puddings, right??

From: Nincakes

No.

From: Darlingtabitha

Come on, have you never seen an issue of Women's
Weekly? Summer Christmas, stirring dried fruit and brandy
into ice cream…

From: Nincakes

you misunderstand me. I meant: no, the world does not
need mince pie ice creams.

From: Darlingtabitha

I'm feeling so judged right now.

From: Nincakes

or candy cane ice cream, roast turkey with stuffing ice

cream, or prawns-on-the-barbie ice cream. At all. Ever. Consider this an intervention

From: Darlingtabitha

I was just going to make a chocolate Christmas pudding cassata. But CANDY CANE ICE CREAM. I love your brain so much I want to squish it between my fingers.

From: Nincakes

I accept no responsibility for anything.

On Christmas Eve, I closed the café at 3PM. Nin was already off on the bus home to her family in Launceston. Lara and Yui had begged off after the lunch rush, or rather the grab-a-tremazzini-to-keep-up-my-strength-while-running-around-like-a-headless-chicken-to-pick-up-the-six-presents-I-forgot-I-was-going-to-need rush.

Xanthippe had disappeared again. The appeal of running a café had definitely worn off her. So it wasn't all bad news. Darrow's regular absences were what had made him such a brilliant business partner, after all. My faith in Xanthippe's short attention span had finally paid off.

I'd be back on Boxing Day, when Hobart exploded in the post Christmas sales. Seriously. Whose bright idea had it been to not only open the shops on Boxing Day, but put everything on sale? After a December of mad shopping-lust, Christmas Day was our single oasis of calm before the madness got madder.

And they were all going to want gluten-free friands with their coffee.

When I got home, I found Darrow, Ceege and Stewart in my living room, trying to get to grips with editing software. An image of Pippa Avery jumped out at me from the monitor, in starkly contrasting black and white.

I eyed the empty snack plates that littered the coffee table. 'You'd better not have touched my tiramisu.'

'Ye mean those WARNING TOUCH ON PAIN OF DEATH WITH SPIKY INSTRUMENTS signs were no' there tae make it taste better?' Stewart said, not looking up from the screen.

'Mmm, forbidden fruit,' said Ceege.

'You think you're funny, but you're not,' I said in a warning voice.

'Relax, Darling,' said Darrow. 'I can keep a lid on the rabble. Despite my sweet tooth.'

'Are we the rabble?' Ceege asked Stewart.

'Aye, must be. I've always wanted tae be rabble.'

'Me too!' They high-fived each other, unironically.

I ran upstairs to get dressed. The black dress was still hanging there, a pointed reminder that I had actually been trying to mould myself into the perfect girlfriend for Bishop, while denying I was his girlfriend. So that was embarrassing.

How did we go from me kissing someone else in public to maybe possibly levelling up to a proper relationship? Damned if I know.

But I'd been expecting anger, jealousy, some kind of deal-breaking ultimatum like telling me I had to cut off being friends with Stewart. Instead I got—warmth and security and unhurried kisses. That's enough to make any girl want to make tiramisu and Swedish potato pancakes topped with sour cream and dill, then gear herself up to impress and/or offend his mother.

I looked at the black dress. Yep. Still not me. Xanthippe was going to laugh at me if I wore it.

On the other hand, since when did Tabitha Darling care about anyone's reaction to something she wore?

I dug through my piles of stray clothing and came up with something festive—a light green frock with sunflowers all over it. It was just begging for my silver daisy chain necklace, and after that … well. Strappy green sandals, hair in bunches, and green ribbons tucked into my hair ties.

'Oh look, it's the Christmas fairy,' crowed Ceege as I made my entrance into the living room.

'Don't mock the elves, or you'll get coal in your stocking,' said Darrow. He wore a green velvet suit, a red silk shirt, and his tie had a holly and ivy pattern on it. It's good to have someone in your life who never makes you feel overdressed.

Stewart looked at me, his eyes warm. He was taking it

suspiciously well, this whole thing where every time we kissed, my relationship with Bishop became just a little bit closer to a relationship.

Xanthippe strolled out of her room. She wore black jeans and a red shirt, and there was nothing out of the ordinary about her, except that all her buttons were done up. I looked closer, wondering what was different. 'You're not wearing makeup,' I said finally, blinking. 'At all.'

'Hush,' said Xanthippe, having the grace to look slightly embarrassed. 'My Mum hassles me about wearing too much. It's not worth the drama.'

I smirked at her.

'Come on,' she said again, more loudly. 'Like you wouldn't do anything differently if we were going to visit your mother.'

'That's assuming anyone can find my mother,' I shot back. 'I think the hippie belly dancing cult has eaten her.'

'I'm pretty sure hippie belly dancing cults tend towards vegetarianism.'

I loaded up my food containers, and we headed out to the car.

'Going somewhere?' said a voice I would recognise anywhere. I glanced along the pavement and saw Bishop leaning against a fence. He always looks good. He is the definition of tall, dark and handsome.

And after crushing on someone for so long, it shouldn't be a shock that he still made me feel slightly melted.

Maybe that's exactly how it should be.

Bishop looked me up and down, a bemused smile crinkling up the corners of his mouth. 'Quite a dress.'

'I thought we were meeting you there.' Arriving with Zee had felt like slightly less of a major personal statement than arriving on Bishop's arm.

'I didn't want to subject you to Xanthippe's driving.'

'Screw you, big brother,' said Zee, and hopped into the driver's seat of her Spider. 'Your loss, both of you. At least I'll turn up in style.'

'Yeah yeah, wear your seatbelt,' Bishop said, and she gave him the finger.

My arms were full of Tupperware, which meant he had no opportunity at all to hold my hand as we walked to his car.

'So, ready to face Nonna Nikolaidis?' he asked.

'Hey, I've spent the last couple of weeks associating with teenage hoodlums, webcam girls and property developers, I think I can handle one elderly Greek grandmother,' I said lightly.

This was a lie.

The Nikolaidis family stronghold was up in Fern Tree, the deep green mountain suburb beyond South Hobart. Bishop and I bickered over our musical choices for the whole drive, which at least felt natural and us.

'Okay, then,' he said when he parked out the front, behind Xanthippe's Spider. She had beaten us there by several minutes, probably because the Spider has little respect for speed limits on mountain roads. There was a statue of Pericles in the front garden, with Christmas lights strung on him. Good to know I wasn't the only one with an embarrassing family. Bishop leaned over. 'You can unbuckle that seatbelt at any time.'

'It makes me feel safe,' I ventured.

'She's only a grandmother, she's not going to eat you. Cannibalism is definitely not an approved Nikolaidis family tradition. It's up there with vampirism and bringing the same dessert as Aunt Pia.'

'Very reassuring,' I said, but I couldn't make myself move from the seat. Not at all. There was a silence that maybe wouldn't have seemed long and awkward with anyone else, but this was me and Bishop, so it did.

'It's not working, is it?' he said finally.

'I'm fine.'

'You're not fine, you've gone as white as a sheet.' He leaned in, and brushed a stray lock of hair from my face. 'Tabitha, this was your idea.'

'I know.'

'I didn't ask you to—girlfriend up, or whatever ridiculous term you have for it. I was fine with the indefinable something we had where I sleep over most weeks, and you don't throw a tantrum if I get too caught up in work to text you.'

I stared at him, panic rising in my chest. 'But that's not what you do. You always do the girlfriend thing.'

Bishop's eyes flared with impatience. 'If I wanted to repeat an old relationship with one of my exes, I would be there right now doing that, instead of here in this car, trying to make sense of anything you say and do.'

Yelling at each other in a car did, admittedly, feel more like the 'relationship conversation' I had expected when he found out about the YouTube kiss.

'So you don't want to get serious? You don't want me here.'

'I didn't say that! I just—' He dragged his hands through his hair, which is the thing he generally does when his brain tells him he wants to strangle me. 'I don't want you to fake us being more serious than we are, especially not for my bloody family. I can wait. We can both wait. We have time.'

I'd been looking at this all wrong. He didn't want to push us forward. I was the only one doing that. And giving myself a minor emotional breakdown in the process. 'So that was why you weren't all jealous about the kissing thing,' I said finally. 'You didn't care.'

His eyes darkened for a moment, and I saw a flash of the angry, frustrated Bishop who used to yell at me to hide that he liked me. Because apparently we're both twelve years old. 'I wasn't happy about it,' he said finally. 'But you're you. I know you, Tish. You flirt and you're all huggy with people, and I can live with pretending some random kiss in a film project didn't happen.'

Some random kiss. Had he not been paying attention? Had he not—oh. 'You haven't seen it? I thought—'

'I've managed to avoid that so far.' Then Bishop gave me a closer look. 'Would you actually feel better if I did?'

'No,' I said quickly. 'This is—so we're good.'

'I thought we were.'

The silence between us stretched beyond the road, beyond the dappled sunshine that squeezed through the thick green trees.

I released my seatbelt finally, but only so I could lean forward and let my head hit the dashboard with a clunk. 'I think it's better if I don't come in to do the family thing.'

Bishop's hand brushed the back of my neck, stroking me there. It made my shoulders relax, like I was a cat. 'It does seem like you've had enough trauma for one month.'

'Have I been acting crazy? With the girlfriend fever.'

'Yes you have,' he said with a low laugh in his voice. 'I could hardly tell the difference, though.'

I leaned back against him, my head fitting neatly under his chin. He smelled good. It was hard to be stressed when you were being cuddled by someone who smelled that good.

'You're still mine, right?' I breathed. 'Not boyfriend, not significant other, not—anything else that needs a Facebook status. But mine.'

He kissed the top of my head. 'Who else is going to keep you out of trouble next time you fall into a crime scene?'

I tipped my mouth up to his and we kissed slowly. It wasn't a goodbye kiss or an 'I can't go five more seconds without touching you' kiss. But it was good, and it was us.

'You should go in,' I said finally, relinquishing him. 'Keep the food—pretend you cooked it. That should give you brownie points.'

'You can't walk back from here,' said Bishop. 'Let me drop you home first.' Oh god, such a gentleman. If I was sensible I would make him take me to his place right now, get naked and sort all our relationship questions out without any words at all.

'It's okay,' I said, sliding out of his arms before I could change my mind. 'I'll steal the Spider. Tell Zee *after* dessert.'

'I suppose I can look the other way for grand theft auto just this once.' Bishop gave me an inscrutable look. 'You're not up to anything, are you?'

There was the Leo Bishop I knew and loved. For the least scary possible definition of 'love'.

'It's Christmas,' I said breathlessly, then threw myself back into the car to kiss him again until we were just that bit more breathless. 'What could I possibly be up to?'

'What are you doing back?' Ceege asked when I walked back into the living room.

'Forgot something.' I picked up the video camera that Stewart had been using in Flynn.

Stewart gave me a suspicious look. 'Do ye know how tae use that?'

I found the reddest, biggest button, switched the camera on

and swung it up to film them both. 'Nope. You'd better come with me.' I turned around, heading back for the Spider.

Stewart caught up to me by the time I got there, having had the presence of mind to grab his jacket, keys and his own camera on the way 'Are ye after an adventure, Tabitha Darling?'

'Yes,' I said breathlessly, and grinned at him as we buckled up. 'Yes I am.' I set off, my hair streaming back as we drove. 'If my phone rings, you get to answer it and listen to Xanthippe abusing me for stealing her car.'

'Ye give me the best jobs,' Stewart said cheerfully, and snapped a picture of me which was probably going to end up as police evidence when Xanthippe killed me dead, some time in the distant future.

I could have done this without him. Of course I could. But he was my favourite partner in crime.

It was fine weather, though the traffic was terrible—everyone was going somewhere, whether it was home or to relatives or whatever. Christmas Eve. Part of me felt very guilty about not being in a certain other place, with a certain other person. Would Bishop feel as relaxed about giving me an out for Christmas if he knew I was running around with Stewart, involving myself in something I shouldn't all over again?

Bishop would never have come with me to do this, not without interrogating me until I couldn't see straight. Right now, therefore, he was not what I needed.

'I still cannae get used tae Christmas in summer,' said Stewart, raising his voice against the growl of the engine. 'Feels wrong. We should be inside, feeling miserable and slagging off *EastEnders* with the thermostat pushed up as high as it can.'

'I don't think Jason killed anyone,' I told him. 'It's been running around and around in my head.'

Stewart glanced across at me, and his voice had that careful pitying tone in it that Xanthippe had been trying out lately. It didn't sound any better in a Scottish accent. 'Tabitha. The lad confessed.'

'I know. I don't believe it. There's something wrong, and I'm going to find out what it is.'

'So we're away tae Flynn?'

'Oh yes,' I said grimly. 'To Flynn.'

Stewart sighed and pushed himself comfortably against the side of the car. 'Wake me when we get there.'

❋

Shay French came out of the back door of his parents' house, and found Stewart and me leaning against his back fence. 'What do you two want?' he said warily.

'Dropped in,' I said.

'On Christmas Eve? It's kind of a bad time for our family, in case you haven't guessed.'

'Yer need a break, then,' said Stewart lightly. 'Get away from it all.'

'What's this about?' Shay folded his arms defensively.

'Tabitha has a theory,' Stewart told him. I was glad he'd come along. Somehow all my ideas seem more sensible when endorsed by him.

'I do,' I said, nodding.

'Going to make things better, is it?' Shay glared at us both. 'The Averys left town, went to a hotel or something. Someone threw a brick through their window.'

'Was it you?'

'No,' he said, coughing on something that wasn't quite a laugh. 'Everyone reckons it was, though. People keep stopping me in the street—a couple of guys congratulated me, and rest of them want me to know how much they *understand*. They don't understand anything. Anna's gone, and Jase didn't do anything to *her*, but no one seems to remember that part. It wasn't his fault.'

'Jason did admit to killing someone,' I said.

'Yeah,' Shay growled. 'Anna's fucken murderer. Wish I had.'

I resisted the urge to roll my eyes about how teenage boys are ridiculous. 'This is serious, Shay. He's in a lot of trouble. He took his father's gun—an unregistered one—and he shot someone.'

'If we were in America they'd give him a fucken medal.'

'Even if they agree it was self-defence, he wasn't supposed

to have that gun, let alone point it at anyone. You know he could get jail time.'

'You came all the way out here to tell me Jase isn't a good bloke?' Shay said, furious with me now as well as the universe.

'No! Something's wrong about the story. Alice's story. Jason's. I don't know why. But I want to figure it out.'

'You'd better not be trying to prove that Jase hurt Anna,' Shay said warily.

'I'm not trying to prove anything. But I have a plan to figure out if we really do know everything about what happened that night.'

'With a camera?'

I nodded grimly. 'With a camera.'

'You people are unbelievable.'

'But no' boring,' Stewart said, grinning over at me. 'Never boring.'

24

Sick of the usual New Year's crap?
Fancy a night with a kick to it instead of a whimper?

Cassidy Crème invites you to join her at Noir
Nights, a new late night cinema club in Salamanca for
a special New Year's Eve event—Le Cabaret Noir!

The theme is 1940s film, so dress to impress.
Featuring the gorgeous DJ CJ, the hot instrumental
vibes of Ljungberg, & the first screening of local film

Flynn by Night

plus a midnight performance by Catfang!

BE THERE OR BE NOBODY

New Year's Eve is big in Hobart. I suppose it's a big night
everywhere, but what do I care about other places? The docks

area turns into one enormous drunken party as the whole city hangs out for the fireworks, and the Taste of Tasmania. There's a swanky affair out on the water, champagne and gourmet local cuisine. There's wall to wall yobbos everywhere else. Much booze. So drunken.

We were crammed into Noir Nights, a new club on an upper floor of one of the sandstone terrace buildings in Salamanca. I could see straight away why the manager was a mate of Darrow's—this place was so stylish it hurt the eyes. The decor was startling black and white, and the ceiling was plastered with a painted montage of images from old movies. I looked more closely. 'Stewart, have you been cheating on me with other murals?'

His involvement in the film project was starting to make sense now.

'Possibly I came back tae town a few weeks earlier than I said I did,' he admitted, with a guilty expression on his face. I smacked him, without serious intent to harm.

Images from the Flynn shoot were projected up on the walls in dizzying fashion—stills of the various members of cast and crew in costume. Loud, boppy music crashed around us, telling everyone it was going to be an amazing night.

I secured a sparkly drink and circulated, looking for familiar faces. Of course, this was a club in Hobart, so I knew almost everyone. But I was particularly looking for—ah, there they were. The Gingerbread women, dressed to the nines.

Alice's soft chestnut brown hair had to be her natural colour—it suited her in a way that the blonde never entirely did. She stood between Libby, who was tall and imposing as she stared around the room like it was offending her, and Melinda, who was curvy and nervous and looking like she might need to hurl her lunch out the nearest window at any moment.

They headed for the bar that was serving vodka-injected oranges, Irish coffees, Dutch lager and pink grapefruit soda. Yes, those were the only options. No one was complaining.

It's amazing, the shit Darrow gets away with in the name of cool.

I kept my eyes on the door, because there was one thing I needed from Shay. The coconut sprinkle on the lamington.

Stewart passed behind me again on his way to help Darrow with the projector. 'Ye get this look on yer face when yer plotting evil,' he said in my ear, and I could feel his laughter against my neck. Was he doing that deliberately? It reminded me that I still had very non-platonic feelings about him, no matter how much I didn't want the complication. 'It's a wee bit scary.'

'Not evil,' I protested. 'All my deeds are virtuous.' But Stewart had already moved on.

I glanced up at the door again. I had almost missed their entrance. Shay stood there, trying to appear relaxed and okay in a borrowed striped suit from the *Flynn by Night* shoot.

Jason slouched in beside him, defensive in jeans and a shirt that had seen better days, his whole body language screaming that he wasn't going to make an effort no matter what.

At least in Hobart, fewer people knew who he was. They might have seen the newspaper articles, but they wouldn't know him personally. If he kept his head down, no one would think of him as the teenager who was out on bail for shooting a bloke.

Well, not right this minute.

The music started thumping. Ljungberg, who was sharing DJ duties with Ceege tonight, was in command of the music. She had bare arms and big hair, and only spoke Swedish. She played some less depressing examples of Aussie indie music mixed up with more obscure European. In between the tracks, she cracked out an actual cello and played retro tunes of the Sinatra vintage.

There was space for dancing, there were big squishy couches to collapse on with your friends, and there were a couple of benches along one side of the room to aid the messy and uproariously funny business of eating vodka-injected oranges.

It was going to be a good night.

I wore a cut off white ball gown with pink Eiffel towers printed all over it, and a hem that trailed threads around my knees. I had found the perfect shoes to match: pink and strappy and not-quite Audrey Hepburn in *Funny Face*, but good enough for me.

The hair was a disaster, far more Audrey Hepburn in *My Fair Lady*, but my battle with hair products had left a tangled mess to which the only solution was to stack it higher, and add glitter.

In this crowd, I wasn't over-dressed.

I felt an odd prickle along my shoulder blades, that sense that someone was looking at me. I turned my head and met Bishop's dark eyes as he stepped into the club. He wore a black shirt and jeans, very casual for him. He raised his eyebrows at me in a 'Well?' kind of way.

Hey, the gang's all here.

As I smiled at him, so glad he had made it, the lights went out. There was an odd sort of embarrassed hush that always happens at moments like this—people don't want to react too extremely in case this is part of the show, and they'll look stupid.

After a good ten seconds of blackness, they were proved right. This was the show.

The projections started up again, bouncing off every wall, a flutter of black and white images. They were still at first, but then the moving film started against the back wall, looping scenes from the *Flynn By Night* shoot. They'd chosen the best stuff. A gangster and his moll having an argument. A couple of hoodlums threatening a shopkeeper. A femme fatale strutting past the camera. A dozen femmes fatales strutting past the camera. Heh, a lot of women got into the whole femme fatale thing, huh?

A guy and a dame exchanging a parcel in a dark alley, shot from a neck-breaking sky angle, and then snogging messily up against a wall. I stared at that one for a long moment before slipping away to do my job.

'Mesdames and Monsieurs,' came a deep, confident voice in a slightly unexpected accent. 'May I present Le Cabaret Noir!'

A spotlight hit the bar, and a buxom figure in a sparkly figure-hugging cocktail dress slithered over the counter, stood up in eight inch heels and threw his arms out in greeting to us all.

Ceege hadn't glammed it like this since his break up. I was glad to see that something was at least a teeny bit back to normal.

'Kick it,' said DJ CJ, and the music exploded around him, vibrating the crowd. Ceege made hushing motions, and Ljundberg brought the music volume down. 'My friends, you are here to drink and dance and experience a masterpiece of modern noir cinema. Who said film noir was dead? Not us!'

There were some cheers from the crowd, which went to show how many film students Darrow had stacked the place with.

'But my friends,' Ceege said in a dramatic voice. 'Noir is about more than criminals, the seedy underbelly, and black and white cinema. At its heart, noir is about murder. And murder can be found anywhere. Only recently, in a sleepy town here in Tasmania, there was a sinister double death. The police think they have the real story, that the culprit has paid the ultimate price. But they are wrong.'

It was too dark to see the expressions on the faces of the people who might actually be alarmed by what Ceege was saying. The audience loved it, crowing and cheering. The whole crowd was buzzed.

I had stationed myself near the exit. I couldn't stop anyone leaving, but I would sure as hell be able to see the face of anyone who tried.

No idea where Bishop was. I had to trust he hadn't turned around and walked right out of here when he saw that kiss up on the screen. I had faith in his protective streak outweighing everything else.

I'd thought of every detail about tonight except for the fact that I had a walk-on (snog-on) role in the movie.

'That's right, peaches,' said Ceege. 'We are here to solve a murder. Tonight, we are the detectives. Watch closely, for all the clues you need to solve the crime are right here, before your eyes.'

Light swirled around the club, flickering and dancing over faces, and then the film changed. Instead of showing clips from *Flynn By Night*, it showed a single track, a camera's eye view of a person—a woman, by the shoes—walking down the path to the lake.

There was a hush over the room. Everyone knew the story by now. How could you not, when the murder and the details of the investigation were a constant topic in the newspapers, on the radio, in the blogosphere.

'Alice,' a voice cried out across the room, a tinny messagebank recording. 'Is that you?'

There were maybe three seconds of silence before the film went back to wise-guys and crooked cops. The bare-armed

Swede cranked the music higher, and the crowd got the idea that it was time to dance.

'More clues to come, cherry pies,' Ceege shrieked. 'All will be revealed before midnight!'

The montage of shots was interspersed with new footage, of the girl by the lake, running, falling. The sound of heavy breath filled the air.

It was creepy enough for me to see the footage under these circumstances, and I knew for a fact that the feet in Annabeth's shoes did not belong to her. They belonged to me.

Someone moved towards the door and I braced myself. An arm caught mine, and a deep voice growled in my ear. 'I have one word for you, Tish. Entrapment.'

'Me?' I said, catching my breath. I was pretty sure I wasn't in danger from Bishop, but I was still running on adrenalin and sparkly drinks. 'It's Darrow's club. Darrow's film. I'm an innocent bystander.'

'Yeah,' said Bishop gruffly. 'Completely innocent.'

Stewart was kissing me again, on one of the walls of the club. Same kiss, different angle. Hell, how many of those cameras had been up there? Were the film students being given extra-curricular tuition in creepy stalkerness?

'Method acting?' I ventured, desperately embarrassed but not wanting to be distracted at this point. 'Anyway, you're not supposed to be here, you're supposed to be…'

'Ha,' said Bishop, his gaze flicking towards the obvious

image, then back to me. His body language had changed—his shoulders were tight and angry. 'I don't actually work for you, Tabitha Darling. In case you'd forgotten.'

Then he was gone, striding on through the crowd and leaving me—well, off kilter. Wishing for a vodka orange. Staring at a kiss on a screen, wondering if it had really gone on that long in real life.

The music was too loud to think, and the victim's eye view of the camera kept returning to the screen, intercut with footage of Greg Avery and his wife playing crime boss and traitorous dame. There was a detective skit or two, and then we saw a horde of teenage boys in nice suits shooting at each other with their fingers as they ran across Main Street.

Some of the best footage had been grabbed when people didn't think they were being filmed. There was a wicked bit of Xanthippe in her full get up, teaching a row of glammed up teenagers how to vamp for the camera, Ingrid Bergman style. Stewart (I knew it was Stewart, he had crowed about it during the editing sessions) had filmed Darrow in his stupid beret, directing the action and having sandwiches thrown at him by a gang of kids in flat caps, dressed up as urban urchins. It was like one enormous gag reel for the cheapest movies ever made.

Then there was the camera-eye view again, down by the lake. The woman with the shoes stopped at the sight of a car parked haphazardly near the water, its boot firmly closed.

'Alice?'

That was the worst of it. It was Annabeth French's real voice, taken from a message on French Vanilla's hidden sim card. I hated myself a bit for that part, but Darrow had insisted on putting it in when he realised what we had. This film wouldn't be forgotten in a hurry. 'Alice, call me back when you can.'

The editing was choppy here and there, but very effective.

Now we were back to the new footage, of my feet down by the lake. The camera swung up, and this time the full message played: 'Alice, call me back when you can. Some people are looking for you—me—well, you. Don't come here, it's the first place they'll look.'

It gave me chills to hear it. Xanthippe had refused to show us any of the text messages she had found on the memory card, insisting they weren't anyone's business, and had nothing to do with Annabeth's death.

I mostly believed her.

But the phone messages, those she had shared.

The camera fell, as if its owner had been hurt. It hit the ground with a shudder and you could see blonde curls and a female shoulder. I knew it was me, I remembered recreating it for the camera, but for a moment all I saw was Annabeth.

The image blurred and jumped, and then everything went black. The lights didn't come on again. The music was dead. And I was too far from the action.

I squeezed and pushed my way through, because I knew exactly where to go. The laptop that fed directly to the screen was in the back room.

Finally people were realising that this was not the show. The lights were really out, the power was dead, and I was still elbowing my way through all of them, in the dark.

I found the door finally, shoving it open just as Darrow reached me with a torch. 'Ceege is checking the power board, no drama.'

The lights came on again, and we stared into the office. The smashed remains of the laptop were scattered across the floor. A table had been overturned. Bishop was securely holding a struggling, furious Libby, AKA Gingernutz of The Gingerbread House.

'Damn,' I said softly. Not who I had expected.

'Tabitha,' Bishop demanded. Fury poured off him. 'What exactly were you hoping to achieve here?'

Not this.

Ceege came in with Melinda in front of him. She looked tear stained and soggy, but at least she hadn't thrown up recently. 'Found this one at the power box,' he said. 'What's going on?'

'We're not going to say anything,' Libby said flatly, crossing her arms.

'I think that comes as a relief,' said Bishop, letting go of her. He was still glaring at me.

'How is this my fault?' I said defensively.

'Oh, I think we'll find a way.' Me getting involved in any kind of police business was his least favourite thing. It was a fair cop. I'd known that he wouldn't approve.

'Where's Alice?' I asked, turning my attention to our culprits instead. Why would they do this for her?

'Alice didn't do anything!' Melinda protested. She didn't look defensive though, but afraid. Interesting. What did she have to be afraid of?

'Yes she did, she really really did, and we have to find her.' I was starting to worry now. Nothing had gone as planned. 'Has anyone seen Jason or Shay?'

'D'ye miss the part with the lights goin' out?' asked Stewart, at my elbow. 'No one's seen anyone.'

'Xanthippe,' I said, appealing to her because—well. She was the person in the room most likely to trust me no matter how stupid I sounded. 'We've been missing something about what happened that night. Even the film didn't get it right.'

'What sort of something?'

'I don't know! I haven't figured it out yet.' I went back to the doorway, surveying the crowd. Certain faces were most definitely not in attendance. 'But I think Jason might have.'

25

From: Darlingtabitha

is it possible to be completely sick of ice cream this early in the summer?

From: Nincakes

believe me, I was over it weeks ago.

From: Darlingtabitha

too early to start experimenting with soups for winter?

From: Nincakes

T, if you start talking about raspberry vinaigrette soup, I will bash you with my rolling pin. Just bake the damn friands.

From: Darlingtabitha

could vegemite friands be a thing?

From: Nincakes

I WILL KILL YOU DEAD.

✺

We spread out to look for them in the street outside. Trouble was, the street outside was typical New Year's madness. There are a lot of pubs along this stretch of Salamanca, and it was about an hour to midnight. There were people everywhere, drinking and messing around and basically being stupid.

You lose points with me when you drink unattractively, and the Hobart waterfront at New Year's is full of unattractive drunkeness. But that wasn't important right now.

'We'll never find them,' I moaned. 'This was a stupid idea.'

'A couple of hours ago ye thought it was a brilliant idea,' said Stewart breathlessly, his camera bag still slung over his arm.

'It would have been if it had worked! Instead we've made everything worse.'

'I'll try the roof,' said Darrow. Bishop nodded curtly and followed him.

Stewart, Xanthippe and I looked at each other.

'Where would I go if I was a *femme fatale* on the run from the law,' mused Xanthippe.

I eyed her. 'You agree Alice has to be in on this too? More than her friends admitted?'

'Up to her neck,' said Xanthippe. 'You can't trust people who seem that nice. Come on, let's see if we can find a quiet corner.' She took off in the direction of the alley leading to Kelly Steps. This was a direct route up to Battery Point, the suburb up the hill behind Salamanca. The fastest way to escape the noise and chaos of the street.

At the end of the alley, the chunky sandstone steps led their way steeply up the hill. Xanthippe ran up them two at a time, then stopped halfway and pirouetted slowly.

There was an old overgrown garden behind a big gate, just there. The wall around it was high, but you could see into it from the steps. I vaguely remembered playing there once as a child, when the building it was attached to was open for dance or drama lessons, or one of the many activities my mother thought would give me something to focus my energy on.

The garden was a bit of a mess. I recalled my first nettle sting, and learning that it really was true you could always find dock leaves nearby, to ease it.

Alice was in there, facing Jason. Shay was there too, hanging back, his arms crossed defensively as per usual. He looked ridiculously cute in his real suit. Like a kid playing dress up.

We were all kids playing dress up.

'What the hell was all that about in there?' Jason hissed. 'What are you running from, Alice? What don't I know?'

Covertly, Stewart slid his video camera out from the bag and took the lens cap off, lining up the shot.

'It won't be admissable as evidence,' I said in a low voice.

'That wasnae something ye were too worried about earlier,' he whispered back, and filmed the scene anyway.

Jason was steaming mad. 'What was in that film that freaked you out? Like, specifically?'

'What do you think?' Alice cried back. 'It was horrible, like they were trying to—'

'Show what really happened?' Shay suggested in a voice much older than his years.

'No,' she said, sounding genuinely shocked. But then, she always sounded genuine. 'They're making some kind of sick game of Anna's death, it's nasty. I don't want to remember that night.' She turned back to Jason, entreating him. 'Of course I wanted to get away.'

'Yeah,' he said flatly. 'But there's a difference between running away from something you don't want to see, and getting your mates to smash up a film and sabotage the lights. Makes you look really bloody guilty about something. So how much do they know?'

'They just—they knew I was upset.'

'I was near enough to you in that club, Alice. I heard you begging them to do it. What was so important?'

Alice bit her lip, tilted her head and basically used every tool in her repertoire to look like the innocent, injured victim all over again. 'I can't stand to see Annabeth being used for tacky entertainment like this. It's cruel to her family and friends.'

'Cruel,' Jason repeated. 'You know what, Alice? I have a really good lawyer. The best money can buy. Turns out that's the one thing my dad is good for. And this lawyer has been asking a lot of questions. Like, what you said to me on the phone that night, to get me to the lake. About whose idea it was for me to bring my dad's gun. How you even knew about the gun in the first place. And it's becoming kind of obvious how good you are at worming information out of people. Out of me. I told you stuff I never should have.'

'We're friends,' she said softly. 'That's what friends do.'

'Friends,' said Jason. 'Yeah. We became friends really fast. I told you everything about me. All because—when I turned up on your doorstep, looking for Annabeth, you couldn't lie and just say you were her flatmate.'

'You wish I'd lied to you? Jason, that's not who I am.'

'You'd been lying for months. To everyone. People you lived with. Why couldn't you lie to me? You never even tried. You wanted me to know the truth. About you pretending to be Anna. And I can't help thinking that...' and his voice shook on the words. 'I think everything that happened this year is something you meant to happen.'

Xanthippe tugged on my sleeve to get my attention, mouthing words at me that I couldn't quite understand. I mouthed 'what?' back at her, and she rolled her eyes and waved her hands, and it was a few minutes before we realised that all three of the young people in the garden below were now looking up at where we stood on the steps overlooking them. Oops.

'Hi?' I ventured.

Stewart gave them a small wave, and didn't lower his camera.

'Come on down, guys,' said Jason, sounding tired and oh so grown up. 'I don't mind an audience, and we all know Alice likes to be watched.'

'Why are you being like this?' Alice shot back at him.

'It's been a rough month,' he snapped back.

Stewart, Xanthippe and I trooped down to the gate and let ourselves in.

'Any insights, Tabitha?' Jason asked me. 'I'm bashing my head against a brick wall in a cardigan here.'

'You're all treating me like I'm the one who did something wrong!' Alice protested, sounding close to the edge. 'I didn't do anything bad! I was in danger, and Jason saved me.'

'Annabeth's boyfriend,' I said quietly. 'That was what got me suspicious all over again.'

'Hang on,' said Xanthippe, frowning. 'Have I missed something here? Annabeth didn't have a boyfriend. Jason's dad gave her the money to go the mainland.'

'That was the weird thing,' I said. 'She told *Shay* she was seeing someone. Before she left. Why would she tell her brother that if it wasn't true?'

'To hide where she got the money from,' said Alice, sounding panicky. Interesting.

'That's what doesn't make sense,' I said. 'Sure, she didn't want Shay to know she was letting Jason's dad pay her to leave. But of all the lies she could have chosen, why that one? Why something that would make Shay think she was a horrible person? She could have pretended she won a scholarship, or got a loan, anything. Why let him think she was cheating on his best mate? Unless it was true.'

'There isn't a boyfriend,' Alice said flatly. 'There … isn't.'

'So where is he, this boyfriend?' Shay asked, speaking up from where he was lurking along the fence line. 'If Anna was telling the truth about him, where the hell is he? The police would have found him.'

'The police did find him,' I said. 'We found him. They dragged him out of the lake.'

Stewart made a thoughtful noise. He nodded, and grinned at me like I was the cleverest person he'd ever met. I loved it when he did that. It made my insides feel like black forest cake.

'Malcolm Drake,' Jason said slowly.

'Malcolm Drake,' I agreed. 'He invited Anna to the city, got her into the film school. The money came from Greg Avery but the idea came from Malcolm Drake.'

'No,' Alice said, and for once she sounded angry instead of meek and battered. 'No.'

'You never did say what you did in Sydney, before you ran away from that terrible but non-specific domestic situation,' I said to her. 'I think you were an actress. I think Anna replaced you in more ways than one. Was Malcolm promising to get her parts instead of you?'

She looked utterly shocked. 'Me? I'm not an actress, I'm…'

'Oh, we know,' I said firmly. 'You're apple pie and cardigans, and reading long books on rainy afternoons. You're vanilla. But it never made sense, Alice. Why would someone like that ever set foot in a house wired with cameras? Why would someone on the run from an abusive boyfriend put herself on display? You had to be either an exhibitionist, or an actor. Pretending to be someone else, twenty-four hours a day, for three quarters of a year, in the face of actual surveillance. That takes work, or skill, or both.'

'Jason, make her stop,' said Alice in a small voice. 'She's trying to make me look bad. No one can prove any of this. It's not true. I'm me. You know me.'

'I don't know who you are,' Jason said quietly. 'But I know Anna is dead, and I know I shot someone, and I know that … I wouldn't have been there that night if you hadn't made me think you were in danger.'

'Jason,' she said, looking devastated. If she was genuinely innocent, we were the worst people in the world to put her through this. 'I'm sorry I brought you into it, you know how sorry I am. But you can't blame me for your actions. You have to take responsibility for pointing the gun, and pulling the trigger…'

'I know I do,' Jason said calmly. 'And I will. But I want you to admit your part in it. And I want to know if…' He hesitated, his voice breaking. 'You told me on the phone that he was violent, that he was coming for you, that he had hurt Anna and you didn't know if she was going to be okay. You sounded so scared. Were you acting? He broke through the trees, coming at me and—after everything you said, I thought he was some kind of maniac. *Were you telling the truth?*'

I hated to say what I had to next, because it might break Jason. I had hoped to make things easier for him, and I had a horrible feeling now that my interference tonight might make his life harder.

'The thing is,' I said in a low voice. 'Alice, if he was the abusive boyfriend out for revenge, and you hit him over the head, almost killed him ... why would he go for Anna first? I can believe he might have hit her, pushed her out of the way, even killed her in a moment of fury, that fits. But Anna's killer held her underwater until she drowned. There were bruises on her arms. She struggled, and someone took the time to hold her there.'

'Oh god,' said Jason faintly.

'That's a lot of trouble for him to go to,' I continued relentlessly, well aware that I was giving us all nightmares for a week. 'For the wrong girl.'

'He did it to make me scared,' said Alice, face drained of blood. 'He wanted me to see what he would do to me next.'

It was a good story, and I was a complete bitch for disbelieving it. Except, it couldn't be true.

'Whoever killed Annabeth French really hated her.'

'Anna was my friend,' Alice protested in a 'see, she's got the wrong idea' kind of voice. 'Jason knows that. I liked her.'

'All I know is what you've told me,' Jason said in a quiet, broken voice.

'You can't PROVE IT,' Alice howled, finally coming apart. 'It's just WORDS.'

She was right. Almost everything I had said was speculation. I had nothing tangible, no evidence for what Alice had done.

'Good words, though,' Stewart told me, patting me on the shoulder. 'Believable words.'

'I agree,' Xanthippe said, standing so close to my other side that her arm brushed mine. I leaned into their touch. 'Really, Tish. I'm impressed. I've been telling you for ages you should do the private detective thing. The little flourishes, making complete leaps of faith about other people's character flaws, the almost paranormal gathering skills when it comes to gossip. Good stuff.'

'Are you being sarcastic?' I demanded.

Xanthippe shrugged. 'I'm not even sure anymore.'

'What do we do now?' Shay asked. He expected me to have the answers. Damn it. Possibly I should. Some answers would be great.

Someone cleared his throat. I looked towards the gate and have never been so pleased to see Bishop in all my life. 'Mind if I join you?' Great, now he was being sarcastic too.

'Please,' I said fervently.

He looked from me to Stewart and Xanthippe, and then the seething teens in the corner. 'If you're finished and everything.

I mean, I'd hate to interrupt by bringing actual professionalism into this.'

'Bishop!' I wailed.

'I want you to make them stop harassing me,' said Alice, every inch the victim. 'They can't do this. I want to go home.'

'I'm afraid I'm going to have to interview you at the station,' said Bishop, his voice as deliberately calm as if this was a Cary Grant movie, and he had just spotted a stray jaguar in a library.

'You can't listen to her,' Alice said, her voice getting higher and more frantic. 'She's making things up, there's no evidence! She's not the police. Arrest her!'

'I don't know what Tabitha has been saying to you,' said Bishop, giving me a stern look. I resisted the urge to stick my tongue out at him.'I missed most of it, probably a good thing. And believe me, arresting her is on my top ten list of things to do in the New Year.'

'Hey,' I protested.

'But I need to talk to you, Alice Conway, about blackmail,' Bishop went on. 'We've been talking to your housemates and some of their statements raise questions.'

'They wouldn't,' Alice said, and her voice had a touch of venom in it. I almost collapsed with relief. The nice façade was cracking, finally

Bishop nodded. 'They both claim that you threatened to expose the history of The Gingerbread House website to their families, and that you used this to force their silence over what happened on the night Malcolm Drake was killed. They also now claim to have witnessed the blow you struck to his head in the driveway of your house. In addition, you compelled Libby Fleming to approach Pippa Avery in order to attempt to extort money from her. There are several other complaints against you, but those will do for starters.'

'I didn't make anyone do anything. If people want to do things for me, it's because I'm a *nice person*,' Alice screeched, all but stamping her foot.

'Yeah,' said Jason sourly. 'Really nice.'

Shay looked at Bishop. 'Detective Sergeant, Tabitha has a theory that Alice killed my sister. That she set Malcolm Drake and Jason up that night. Oh, and that Drake was Annabeth's bloke.'

Bishop just looked at Shay. And then he looked at me. His face showed nothing—no approval nor disapproval. I smiled my best smile.

'Did it have to be New Year's Eve?' was all he said, finally.

'Timing's everything?' I ventured.

He made a noise under his breath. It was probably best that I couldn't translate.

26

I'm glad you asked. The official method in the early days of ice cream pioneers in Philadelphia was to mix cream and sugar together, and freeze. As sophisticated recipes go, it's only one step up from adding Milo to a cup full of snow. Their first favourite flavour in Philly was lemon. US President Thomas Jefferson (who apparently didn't have anything better to do) and/or his private French chef, introduced two revolutionary concepts: eggs (by way of the frozen custard method preferred today) and vanilla (the pods were imported from France, despite the fact that he could have saved money getting them directly from Mexico. Especially as this was the time of the French Revolution).

How do you make vanilla ice cream as interesting as its origin story? I decided finally that if you're going to go with vanilla, you might as well use both boots. And there's more than one culinary association with 'Philadelphia'.

LIVIA DAY

PHILLY VANILLA SUNDAES

(AKA FRENCH VANILLA WARFARE)

Ingredients:

2 cups cream

500g Philadelphia Cream Cheese (NOT the low fat variety)

1 cup caster sugar

4 teaspoons pure vanilla essence

Instructions:

Heat cream and sugar in small saucepan over low heat until sugar has dissolved. Chill to room temperature. Add to cream cheese and vanilla essence, puree until fully blended, and chill in fridge overnight or for at least 3 hours.

Scoop out balls with an ice cream scoop or melon baller, depending on preferred size, then roll in biscuit crumbs, crushed nuts, crumbled chocolate, poppy seeds or fairy sprinkles before freezing.

Serve ice cream 'truffles' in sundae glasses with vanilla custard and whipped cream. Fresh strawberries and blueberries would save it from being insanely over-vanilla, but if certain people have been going on about how marvellous and unparallelled vanilla is as a flavour? They don't deserve to be saved from themselves.

New Year's Day is one of the few days of the year when it is not only understandable but practically compulsory to avoid work of any kind. So against all logic and reason I always go to the café and cook brunch for my staff, business associates and random mates who fancy a feed.

Darrow refers to it as the gathering of the suspects—a rather less funny joke this year.

This was a better turnout than the previous New Year's, which was just Darrow, Nin, and Ceege with his then-girlfriend Katie. I had just returned from my dad's funeral in Queensland. Cooking had helped me feel slightly less crappy, as had the company. But that was a year ago, and much has changed since then.

I hadn't slept. The previous night's events with Jason and French Vanilla and Bishop kept swirling around in my head. When I finally got up, let myself into the café and started to make berry and white chocolate croissants, as well as muffins so heavy with chocolate chips that they practically qualified as fudge, I began to feel better.

I always feel more human in my kitchen.

Nin turned up about ten, and I repeatedly had to beat her out of the kitchen with a broom in order to make her put her feet up and relax. It was easier once Stewart arrived, because he took charge of the coffee making, and chatted to her in that devastating Scottish accent of his until she relented, and put her feet up.

I fried bacon, mushrooms, and French toast.

When Darrow turned up, I threw on some sausages, and told him if he wanted pancakes, he would have to make his own.

It took an hour before he let me back into my own kitchen, and when he emerged he had used up my entire blueberry supply on a high stack of lopsided but scrummily thick pancakes that made us all deeply happy for some time.

Lara and Yui managed to drag themselves out of bed before noon, so they scored blueberry pancakes too, but we'd eaten the last of them by the time Xanthippe and Ceege made a bleary appearance. They had gone on somewhere after Noir Nights closed, and both of them had glitter in their hair.

I reclaimed my kitchen, and started cooking more bacon. There's never enough bacon.

'Room for one more?' said a voice at my doorway.

I turned, and saw Leo Bishop. Still one of my favourite people, whether he's cranky at me for interfering with police business or kissing me breathless.

I offered him my cheek, and he kissed me lightly.

'Long night?' I asked, pouring him a coffee from the chef's pot. I wasn't willing to share him with the others quite yet. I went to the station when he took in Alice, and Bishop had spared a few minutes to listen to my theory. It was more than I had expected.

I hadn't kissed anyone at midnight, being too wrapped up in other things. But Stewart had sent me a 'happy new year fistbump' via text, which made me smile.

Bishop sat at the table now and stretched out those long legs of his. 'I haven't been to bed yet. I hate cases like this.

Compulsive liars are the hardest to crack, especially when they believe their own narrative.'

I blinked. 'Alice is still sticking to her story?'

'Stories. She's long past lost any continuity or logic. We sent in new people to interview her, and she started over with an entirely different version.'

'That's good news, right? It's proof she's lying. No gaslighting us all into thinking she's the wide-eyed victim.'

'Suspicious,' Bishop agreed. 'We'll get to the bottom of it. Police in Sydney are working to gather evidence that Annabeth French and Malcolm Drake knew each other. Libby and Melinda will both receive counselling. They're still making excuses for Alice—she did as good a number on them as she did on Jason Avery. So much for Little Miss Innocent.'

'Dad always said that no one was innocent,' I said, putting bacon on a plate for him with the last piece of French toast and a good heap of mushrooms.

'I don't know if you've noticed, but your dad was deeply cynical about the world. How on earth did you turn out the way you did? All bubbly and full of hope. Well, hope and pastry and coffee and designer salads and...'

'I'm cynical too,' I protested. 'I changed, this year. After everything that happened last time, I stopped trusting people.'

Bishop smiled at me, a deep smile that curled my toes. 'You didn't, though, did you? If you'd stopped trusting people, you wouldn't have cared what happened to Jason. You believed in him when everyone else had written him off. You trusted your instincts. You're still the same squishy-hearted Tabitha. And you make no sense to me whatsoever.'

My instinct was to sit in his lap and forget about the rest of the world. But I didn't think we were there yet. Instead I asked, 'What is going to happen to Jason? If you can prove that Alice manipulated the situation, to make him shoot Drake...'

Bishop kept his eyes on me a little longer. He was well aware there was more than one thing going on in my head right now. He was good at knowing that sort of thing. 'That's up to his lawyer. I think it's likely that it will help his defence. Though, the fact that his father has confessed to the unlicensed possession and taken all the blame for ownership of the gun isn't hurting matters. I don't know if he'll get away without jail time, it depends on the judge, but a suspended sentence seems likely to me.'

'That's still bad,' I protested. 'It goes on his record or whatever, right?'

Bishop rolled his eyes. 'Jason pointed a gun at someone and pulled the trigger—he caused a man's death. Self-defence isn't a magical excuse that erases that. It becomes even more complicated if it was only perceived self-defence. If it's true that Alice Conway set up Malcolm Drake to appear to be a predator when he was just some bloke panicking with head injuries ... you never know with these things. One way or another, it will go to trial. Jason will have at least a year before he finds out how it's going to end up.'

That poor kid. It burned me that Alice could have put him in that situation, screwed his life up so effectively, to get revenge on her boyfriend and his other girlfriend. 'You will prosecute her,' I said fiercely.

'We will,' Bishop said, cutting into the bacon and toast. 'For anything and everything we can. But Tabitha, I have to ask. Is this … mystery solving thing going to be habitual with you? It's bloody hard on my nerves. Am I going to be picking up the pieces of your investigations on a regular basis? It's more interesting than attending car crashes and minor burglaries, but I need some warning if I have to face elaborate plots and diabolical masterminds more than once or twice in a lifetime.'

'I didn't mean to,' I said, leaning my chin on my hands. 'It's always an accident.'

Bishop nodded solemnly. 'That's what scares me.'

I paused before saying the thing that had been bothering me most. 'Do you think Alice might be a victim in this after all? I mean, I could be completely wrong. Maybe Drake did abuse her, that kind of thing can mess people up for life—she could be a compulsive liar and still not have actually killed Annabeth.'

'You could be wrong,' said Bishop, filling his mouth with mushrooms. 'But I don't think you are. When it comes to people, Tish, I trust your instincts above mine. Above just about anybody's.'

'Really?' I stared at him. 'But sometimes I get it completely and utterly wrong.'

'You have a better hit rate than most.'

'I do?' This was news to me.

'Comes from listening to people's problems all the time, I guess. You've been paying attention to other humans your whole life.'

'You make it sound like a superpower. Mostly I anticipate what kind of coffee my customers want. Or what kind of ice cream might cheer them up.'

Ooh, that reminded me. 'Okay, pick up your plate. You have to come join the party. There's something you won't want to miss.'

By the time I dragged Bishop into my brunch, Darrow had produced several bottles of champagne. That's what friends are for.

Xanthippe and Ceege were deep in a conversation about committing perfect crimes, and how they would do it if they wanted to bump someone off without getting themselves arrested.

If Bishop was going to be scared by something, it should be his sister's imagination.

'See, being online should be the perfect alibi, but it's not,' said Ceege. 'I mean, my Guild would know if someone logged on to *World of Warcraft* pretending to be me. It wouldn't be me. Like, if Tabs tried to do it, she'd screw up royally in the first five minutes.'

'Thank you,' I said, accepting my glass of champagne.

'Well, you would, babe. It's a whole different language. Catch-phrases. Greetings. We have a code. You wouldn't pass the first conversation with Dweeb the Destroyer, or Darkest Helena.'

'No alibi is perfect,' said Bishop thoughtfully.

'But someone like Dark Dweeb or Helen the Destroyer could pretend to be you,' Xanthippe said, pointing a long manicured finger at Ceege. 'To set up the perfect alibi.'

'Nah, the ISPs would be wrong.' Ceege looked at Bishop. 'You have cops who understand about ISPs, right?'

Bishop looked alarmed. 'Yes, yes we do,' he said, not sounding overly convincing. We all took pity on him by not asking if he knew what an ISP was.

'Anyway,' Ceege went on. 'They're all living in California and Bulgaria. The rest of my Guild.'

'They say they are,' said Xanthippe. 'In reality they could all be twelve-year-olds who live down the road from you. And they could be plotting your death as we speak.'

I left them to their plans, and went to fetch my *pièce de résistance*. As I pulled the carton out of the freezer, the door swung open and Stewart followed me in. 'Dessert? Brunch comes with dessert? Yer breaking all the food rules left, right and centre, as ever.'

'Ice cream laughs in the face of rules.'

'Aye, whatever helps ye sleep at night.'

Stewart went for the right cupboard without asking, and loaded up a tray with sundae glasses. 'So Bishop is here. As a…'

'Friend,' I admitted, though my voice went up at the end of the word and hovered.

Stewart raised his eyebrows. 'No' going with a different noun these days?'

'Tried at Christmas. It didn't quite stick.'

Not having a formally defined boyfriend was of course not the same thing as being available. Because … the thing with Bishop was still a thing. At least, I was pretty sure it had been, up until last night when he saw the *Flynn By Night* kiss up on the screens.

It had occurred to me way too late that while Bishop had known about the kiss and its existence, he might not have actually known who it was I had been kissing. And that might make a difference.

Stewart was smiling, a certain kind of smile that made me want to smack him just a little bit. 'Redefining a relationship is not the same thing as breaking up,' I said firmly. 'And none of it was because of you.'

'Aye right.' He was still smiling. Possibly there was now smirking.

'It was a necessary step on my personal journey, and that whole … thing about kissing you was a symptom, not a cause.' If I said it firmly enough, I might believe it.

Stewart shrugged. 'Eh, I've been called worse.'

I set the tub on the table with a thump along with my candy pink retro ice cream spoon. 'I'm serious.'

He leaned down and kissed me. I wasn't prepared for it at all, but Stewart kept kissing me until I caught up. I was surprised and flustered and he tasted of blueberry pancakes and coffee (always coffee, with Stewart). By the time he let me think again, I had my arms around his neck, and was completely failing to play hard to get.

'Damn,' I said breathlessly.

Stewart reached out, and picked up the ice cream spoon. 'Just so ye know, tha' had nothing to do wi' *ye*. It's all about my own personal journey.'

'I hate you right now.'

'Could as easily hae been Xanthippe, or Ceege. Ye happened tae be there.'

I took the ice cream spoon off him, and hit him on the nose with it. 'I missed you when you went away,' I said grumpily. 'Don't let it go to your head. And don't do it again.'

'Oh, I'm sticking around,' he said lightly. 'Marshmallows?'

'This is death by vanilla, and it is not to be served with marshmallows.'

'What if my personal journey requires marshmallows?'

I stepped on his foot, accidentally on purpose. 'I think you'll survive.'

Later that day, once my crowd of decadent brunch eaters had rolled off to their own homes to spend the afternoon napping or working (Stewart claimed he had three chapters to catch up on, and I was only allowed to come bother him when he was up to date with his word count, honestly, writers) I drove my own little car out in the direction of Flynn.

It was a stinker of a hot day, and after a morning in the kitchen it was rather lovely to be out in the country where the green overhanging trees provided shade from the glare.

I parked near the precipice where I had found Jason Avery, and sent a text message. Twenty minutes or so later, his Holden pulled up behind me, and he came over to sit in my passenger seat. 'Don't do it, Tabs. You have so much to live for.' He had been spending way too much time with Ceege lately.

'Funny,' I said, grabbing a bag of leftover pastries from the backseat, and throwing them at him. Gotta feed the teenagers. They've got growing to do.

'Huh, these are good,' he said, eyeing one of the chocolate ones and then demolishing it in two bites.

'I could teach you how to make them,' I said. I'd made a flask of coffee, and poured a cup for each of us. I do good picnic.

Jason gave me a suspicious look. 'Oh yeah?'

'My waitresses are very unreliable. Especially in summer when the surf is up and holiday romances are calling. I could do with another pair of hands around the café. If you like it, you could look at catering college next year, once you know what your plans are.'

He laughed. 'Dad would kill me. I can't leave Flynn.'

'You wanted to get out of this town because of what people thought of you before. Won't things be worse now? You could be waiting up to a year before the trial. Besides, anything you can do to show that you're making a go of your life will help your case.'

'What if I have to go to jail?'

'You won't,' I said firmly.

'Know that for sure, do you?' Jason shook his head. 'Look, Tabs, you're a top chick and I appreciate it. Believe me, I do. But I have to stick with my family right now. With Dad paying my lawyer's bills I can't afford to go against him.'

'Jason,' I said softly. 'You have to get out of this town. We're only an hour up the highway, but it could make all the difference to you.'

'Yeah, well. Maybe someday.' He did another one of those boy shrugs I was getting so used to. 'Sorry about the firework, by the way. Since you gave me pastries.'

That was one detail I had forgotten about. I gaped. 'That was you? You blew up my kitchen?'

He winced. 'Burgers McCall showed me and Shay how to make sparkler bombs, back in grade seven. He always had this theory about what would happen if you put one in a microwave, but never tested it. I really didn't think it would make that much mess,' he added, all in a rush. 'I didn't think about it much at all, actually. Alice kind of—she was good at that. She'd say stuff, and it made sense. I wanted to help her.'

ASIO should be recruiting Burgers McCall for their espionage equipment department. As for Alice—that woman was good. Or bad, more to the point. Her ability to manipulate people was pathological. 'She wasn't even using sex,' I said in awe, shaking my head. 'Just niceness.'

Jason looked amused—and possibly relieved that I wasn't angry about it. Of course if he did come to work in my kitchen, I'd have to dye his hair before Nin set eyes on him again, maybe provide some kind of costume that covered his entire face…

'Nah, she wasn't,' he admitted with a grin. Then looked at me, troubled. 'How'd you know she didn't use sex?'

I hesitated then, because I hadn't been sure I would raise this last part. 'Xanthippe found the card from Alice's phone a while back. Including some texts that showed—that you definitely weren't romantically involved with her.'

Jason's eyes flicked to me, and then he hunched over, avoiding my gaze. 'Is that going to go public, do you reckon?'

'Xanthippe gave the memory card to the police,' I admitted. 'But she deleted quite a lot of the messages first.'

Jason nodded, though there was a definite 'freaked out' look about the eyes. 'That's good, I suppose.'

I could tell he was trying to figure out which messages Alice might have kept, and which might be the worst for anyone to read. 'I don't think it's anyone's business what you talked about with her. But I'd lay off the line about having a romantic thing going with Alice. It's not going to help.'

Xanthippe had never actually told me what was in the messages she deleted, but I'd figured it out for myself. She's not someone who gets squeamish about violating privacy most of the time, so I was assuming a don't ask, don't tell kind of situation.

Damn it, what had that small town done to him that he thought he had anything to be ashamed of?

Jason shook his head, almost laughing, though there was nothing funny about the expression on his face. 'You know, you're the one who assumed that me and Alice had a thing. I let you cos it was easier.'

'You have to stop lying, Jason. You're in enough trouble.' I paused. 'Of course, a few deleted messages aren't going to change the fact that you told Alice all your secrets. I don't know that you can trust her to keep confidences at this point.'

Jason groaned faintly. 'Yeah. I'd figured that already. Is this why you made me that offer? The kitchen thing?'

'One of the reasons. It's easier to stop pretending you're something you're not when you leave home.'

'Yeah,' Jason said, not sounding convinced. 'Hobart isn't the big smoke, Tabitha.'

'It's a start. Or, you know. You could tell him.'

'Tell my dad I fancy blokes now? Yeah. That will really perk up his week.'

I gave him a withering look. People had been giving me enough of them lately. About time I gave back to the community.

'Tell your best friend you're in love with him.'

'Bloody hell.' Jason slumped lower in the car seat. 'You are such a *girl*, Tabitha.'

'Get over yourself, Jason. I live with an engineering student who wears frocks on the weekend. You're not that weird.'

He ground his teeth. 'I don't feel like seeing Shay's face at the exact moment he starts to hate me.'

'He didn't hate you when everyone was saying you killed his sister. Which is way worse, right?'

Jason shrugged, defeated. 'He's not going to be okay with this. I know you live in a shiny little world where—everyone wears glitter and goes to awesome parties and uses words like *genderqueer*. But I live in the real world. I'm going to stay in Flynn and keep my fucking chin up and do everything my dad tells me to, and pretend to fancy girls until—I don't know. Forever, maybe. That's my life.'

It didn't sound like much of a life to me. 'Shay might...'

'Don't,' Jason said, eyes blazing fiercely. 'Don't patronise me. They don't come any straighter than him.'

'You're the one who had a steady girlfriend,' I pointed out. 'He might think the same about you.' And then, being the person I was, I decided to strike the really low blow. 'Shay still thinks his dead sister was cheating on you. Don't you think it would be fair to let him know you weren't that bothered?'

Jason took another pastry out of the bag, and bit savagely into it, sending broken bits of white chocolate and blueberry juice everywhere. 'Do you try to win every conversation?'

'I'm always right when I'm talking about choux pastry. The rest of the time—I'm only mostly right. Think about the job offer, yeah?'

'Oh yeah,' he said, staring out at the criminally beautiful view before us—trees and valley and the illusion of tranquility. 'I'll be thinking about it.'

It was the best I could do.

I should have gone home after that, curled up in bed and just let my body recover from the emotional drama of the last ... well. Not the last few days. The month. The year. My life.

Instead, I kept driving into the inner city streets of Hobart. New Year's Day was maybe the one time of year I could get a parking spot right outside Stewart's flat.

My New Year's Resolution? Stop bribing parking inspectors with delicious baked goods. Mostly.

I ran up the stairs and knocked on his door. 'Have you finished your word count for the day yet?' I yelled through it.

'No, go away!' he yelled back.

'I can be inspiring!'

He opened the door, looking skeptically at me, though he couldn't stop that grin that tugged at the corner of his mouth. 'How inspiring are we talking here, Tabitha? A bit o' plot advice, or full on Muse duties?'

'I have a café to open tomorrow. I could be doing prep work. I could be baking or chopping or boiling, or...'

'Or grabbing random passersby tae demand they tell ye their favourite flavour of ice cream?'

'Everyone should have a hobby. You never said what you thought about my Philadelphia vanilla sundaes?'

Stewart's mouth twitched again. 'Serving them up was fun. The eating... meh.'

'Meh?' Flirting forgotten, I glared at him. 'That was my masterpiece!'

'Couldae done wi' chocolate. Or ... I dunno. Some flavour other than vanilla.'

'There were strawberries on the side,' I pouted.

'You dinnae do vanilla very well, Tabitha. Tha's okay. No one's perfect.'

I narrowed my eyes at him, but let it drop. Right now, I needed not to think, and talking nonsense with him was the fastest way to get there. 'So what are you working on?'

'Love scene,' Stewart said, his eyes on mine. 'Big finale.'

'How's it going for you?'

'It's lacking something.' He motioned me in, and I took a step or two. Stewart closed the door behind me. 'I have my hero and heroine in a room together. All the misunderstandings are resolved, the plot strands are tied up, and if they fall intae each other's arms I can wrap this baby up before dinner. No' that I need dinner after eating my own weight in bacon, mushrooms, pancakes, and the most boring ice cream sundaes ever devised.'

If I hit him, he might stop talking. Right now I really wanted to hear him talk. 'So what's the problem?'

Stewart shook his head slowly, his gaze still steady. 'Nae idea. For some reason they keep talking. Neither of them makes the first move.'

'I think—' I said hesitantly, and then stopped. 'You're screwing with me, are you?'

'Oh aye. Finished my chapters half an hour ago. I was on the phone tae my agent, actually.' He gave me an odd look. 'She wants me tae come out.'

There were two ways I could take that, but I decided to go for the more obvious one. 'As a male romantic novelist? Is that even allowed?'

'Aye. She seems tae think now would be the perfect time. Something about a snog going viral on YouTube. Up to 10,000 hits and rising. If we link it to my books—could be a publicity winner.'

'Show me,' I said in a deadly voice.

Stewart snapped open his laptop, called up the YouTube page, and we watched in silence on the couch as a re-edited, shorter version of Darrow's *Flynn By Night* film played with an indie rock soundtrack running in the background.

The vid of just our kiss had built more slowly, but this one had skyrocketed since Darrow had posted it in the early hours.

13,588 views and counting. Bloody hell. The comments were full of speculation and discussion about the people involved in the film, including me. Me and Stewart and Darrow and everyone. But mostly That Kiss.

Ninety seconds into the vid, the guy's hat fell off as he kissed the dame against a wall. The best kiss of my life, on YouTube for the world to see.

'Tabitha,' Stewart said quietly. 'It doesnae have tae mean anything.'

'The kiss, or the film?' I felt a long way away from myself. But I was finding my way back.

'Either. Ye dinnae have tae make some grand, life-altering decision about us, no' right this second.' There was a silence after that, though, and I knew it had a question in it.

'I know,' I said finally, leaning comfortably against Stewart on the couch as the vid came to an end. 'Shut up. Play it again.'

THE END
(almost)

JASE AND SHAY'S BEER SORBET*

(TRULY AS BAD AS IT SOUNDS)**

375 ml beer of choice, chilled

625 ml ice water (or if you have machinery capable of blending ice cubes into tiny tiny ice shards, then 500g of ice cubes and 125 ml water)

300 ml icing sugar

Combine ingredients. Turn into granita by preferred method—freeze stir freeze or trusty ice cream maker.

Drink.

Apparently it seemed like a good idea at the time. The boys were insanely pleased with themselves and claimed it was the best thing ever. Then they went to throw up in the garden.***

*Recipe not endorsed by Tabitha, whose ice cream maker was boarded by PIRATES. Sneaky, sneaky pirates.

**Xanthippe claimed it wasn't too bad, but I suspect she was lying for the sake of the children.

Ceege has vowed to introduce the world to the perfect Guinness icypole. The world may never recover.*

****Stewart is sticking to his coffee, thank you very much.

[REALLY THE END]

THE BLACKMAIL BLEND

BY LIVIA DAY

Six romance writers.

Five secrets.

Four poison pen letters.

Three stolen manuscripts.

Two undercover journalists.

One over-complicated love life.

Way too many teacups and tiny sandwiches.

This shouldn't be a recipe for mayhem and murder, but Tabitha Darling has been burned once before and she knows the signs that she's about to fall into another crime scene.

At least she doesn't have to worry about love triangles any more. Right? RIGHT?

Stewart looked as if he was going to say something else, but at that moment, Xanthippe emerged from the kitchen. 'Tish,' she said to me, and rolled her eyes at Stewart as he gave her Regency Rake costume an ironic wolf whistle. 'Oh very twenty-first century male, that is, I swoon in your general direction. Tish, there's a problem with Queen Beatie.'

I hurried over to her. 'Is she offended by something else? Did she find out about the Duchess of Bedford? Is the tea too cold? Too hot? Are the sandwiches the wrong shape? Did she make more people cry?' Stewart and I exchanged a brief glance, and the question 'Did she find out there's a conspiracy to blackmail her over tea and cakes' rose to my tongue, but did not emerge.

'No, none of those things,' Xanthippe said impatiently.

I eyed her suspiciously. 'Then what's she in a strop about?'

A light went off in Xanthippe's eyes as if she had spotted the perfect way to present me with bad news as if it was good news. 'Oh, she's definitely not in a strop. This is a strop-free situation.'

'Brilliant!'

'And the ambulance will be here any minute.'

The courtyard swam around me, and then snapped into focus. 'Ambulance, like ... actually what?'

'It's all going to be fine,' said Xanthippe. 'Though when I say fine, she is in fact not very fine at the moment. Still breathing, though, so there's that.'

I opened and shut my mouth and nothing came out. 'Did someone stab her with a cake fork? I hid the cake forks to avoid that very specific situation!'

'No, I reckon she was poisoned.'

Stewart was standing right behind me, and I felt him take my hand.

'What kind of poison?' I said in a small voice. 'Not—allergies? She's allergic to a lot of things. There was a list.' Had I missed something? Was this my fault? 'Is she going to be okay?'

I could hear them now, the ambulance sirens, getting closer.

Stewart guided me into the kitchen, where I could sit down. Poison. Thoughts of my café's reputation flooded through my brain. Poison was bad. Hard to come back from poison. 'You don't mean food poisoning?' I said in an even smaller voice. Salmonella in the quiches. Egg white in the chocolate mousse. This could be the end of Café La Femme.

'To be honest,' said Xanthippe. 'I'm pretty sure it was attempted murder.'

'Oh, thank goodness,' I said, and then realised a beat later that it was the wrong thing to say.

A Cafe La Femme mini-mystery set between *A Trifle Dead* and *Drowned Vanilla*.

E-book only. To be released October 2014.

Available at www.twelfthplanetpress.com and all good ebookstores.

ABOUT THE AUTHOR

Livia Day is a stylish, murder-obsessed fashionista who lives inside the head of someone else entirely. Tansy Rayner Roberts is a mother, a blogger, a podcaster, and a Hugo-award winning critic. Together they WRITE CRIME. And sometimes they invent ice cream recipes. Livia is the author of the Café La Femme series of cozy mystery novels, including A Trifle Dead and new release Drowned Vanilla. Warning: reading these books will make you crave dessert.

LIVIA DAY

A TRIFLE DEAD

A CULINARY CRIME NOVEL

BOOK 1 IN
THE CAFE LA FEMME SERIES

LIVIA DAY

A TRIFLE DEAD

Available in paperback and ebook

Tabitha Darling has always had a dab hand for pastry and a knack for getting into trouble. Which was fine when she was a tearaway teen, but not so useful now she's trying to run a hipster urban cafe, invent the perfect trendy dessert, and stop feeding the many (oh so unfashionable) policemen in her life.

When a dead muso is found in the flat upstairs, Tabitha does her best (honestly) not to interfere with the investigation, despite the cute Scottish blogger who keeps angling for her help. Her superpower is gossip, not solving murder mysteries, and those are totally not the same thing, right?

But as that strange death turns into a string of random crimes across the city of Hobart, Tabitha can't shake the unsettling feeling that maybe, for once, it really is ALL ABOUT HER.

And maybe she's figured out the deadly truth a trifle late…

**Shortlisted for Best Debut Book, Davitt Awards
for Australian Women's Crime Writing**

deadlines✳

PERFECTIONS

KIRSTYN McDERMOTT

PERFECTIONS

KIRSTYN McDERMOTT

Two sisters. One wish. Unimaginable consequences.

Not all fairytales are for children.

Antoinette and Jacqueline have little in common beyond a mutual antipathy for their paranoid, domineering mother, a bond which has united them since childhood. In the aftermath of a savage betrayal, Antoinette lands on her sister's doorstep bearing a suitcase and a broken heart. But Jacqueline, the ambitious would-be manager of a trendy Melbourne art gallery, has her own problems – chasing down a delinquent painter in the sweltering heat of a Brisbane summer. Abandoned, armed with a bottle of vodka and her own grief-spun desires, Antoinette weaves a dark and desperate magic that can never, ever be undone.

Their lives swiftly unravelling, the two sisters find themselves drawn into a tangle of lies, manipulations and the most terrible of family secrets.

The Aurealis and Australian Shadows award-winning novel by the author of Madigan Mine and Caution: Contains Small Parts.

"Perfections sings from the page. It is dark, compelling and monstrously beautiful."
— *Alison Goodman, New York Times bestselling author of Eon and Eona.*

"Kirstyn McDermott's prose is darkly magical, insidious and insistent. Once her words get under your skin, they are there to stay."
— *Angela Slatter, British Fantasy Award-winning author of Sourdough and Other Stories.*

"Perfections is a sharp, creepy and deeply discomfiting novel full of awkward truths and raw emotions."
— *Tansy Rayner Roberts, author of the Creature Court Trilogy and Love and Romanpunk.*

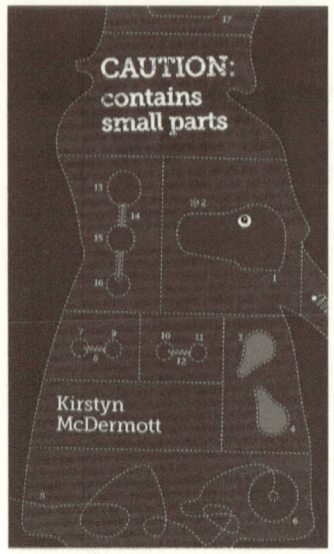

Caution:
Contains Small Parts

Kirstyn McDermott

Caution: Contains Small Parts is an intimate, unsettling collection from award-winning author Kirstyn McDermott.

A creepy wooden dog that refuses to play dead.

A gifted crisis counsellor and the mysterious, melancholy girl she cannot seem to reach.

A once-successful fantasy author whose life has become a horror story—now with added unicorns.

An isolated woman whose obsession with sex dolls takes a harrowing, unexpected turn.

'Kirstyn McDermott's prose is darkly magical, insidious and insistent. Once her words get under your skin, they are there to stay.' — *Angela Slatter*

'Kirstyn is an exciting writer in an exciting place. It's a pleasure to discover her.' — *Kij Johnson*

Twelve Planets

Locus Recommended Reading List for Best Collection in 2011

aurealis awards

FINALIST

Love and Romanpunk

Tansy Rayner Roberts

Thousands of years ago, Julia Agrippina wrote the true history of her family, the Caesars. The document was lost, or destroyed, almost immediately.

(It included more monsters than you might think.)

Hundreds of years ago, Fanny and Mary ran away from London with a debauched poet and his sister.

(If it was the poet you are thinking of, the story would have ended far more happily, and fewer people having their throats bitten out.)

Sometime in the near future, a community will live in a replica Roman city built in the Australian bush. It's a sight to behold.

(Shame about the manticores.)

Further in the future, the last man who guards the secret history of the world will discover that the past has a way of coming around to bite you.

(He didn't even know she had a thing for pointy teeth.)

History is not what you think it is.

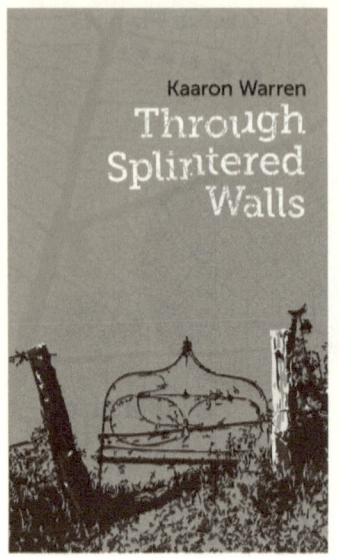

Twelve Planets

Locus Recommended Reading List for Best Collection in 2012

aurealis awards FINALIST

2013 DITMAR AWARD winner

Through Splintered Walls

Kaaron Warren

From Bram Stoker Award nominated author Kaaron Warren, comes Book 6 in the Twelve Planets collection series, including the Shirley Jackson Award winning 'Sky'.

Country road, city street, mountain, creek.

These are stories inspired by the beauty, the danger, the cruelty, emptiness, loneliness and perfection of the Australian landscape.

'Kaaron Warren is a powerful, take-no-prisoners author with an uncanny talent, a deliciously depraved flair for black comedy and a twisted nerve.' — *Alan Kelly*

Twelve Planets

aurealis awards
FINALIST

Bad Power

Deborah Biancotti

Hate superheroes? Yeah. They probably hate you, too.

'There are two kinds of people with lawyers on tap, Mr Grey. The powerful and the corrupt.'

'Thank you.'

'For implying you're powerful?'

'For imagining those are two different groups.'

From Crawford Award nominee Deborah Biancotti comes this sinister short story suite, a pocketbook police procedural set in a world where the victories are relative and the defeats are absolute. Bad Power celebrates the worst kind of powers both supernatural and otherwise, in the interlinked tales of five people—and how far they'll go.

If you like Haven and Heroes, you'll love Bad Power.

'These appetisingly wicked stories give you the perfect taste of Biancotti's talents.' — *Ann VanderMeer*

Twelve Planets

aurealis
awards
FINALIST

Nightsiders
Sue Isle

In a future world of extreme climate change, the western coast of Australia has been abandoned. A few thousand obstinate, independent souls cling to the southern towns and cities, living mostly by night to endure the fierce temperatures and creating a new culture in defiance of official expectations.

A teenage girl stolen from her family as a child, a troupe of street actors who affects the new with memories of the old, a boy born into the wrong body, and a teacher pushed into the role of guide, all tell the story of The Nightside.

'… [Isle's] writing is uniquely hers, direct and honest and crowned by a deft ear for dialogue.' – *Marianne de Pierres*

2012 Tiptree Long List Finalist
2012 Norma Hemming shortlist